PIGEON

The River Bend Series

TJ MAKKAI

For information contact:

info@makkaibooks.com
makkaibooks.com

Editing: Starr Waddell with Quiethouse Editing
Cover: Jason Van Winkle
Formatting: Bad Doggie Designs
Website: Scott Oine with LittleBox Social

ISBN: 979-89864683-4-1

BOOKS BY TJ MAKKAI

River Bend Series
Crow September 2020
Hawk October 2021

Go to www.tjmakkai.com for more information
about up coming releases.

To my son,
Alex
My favorite pigeon stories are the ones we created.

CHAPTER ONE

Claudia
River Bend, WI
The Saturday Before Thanksgiving

Maddie looked a little shaken and seemed to be trying to gain control. "Nah, Norm will be fine," she said, assuring me.

I wasn't sure she believed her own words.

She didn't stop there. "We got him help in time. The paramedics will do their job. C'mon, make the delivery and the victory will be yours."

"We *both* promised the old man. Let's play rock, paper, scissors to see who finishes Norm's delivery." I stuck out my fist, getting ready for the duel.

Maddie didn't raise her arm. "You took his

keys and shook his hand; you have to make the delivery."

My arm still stretched out, I bounced back. "*You* made the same promise. You have seniority."

"Only by two weeks. Four months on the job for both of us, so seniority means nothing. I could say you're older, six years is a lot, especially to a seventeen-year-old like me. You have management aspirations." Maddie seemed proud of her last conclusion. She opened the folded paper that had fallen from Norm's hands as the paramedics rolled him away. Her eyes grew wide with delight. She'd found the nail in the coffin to make me the driver. "The address is 605 Wilson Avenue."

"So? I think that's a couple blocks off the town square, but I don't know it. Why does that make me the driver?" I asked, my arm still hanging in the air, ready to settle this the way most arguments should be decided. "Let's do this—rock, paper, scissors."

"That address might not be yours but . . ." Maddie approached and gave me a victorious smile.

I wanted to punch it off her face with my still-outstretched arm. Maybe not really punch her, but I wanted her confidence to go away.

Her smile got even bigger. "You have to make the delivery. The name on the paper is your roommate Sherrie." She casually placed the paper on my fist and walked away. "Paper covers rock!"

"What? I don't understand." Baffled, I looked at the paper and then at Maddie, who shrugged and went to assist other guests checking in.

I walked through the hotel's front doors, easily spotting Norm's vehicle near the front entrance. I approached the funny-looking minivan, shuffling my feet so I wouldn't fall on the icy walkway.

The cold air blasted my lungs, and the freezing rain pelted my face. I tried clutching my bag for warmth. "For shit's sake, I am going to kill myself driving on these icy roads," I said to no one, looking in the back of the van.

A shiver tingled down my spine.

A dead body stared back at me.

Body Count: One

CHAPTER TWO

FORTY-EIGHT HOURS EARLIER
THURSDAY, ONE WEEK PRIOR TO THANKSGIVING

It was too early to be singing Christmas carols, but with snow in the forecast, I couldn't help but sing "Let It Snow, Let It Snow." I am a firm believer in no Christmas music before Thanksgiving. The holiday was just six days away, and the early November storm was a mixed bag of emotions.

The prospect of a crisp white blanket covering the last of the fallen leaves, the dead grass, and the murky haze hanging over River Bend was making me giddy, but the forecasted freezing temperatures and soon-to-be bad roads kept me from dancing across the hotel lobby where I'd worked for four months.

Today was one of those days where all the employees showed up and were doing their jobs as expected, and that made for a dull afternoon, so I could have used some dancing.

When I was a kid, I used to think adults were boring when they talked about the weather. I believe some of that holds true today, but it is a great determiner about a person. You can tell a lot about someone's personality based on how they react to the weather forecast. Do they complain regardless of its effects on their plans; do they overreact to things out of their control; do they fail to plan; or my favorite, do they use it as an excuse not to participate in life?

Because of that weather forecast, I was using my downtime to play puppet master with my family's and friends' schedules for the week. We had planned to celebrate Thanksgiving on Wednesday to accommodate everyone's work, volunteer, or travel schedules, but Mother Nature decided to toy with us.

I can't help but think about what made the following week play out as it did. Did Mother Nature put everyone where they were, or did I schedule people to be in the wrong spot at the wrong time? Maybe a little bit of both. Does that make me responsible for what happened to everyone, or was it just unfortunate timing for them?

If multiple terrible events collide, people call it bad luck. If multiple good events come together, people call it serendipitous. I am still waiting for a name for what happened. In one day, we had it all—good, bad, and the ugly.

Body count: Soon to be one

CHAPTER THREE

Two months ago, just before my twenty-third birthday, I had a moment of self-doubt about my career, and I was letting it show at work.

I realized my college degree was earning me a slightly above minimum wage job at a hotel in a small town. I had taken this job with the hope of transferring to a larger hotel in the Twin Cities or Chicago, but that was a year away.

Low pay wasn't a problem. I lived rent-free with my Aunt EG, and I had no car payment. The problem was a lack of check marks. During the last four years at college, I'd had a plan, and graduation was the prize.

The degree program had courses that must be completed to earn the diploma. Study, follow the course syllabus, get good grades, and move on to the next course. Keep going until each required course was complete. Each course was another check mark towards graduation.

It was clear and defined, and I could easily check off something each day from my to-do list: study — check; write a paper — check; research — check. Unlike now, when the only checking I did was checking in and checking out guests. I didn't get to check them off any list of mine.

I was going through the motions at work with the excitement of a paper clip.

Gloria, my boss, called me to her office. She asked if I was happy. I gave some mundane answer that I thought she wanted to hear. She asked me my job title and then asked about all the things I'd learned while working there.

While I gave my five-minute answer, she held back her smile. I had managed to list almost every position in the hotel. Without acknowledging my sullen mood directly, she told me, while my job title was one thing, my job training was something else. She also said Scott, my coworker, was about to move, and I would be ready to take his supervisory job. More money, better title and ahead of schedule, she promised me. She parlayed this notion into motivating me to make the most of each shift.

I had one foot out of her office door before she told me to wait.

"Listen, Claudia, I think you understood

everything I just said, but I want to say more. Forget the polite pep talk. I could suggest a dozen how-to-be-a-better-person books or have you spend a hundred dollars on a business seminar, but here's the thing. If you want to get ahead, don't just do your job and punch out at the end of the shift. Learn. Watch. Listen. Who cares about a job title? I don't care what you tell your friends your job title is, but I care about the work you do and so should you.

"I told you from the beginning, this small hotel is a great stepping-stone for bigger things. Make the most of everyone. Learn from everyone. Catherine, working four days a week as a Housekeeping supervisor, is the best person you can learn from.

"She knows more about the building and how to keep it running when the weather gets below freezing. Last winter, when we had a boiler issue and hot water problems in the guest rooms, I called her first before I called Roy in Maintenance. When the food deliveries were late for a month, I had Ken, who works third shift at the front desk, fix it because I knew he had a better relationship with the driver than Monica from the restaurant had with anyone from that company."

My cheeks grew warm. I saw them turning pink in the wall mirror. Gloria was smart, kind, and this was the gentlest beating I'd ever received.

"Thank you. I'm embarrassed that I had to be told all that. I understand everything you said."

From that moment on, I took every opportunity to learn. I was done with college now, and no course curriculum was guiding my life. I had to make my own. If a formal training schedule for me to be ready to leave in one year wasn't available, I would figure one out myself.

The first time the morning Housekeeping supervisor was late, I'd told the staff just to start knocking on doors. Last week, when she was late again, I had been able to run the reports so the Housekeeping staff knew what rooms to clean.. Employees now came to me with problems, and I had proper solutions.

I did not feel bad taking ten minutes of my shift to figure out if we should change our family Thanksgiving celebration from Wednesday to Tuesday. It had been almost ten years since we had our family Thanksgiving meal on Thanksgiving Day. I was having a bit of a struggle juggling multiple schedules, and I did not want to have to leave somebody out.

My parents, Katie Lyn and Matthew, would be coming in from St. Paul, MN, with my brother, Connor. My parents' schedules were flexible, but so far, the biggest obstacle to finding a day to celebrate was my brother, who's a junior in high school. He had classes on Monday and Tuesday and then was off for the long holiday weekend. My parents were ok if he missed school during the holiday week, but he worked at a local home-improvement store and had to help them get the lot ready for the Christmas trees. Our parents had always installed in Connor and me that work was important and we shouldn't let down your boss, coworkers, or ourselves. I had let that lesson slip, but I was back on track now.

While I waited for a text from Connor about his schedule, I thought about the last time my parents had been in town.

It had been a couple of weeks ago, and we were having breakfast at Peach's, Aaron's aunt's café. I was elbow-deep in an apple fritter, wiping the powdered sugar off my blouse, when my mother suggested we have Thanksgiving with Aaron's family. I nearly choked on a chunk of apple.

My dad saw my reaction and raised an eyebrow. He started humming and fingering-drumming "We Are Family" by Sister Sledge, but he softly modified the lyrics. "We Aren't Family." My mother then suggested just inviting Aaron.

Our families were becoming so intertwined between Aaron and me dating and the once-possible business venture, which was now called off because Aaron's aunt, Jan, had changed her mind about going into business with my parents.

I would have been fine with a Fourth of July

barbecue or New Year's Eve party with both families. But sharing a special meal can be an intimate affair. If our families came together because of us, a significant step in our relationship would be taken, and I was not sure I wanted to take that step at the moment.

Sherrie, my college roommate, and I lived together at Aunt EG's house. Sherrie's schedule was also flexible, but she had to leave no later than Thursday at 2 p.m. for her family's dinner. She worked part-time for Aaron at his bar, and recently, she had started working in the main office at C&C Companies and occasionally picked up shifts at Bumbles, another bar, if they were in a jam.

I had volunteered to work at the hotel on Thanksgiving and the two days following. Several of my coworkers saw me as a hero for that. I figured I would have been scheduled anyway since I have little seniority, but I was angling to get three days off at Christmas.

Aunt EG, a successful fiction writer, was in Chicago and would make her way to River Bend for our holiday celebration before leaving for the airport late Wednesday. She had gone on a cruise several months ago and met the ship's captain, who has turned into her latest romantic interest. On Thursday, she would depart on her third cruise with this captain. She was presenting an easy, flexible component but with a hard deadline for departure.

Aaron was flexible for dinner anytime, since he owned a bar and had staff working. He hoped the holiday feast would not interfere with watching football on Sunday day and evening, Monday night, and Thursday. And more games during the week were possible. I had mentally tuned out that conversation. If I had to worry about kickoff time and possible overtimes, we may not have eaten until Pearl Harbor Day.

I rechecked the forecast. Sunday, sleet and ice were expected. Heavy snow would hit Wednesday. *Our Wednesday celebration may have to move to Tuesday*, I thought.

I sent a text asking if Tuesday worked for everyone and to confirm the dish they were bringing. That text started a puzzle, and the pieces began to fly.

I had to get EG north ninety minutes on Wednesday and Sherrie ninety minutes south on Thursday or before. They presented the hard deadlines, and Connor was the current roadblock.

EG: *Tuesday good. Booze and the house. Add Jorge and Addie to the guest list.*

Running Tally: Me, Aaron, EG, Jorge, Addie
Guest Count: 5

Sherrie: *Tuesday good. Need time—got more hours from C&C but flexible. Pete is in too if not during his shift or Thursday afternoon.*

Guest Count: 7

EG: *No Jorge and Addie*

Guest Count: 5

Sherrie again: *Forgot to mention potatoes. Two ways. Mashed and TBD*

Guest Count: Still 5

Aaron: *Phil is in. Assuming you want me to bring pie*

Guest Count: 6 or 7

I need to write this down, mental math is not my thing.

Aaron again: *I can tell you're thinking. I see the dots ticking. Pie, both pumpkin and pecan. Whipped cream and bread for leftover turkey sandwiches.*

Guest Count: 6

I was pretty sure it was six confirmed.

Jorge: *I will be there. Don't tell anyone. I got booze. Good booze. Extra tables and chairs. Fridge and oven are available if needed.*

Guest count: 6 (plus Jorge)

EG: *Storm is looking bad. Are we doing this? Can your parents and Connor make it? I can change my flight and fly out of O'Hare. Good either way. Invite anyone you want. I got enough china.*

Mom: *Just a warning, your father is experimenting with the cranberry sauce. He wants to make it memorable this year.* [Eye roll emoji] *Are you good with cooking the turkey? I like lots of gravy—ask Aaron if you have to. Sorry, hon, you know I like my*

16

gravy. Love, Mom

Mom again: *still waiting on Connor and his work schedule*

Guest Count: 6 (plus Jorge) (but assuming Mom, Dad, Connor)

Aaron: *Dessert is all set. When are we doing this*

Guest Count: Same

Dad: *Ignore your mom. I got the cranberry sauce!!!!! and salads. All will be fine.*

Mom: *Cheese, crackers, sausage. And two other appetizers—TBD. Probably something cold unless I use Jorge's oven*

Aaron: *Jenna and Kay were just here. Kay in, Jenna out*

All that information coming in, and nothing from my brother. My head was swirling. I wasn't sure if I'd gotten the head count right or if I was missing someone.

Agh, what about Phil's wife, Patty?

I was thankful guests walked in and needed some help.

Guest Count: 12—assuming Mom, Dad, and Connor could make it with Connor's schedule and the weather (plus Jorge) (maybe Patty).

CHAPTER FOUR

Work wrapped up slowly. My phone traffic had also mellowed since everyone was in a holding pattern, waiting for me to make a decision. Instead of heading back to the house, I went to see Aaron and Sherrie at the bar, two-and-a-quarter miles from the hotel. I knew that because back in August, I had started running, having set a goal to run a marathon early next year. I had jumped into the sport to mark something off my bucket list and had fallen in love with it.

My favorite time to run was early morning, before the sun came up and the town was still sleeping. I loved running on the path along the Mississippi River and through trails in the parks and woods. The path I mostly ran was on the Wisconsin side of the river. Occasionally, I changed my route.

Early one morning, after watching a slasher horror movie the night before, I had my fastest time, freaking out while running along the dark river path. That run was short in distance but fierce in record speed.

Now, when I ran in the dark, I stuck to major streets. Most mornings, I loved it, but occasionally, I had days where no music, serene predawn mornings, or fear of a sucky marathon time could push me. Those mornings, I used my watch's GPS and guessed the distance between different points in town. I became full of useless information, like the three dry cleaners in town were less than a half mile apart. The two car washes were one-and-a-quarter mile apart. I could go on, but no one needs to know that type of information.

River Bend, population twenty thousand, started at the freeway off-ramp and ended at the Mississippi River. In between were hotels, shops, a large park, the town square, and Jameson College. I'd thought that was all there was to River Bend but soon learned there was a lot more to discover. I'd tried running through the beautiful campus but felt like such an interloper, never having attended the private college, until I befriended the night security guard, Richard, whom I'd met at Aaron's bar.

He'd been eating pizza with his wife, Emma, who was a former runner. They were a sweet couple. He was native to River Bend, and they knew the area well. They gave me a few pointers of where to run. He encouraged me to run through the campus because it was beautiful and safe, no matter if I was a student there or not. All were welcome. Emma suggested several routes outside of town that I hadn't known existed.

Three days later, Sherrie had come home with a map that Emma had personalized with highlighted areas of places I could run. She had been delighted to pass on her knowledge of the town.

Sherrie had taken it upon herself to place stars on all the businesses where she was working or had worked since moving to River Bend in June, including Aaron's bar, Bumbles Restaurant, and even her once-a-month weekend job at a recycling center. By far, the most stars came from her current employer, Carlin & Cole Companies. They owned a billboard-printing factory, one apartment complex, three commercial building warehouses, a funeral home, a tractor dealership, and a root beer stand. She had been filling in for Eva Reiner—who was preparing to move from her twenty-acre farm to the city—as the executive administrative assistant at the printing factory in the main office and was already thinking of possibly transitioning to full-time after completing her master's degree. Harold Carlin, the president of Carlin & Cole (or

C&C), had taken a liking to Sherrie and gave her various jobs throughout the company to help her earn money for school. Eva was pleased to have someone reliable to do her job, but not someone who wanted her job.

Sherrie wasn't sure what she wanted to do with her degree, but she loved learning new things. She also loved sharing what she learned, and therefore, I had gained too much knowledge about the materials used to make billboards. I could no longer drive on I-94 and look at one of those billboards without wondering if it was wood, metal, or a special type of wrap designed and manufactured in River Bend.

One of Sherrie's favorite shows, and now mine, was "How It's Made." I had once stayed up until one in the morning to watch how car dashboards are made. I'd never known that I wanted to know about that, but I could not stop watching.

As I walked to the bar, Sherrie texted: *if Tuesday Wednesday evening add Eva and Charlie.*

I was losing count, but it didn't matter. My mom, dad, and EG all believed the more the merrier.

Guest Count: 12 (plus Jorge) (maybe Eva, Charlie, and Phil's wife, Patty)

CHAPTER FIVE

The cold air whooshing in when I opened the door to the bar drew everyone's attention, and as they realized it was me, the whispers started. The pointing and whispering had lessened some, and I had learned to ignore it, mostly.

The bar was filled with some locals and the last of the Jameson College kids before they headed back home for the holiday week.

Back in August, I had fatally shot a man in this bar. The police had called it a justified shooting, and I'd been cleared of any criminal charges. I was still dealing with the emotional toll of killing someone. Most of the locals had gotten past what happened, but it was a novelty and tourist point for the collegiate congregation.

Aaron had been injured—shot in the

shoulder—that night, but I had never doubted he would reopen the bar. But, having been deployed several times with the army, he had experienced much worse emotionally, yet he was unsure about reopening.

I hadn't wanted to be haunted by a location. My memories spooked me enough. I'd wanted the bar to remain a place of joy where people could gather. I said if he closed permanently, someone would open it up and try to cash in on the notoriety. I said I preferred he make money off it, and that each time I walked in, I'd know I was strong and could face whatever obstacles I was confronted with.

I still twitched a little when I looked down the hallway towards the back door where everything had taken place, but I wouldn't run from it.

I unwrapped my fuzzy peach scarf, revealing my prized purple sweatshirt featuring the cast of *High School Musical*. My college roommates had given it to me as a gag gift, but the joke was on them. It is my favorite go-to top on rainy days, better than the sweatshirt I'd paid $137 for.

I'd paired the sweatshirt with baggy green camo pants, socks so thick my feet barely fit in my canvas high-top tennis shoes. No glamour but all comfort, a perfect match for the bar. The walls were decorated in a sports theme, but it was anything but a typical sports bar. It felt like the best rec room, missing only a fireplace, like visiting with friends in a log cabin.

Aaron was talking to a woman—not a girl, a woman. He looked my way, waving and giving me a smile that made my stomach flip. Dating almost five months, and I was still giddy each time I saw him.

The woman's gaze did not follow his wave. She kept her focus on him.

She had perfect blemish-free white skin and a slim jawline. Her hair was long and brown, flowing over a leather jacket that looked as old as River Bend but as cool as all the members of *High School Musical* combined. She looked to be about the same age as Aaron.

He walked away while she was still talking. She plastered a stiff smile on her face, grabbed her leather bag, and headed towards the door. Her jeans hugged her butt, extending her legs to the moon, and the highly polished black knee-high boots contrasted provocatively with the leather jacket.

We crossed paths a few feet from the door.

She looked at me and said, "My little cousin loves *High School Musical*. It looks comfortable" She kept walking and was gone before I could say anything.

I suddenly felt nine years old, dressed for a sleepover with my BFF, and briefly considered going upstairs to Aaron's apartment above the bar to change clothes.

Between Aaron's two places, EG's home, and our non-nine-to-five jobs, I never knew where we would end up, so I always brought my overnight bag—which Sherrie had dubbed Wilbur—everywhere I went so I could look like a human and forgo the walk of shame when I left Aaron's place in the morning.

She had affectionately named the bag after the pig from *Charlotte's Web* because she thought it should have been donated or put to the slaughter over a decade ago, but I thought everything classic should be saved. It wasn't pretty, but the style had grown on me. Wilbur wasn't a large sack, but it grew in size each time I fed it more clothes and toiletries.

Aaron had suggested I leave stuff at his apartment and also at the house he owned out in the sticks—a sweet gesture, but one I was not quite ready for. That step in the relationship scared me. I had been staying at one too many houses as an excuse not to plant roots too soon. That had not stopped me from taking Aaron's sweatshirt yesterday, which he'd worn the day before, and wearing it as I'd cuddled on the porch with a book last night. Taking in his scent as I turned pages, I'd been swept away to another world, onto a book barge floating down the River Seine in France, arguably the most romantic river in the world.

I decided against going to Aaron's apartment to change. *I like this outfit*, I thought, embracing the evening and my choice of wardrobe.

I scanned the bar looking for friendlier faces. At least One-Way-Talkie wasn't there. He had been in several times over the last few weeks, asking one too many questions. One-Way-Talkie was nice enough but pushed our buttons with all the questions. He had stopped talking to me when I asked if his thick black glasses were inspired by Buddy Holly or Elvis Costello. Hence the name One-Way-Talkie, instead of Walkie-Talkie since he didn't respond to questions asked of him.

Three people working at the bar was typically sufficient, but ever since the bar had reopened, business had grown each week. Earlier that day, Aaron had said he was unsure what that night would be like since many college kids had already left town.

Along with Sherrie working tonight were Pete and Jacob, a money-hungry twenty-two-year-old fourth-year student at Jameson College. I watched them carrying cases of beer from the walk-in cooler to the bar. Pete gave me a head nod, and Jacob scurried around him hustling to put the beer away.

Pete had been with me the night I killed the man. He'd been knocked unconscious, but I felt as though we'd been through the ordeal together, bonded for life through a tragic event.

I was not sure if he'd ever played football or not, but I would have described him as the guy on the offensive line protecting the quarterback and working just as hard as the quarterback with none of the glory, which was the way he preferred it.

Before Aaron had decided to reopen the bar, Pete was there with Aaron's brother, Chuck, cleaning up the mess, refusing to speak to the press. He said it was not his story to tell. At six feet tall and shoulders as wide, he was a perfect mix of security and security blanket.

I surveyed the rest of the bar.

Hailey Carlin—twenty-one and Sherrie's boss's granddaughter—sat with her best friend, Anna, at a table between me and the front door. We only tolerated Hailey because Anna, was Pete's girlfriend. She walked around town as if she had personally built the C&C companies herself.

Usually, she was at a private college in Chicago, but she returned on school breaks, hoping to snag a husband. Anna, on the other hand, always had a kind hello for everyone and seemed genuinely interested when she asked how you are doing.

Sherrie was behind the bar. She saw me walk

in, and looking at the two guys who had just sat at my usual spot, she pointed to a nearby table. "I'll bring your drinks over to *that* table. Better hurry before someone gets that spot." She knew how to use her power wisely.

I walked to the end of the long bar, which ran along the right side of the room. I grabbed my favorite spot—the last seat, right by the wall—next to Earl, a regular who Sherrie and I had guessed to be between sixty-five and one hundred and five years old.

"Hey, Earl," I said.

"Evening, Ms. Claudia," Earl said.

Earl wore his usual uniform of jeans, a plaid button-down shirt, work boots older than Sherrie and me. The uniform never changed unless his wife made him carry a coat because it was below zero. He never wore the coat. He came to the bar several days a week, and the first thing everyone did when they walked in was to say hello to him. He had become somewhat of a minor celebrity with the college kids, who had started a tradition of having their first drink with him when they turned twenty-one.

From my vantage point at the end of the bar, I could lean on the wall and watch just about everyone in the place while talking to Sherrie behind the bar.

She wiped the bar down where the two guys

had vacated. "Beer or vodka? Pete made fresh-squeezed lemonade, and with a little vodka, apple schnapps, and some other liquid, it's delightful."

"Some other liquid?"

She bounced on her toes. "Pete's secret mix. He refused to divulge. I saw him with the schnapps but don't know the rest."

"That sounds refreshing but dangerous. It's probably something we need in July. I'll take a pint," I said.

Aaron came up behind Sherrie and set a bottle of beer in front of me. "Give this a try and tell me what you think. It's a new seasonal flavor."

Sherrie threw down the towel she was holding. "That's cheating!"

Jacob appeared by my side from out of nowhere. "No way. She asked for a beer."

"Correction, a pint. Not that fruity hipster crap they're trying to call a microbrew," Sherrie shot back.

I could hardly keep up with the conversation, my attention bouncing between each of them.

Pete strode up behind Aaron, who was behind Sherrie. He reached over them and put a glass of what looked like summer sunshine next to the beer. It had ice chips, a cherry floating in mellow yellow nectar with a green and blue straw climbing out of it. All four looked at me like I was holding the key to a locked door I hadn't know existed.

I looked at them one at a time. "What is going on here?"

The four of them remained silent.

Finally, Earl spoke up. "It's a competition that failed. You're the last hope of a win."

"Are you the judge of this competition?" I asked.

"Nah, Sophie and the ladies are at the church settin' up for the pancake breakfast on Saturday. Just waiting for her so we can walk home together. These four snippets here are worse than the ladies chatting up at church. I would've had more peace sitting on a cold chair drinking old coffee."

"You can leave anytime?" Aaron jabbed, but with a smile.

Earl waved him off. "The boys there tried a little competition, but no one bought either drink."

"I'm the pity vote?" I asked.

"I can vote. I can vote!" a voice behind me screeched, like a Styrofoam cooler bouncing on the seat of a truck.

The tiny blonde hairs on the back of my neck stood up. I wished the damn vehicle would stop bouncing. It was the one time in life I would have been ok tossing something out the car window.

Hailey Carlin.

Anna did a drumroll on her legs. The group

looked at me as if I was on the cusp of correctly answering the final *Jeopardy* question.

Hailey tried her best to reach in for a drink. Jacob blocked her.

I pushed my hair behind my ear, put my hands on the bar, and leaned over. "What do you think, Earl?"

"Give 'em hell, and let me have my bourbon." He winked and raised his glass to me.

"Got it! Diplomacy!" I picked up both drinks. I turned and handed one to Hailey and one to Anna.

Each took a sip and swapped beverages.

Anna cheered. "Umbrella wins."

"No way, definitely this one!" Hailey said, giving eyes to Aaron.

I didn't need to see Hailey flash her smile. Aaron turned pink and shifted awkwardly away. Girls flirted with him all the time at the bar, and it made him uncomfortable. He was just not the kind of man to mess with other women. If he'd wanted to date other women, he would have broken up with me. He was one of the good guys in the world.

I didn't understand Pete's reaction when Anna voted. I would have thought that would put at least half a smile on his face, but it seemed to irk him.

Maybe a girlfriend pity vote is worse than no vote at all.

Everyone except Aaron walked away, leaving Earl and me in peace. Aaron grabbed a pint glass, tapped a beer, and placed it in front of me.

Earl pounded his skinny little arm on the bar. "Kiss her. Men these days are weak. Your woman walks in; you treat her like a lady. Now lean over and give her a peck on the cheek."

"Of course, where are my manners? Thank you, Earl." Aaron stepped on something behind the bar to give him a boost. He winced when he grabbed the bar.

The night I had shot a man, in August, Aaron had taken a bullet to the shoulder. He was still in physical therapy and progressing nicely, but he had his moments from time to time.

He threw half his body over the bar so he could reach me. At the last moment, as he was leaning in, he turned his head and pecked Earl on the cheek.

"Damn fool!" Earl shouted in a gravelly voice, but I swear he chuckled under the attitude. "I think it's best if I head to church before things get too wild in here." He stood and tipped his imaginary hat to me.

Aaron shouted, "Earl," and the rest of the bar chorused, "Earl," raising their glasses to him as he shuffled out.

Aaron stayed where he was on the other side of the bar. "How about I take you to breakfast on

Saturday?"

"I would prefer popcorn and a movie tonight."

He cocked his head towards the door. "Earl gave me two tickets for the pancake breakfast."

"Have we come to that point in our relationship that I don't get breakfast in bed but a free meal in a church basement?"

He began cleaning the bar area. "I see nothing wrong with it."

I looked down the bar. Sherrie was a spitball of energy—more than usual. She was naturally chatty, but talked to Pete nonstop.

I suddenly realized something Sherrie did not. "I have a better idea. Don't say anything and just go along with it."

He nodded, and I started playing puppet master again.

I yelled down the bar, "Hey, Pete, come over here."

After making two cocktails and cashing out a check, he walked over. "What's up?"

"Aaron is busy Saturday and can't take me to the charity pancake breakfast. He wants to make sure someone from the bar is there, so are you willing to escort me?"

"Sure, as long as we're out of there by nine. Shall I pick you up?"

"Let's meet here at eight and walk over," I

said.

He nodded and left to take more drink orders.

Aaron had a slightly confused look on his face.

I smirked. "I won't be the one standing here Saturday at eight. I'll make up some story, and Sherrie will take my place. She'll expect you but will be pleasantly surprised when it's Pete."

Aaron's eyebrow went up. He gave me a slight frown, and his forehead wrinkled. It was fun watching him tabulate what I was conspiring.

"I want no part of this. No way. No how," he said, shaking his head. "I am not playing matchmaker, especially with two of my employees. Plus, isn't she seeing Holton?"

"Shh, keep your voice down. Nothing ever really happened with them. He took her to two awkward and formal community events, acting like he was auditioning her for the role of his wife and not dating. She's over it—said there was no need to break up since they weren't even dating. Plus, how many hours is she really working here? She's scheduled one or two shifts a week and then just picks up other shifts as needed, and even those shifts have dwindled with money-hungry Jacob around. Since her classes started in September, she's working more at C&C than for you."

"Easy there. I'm staying out of it. A warning:

this might be a really bad idea."

"She is already smitten with him. Although she'll never admit it."

"You forgot one important thing that makes this even trickier. He has a girlfriend. One that you like."

"I get that, but something seems to be not right with them. So I want to lay the foundation of a friendship between Pete and Sherrie outside of this building. I've got a good feeling about this. Plus, do you hear the music?"

"Coldplay, some live bootleg version. What's your point?"

I was triumphant in my answer. "What are Pete's rules when he's the lead bartender on duty?"

"No clue," Aaron answered. "What? Wait. They have their own rules?"

I waved my hand, telling him not to worry. "First rule, you are always the boss, even when you are not here. Always act like the boss is here. Second and final rule, he is always in charge of the music. Do you think Coldplay is his doing? That has Sherrie written all over it, and Pete is letting it go."

Aaron rolled his eyes, smiling, put up his hands in surrender. "Leave me out of this."

"Ok, just don't show up here Saturday at eight, and all is good." I motioned for Aaron to lean in and I whispered, "What's the story with Phil and

Patty? Why is she not invited, or are you just counting them as one?"

"Her sister in Green Bay had foot surgery. Patty's there for two weeks. He's heading to his sister's on Thursday, but I don't think she's much of a cook. Patty would be relieved to know Phil is getting a decent holiday meal even if it's not on Thanksgiving."

"Good to know there are no marital issues. As much as I love Phil, Patty is a hoot. It would have been fun having her at the dinner table."

My phone beeped. It was my brother.

No work Tuesday. Mom and Dad said I can skip school so we can all be together for thanksgiving break . . .

He tended to ramble when he lied, and it was a rather lengthy text. *I should really verify the last part with Mom and Dad*, I thought, but instead, I took a screenshot as evidence it was Connor with this declaration. I decided to change our Thanksgiving dinner to Tuesday and sent the message to the group.

Kay: *I'm out, but Jenna's is in.*

I rolled my eyes to no one and looked up, smiling at Aaron as he chatted with two guys drinking at the other end of the bar.

A shrill voice behind me asked, "Who is Kay?"

"Hi, Hailey. What happened to Anna?"

"She went to the restroom and to say goodbye to Pete. We're headed over to check out what's going on at the bars over on Broadway. So, who is Kay?"

"Isn't that a special talent? Reading someone's phone over their shoulder. Kay and Jenna are friends."

"Friends? Or *work* friends? *Drinking* friends? Can't be local. I don't know them."

It felt like an interrogation. I wanted to drop my beer on her fuzzy boots.

"I used to work with Kay at Chambray Senior Center, and Jenna works for a judge while going to school," I said, irritated with myself for answering.

Anna joined us. "Is Hailey grilling you for information? She has a way of pulling stuff out of people. Best to ignore her sometimes, but I don't have to since she knows all about me."

"Is that how you two are friends? Opposites attract: you are kind, and she is brash."

They swung their arms around each other and together answered, "Yes," as they walked away.

Maybe I'm wrong about them. My head cocked involuntarily. *Maybe it's Anna I'm mistaken about. A person's choice of friends says a lot about them.*

Guest Count: 12 (plus Jorge)

CHAPTER SIX

Sherrie was supposed to work until closing, but she let Jacob stay because he needed the money more than she did. She was due at C&C at eight the following morning and wanted more than five hours of sleep.

Twenty minutes later, she finished, so we walked over to Draw Bar for a beer. Sherrie didn't feel comfortable drinking where she worked. She said she could never completely relax, always thinking she should be cleaning. Kind of like Aaron and me—we never had public displays of affection in the bar while it was open for business. I always felt like we were in a department store window display while in his bar.

Aaron was hopefully going to join us but wouldn't commit until he saw how busy his bar got.

We stopped at my car so she could grab a sweater out of my always-with-me-overnight bag, Wilbur. We stood on the sidewalk, and I shivered when a blast of cold air swirled in under my jacket. My cropped sweatshirt and jean jacket cut the wind, but the wide cut in the sweatshirt allowed for a breeze to climb up my spine. The fierce cold air coming over the Mississippi River was a prelude to the winter storm headed for River Bend.

I held her purse and jacket as she took off the old aqua-and-pink flannel uniform shirt. A button popped off and fell into the back seat. There were maybe two buttons left, but she would make the shirt last another four months. She threw on my sweater, then dug in her purse for a scarf. With jeans and ankle boots, she totally rocked this impromptu outfit.

That reminded me of something. "Who was Aaron talking to when I walked in?"

"You have to be a little more specific. The bar was busy."

"She-ee-ee . . ." My teeth chattered so hard I could barely speak.

"You gotta narrow that down. If you say she was white, I'm walking away. Besides me and two students from Jameson representing the Black community, you got it down. Being white and female you are at fifty percent of the people in there."

"Long brown hair, flawless skin, leather jacket, and—"

"Ohhhh, the jacket. I have been eyeing that beauty for a few days. One-Way-Talkie calls her Dougie."

"They know each other?" I had no idea why I was interested.

"I don't know how well they know each other, but I've seen them chatting. It seems like she knows Aaron. Pete seemed to know her so just guessing. she might have been local at one point, and I think One-Way-Talkie just annoys the locals. What are we going to do about your outfit?"

"I'm comfy," I said in protest.

"You look like a rag doll. Just because you have a boyfriend does not mean you need to stop dressing up when we go out. I need a better-looking wingman."

"I need a friend that does not sound like my mother. EG would like the outfit."

"EG would not let you out of the house. What do you think happened to your straw cowboy hat that"—she used air quotes—"*accidentally* got misplaced."

"What!" I laughed. "She probably put it with your purple-and-orange-checkered shoes you can't find."

"How much stuff do you think she's stashed

away? Maybe that's what happened to your brother's jeans with one too many holes in them. The pair he keeps accusing you of stealing."

We laughed as we walked with our backs to the river and hurried along the sidewalk.

Sherrie elbowed me, and I looked up. Hailey was coming down the street by herself, her head in her phone. We stepped into the street between two parked cars and waited longer than normal after cars passed in order to jaywalk to Draw Bar.

We were only two years older than Hailey, but I always found myself questioning what she was doing. It was rare to have a conversation with her without her phone in her hand. The few times I had seen her without her face plastered to her phone was when she was talking to guys in the bar.

We saw our opportunity to cross after a truck passed and blocked us from her view. We swiftly and quietly crossed the street and slipped into the bar. The heat of the indoors blasted our faces, and we took off our jackets, giggling with the excitement of escaping from Hailey.

Jim, the owner, was behind the bar and gave us a nod, and we looked for seats.

The bar was half-full with what appeared to be Jameson students.

Jim swung by our table. "Hi, ladies, Thursday night special—twenty-ounce Long Island iced teas for three dollars. Two teas, or got something else in mind?"

Sherrie and I looked at our phones to check the time, and we shook our heads.

"Got any beer specials?" I asked.

We were not in for a long night out—or at least that was our thought in the moment.

"One pitcher, three glasses?" Jim asked.

Our eyes followed Jim's, and we sighed, dropping our shoulders.

Hailey was taking a barstool from another table. She slid it up to our table.

He mouthed, *Have fun* before turning to Hailey. "I'll have the pitcher and some chilled glasses here in a minute."

"No beer for me. I will have vodka cranberry, extra lime, thanks," Hailey said, dismissing Jim. She tossed her purse on the table and looked around the room. "Another bummer of a bar. There seems to be no guys out tonight."

"Half this place is full of guys. Almost all are Jameson students? Not good enough for you?"

"You sound like Anna." She put on lipstick and scanned the room again.

"What happened to her?" I asked.

"Oh, a, um, she wasn't in the mood to be out, so we decided to call it a night. I saw you guys come in and figured I would join you for one more look around. What's the story with Aaron's brother? Is he around? Man, he is hot. You still living at his place?"

Aaron's brother, Chuck, was in the Middle East on a six-month assignment with the private pseudo-military security firm he worked for. Before he left, EG's house had caught on fire, and he let us stay in his house for three weeks since he wasn't there. The damage was minor, and once it was fixed up, we were allowed to move back in.

"We have been back at EG's for three months. I don't think he's supposed to return until after the new year. Plus, do you want to date someone who's almost thirty?" I asked, knowing if a guy was cute or rich, age didn't matter to Hailey.

Thankfully, we didn't have to hear her answer because Jim dropped off our drinks.

After pouring our beers, we clinked our glasses together and said, "Cheers."

Sherrie turned to Hailey. "Am I going to see you in the office tomorrow?"

Hailey was slow to respond. "Are you asking me?" She pointed to her chest. "I'm not working while I'm on break. I got lucky being able to come home tonight. Most of the others still have class tomorrow. I am not wasting my break working for my grandfather." Her eyes continued to scan the room, but at least now, her phone was down.

Sherrie made a pouty face. "That's too bad. I was hoping you would be there. I made a mistake yesterday. Your grandfather was *maaad*! I have never seen him act that way. He asked me to put away some files on his desk, and I guess I grabbed the wrong stack. I started to read a file so I would know what to do with them. He grabbed the papers from my hand, threw them in his desk-side drawer all crazy, with a paper still sticking out. He locked the desk and left. He was furious. I'm only telling you this because he adores you so, and it would have been a nice distraction having you there tomorrow."

Hailey snorted a laugh. "That's generous. He doesn't adore me. He *tolerates* me. Grandad thinks I have not lived up to my potential. Always poking at me to do something." She stopped scanning the room and picked up her phone.

"What do you think made him mad?" I asked.

"I screwed up. How can I explain it to you any better? Maybe you should have another drink." If she was not my best friend, her condescending tone would have been insulting instead of endearing.

"I mean, was it the fact you didn't hear the instructions correctly, or did you grab the super-secret company formula? Do you know the original recipe for Coke, or was there a map of buried treasure in the file you picked up? Give me something juicy to feed off of. My job has been

45

boring lately, so I could use something spicy."

Sherrie thought for a second before answering. "I think it was the file itself that I grabbed. From what I could tell, it was some official documents and also some handwritten notes. The papers were thick, and a few sheets had a government seal on them. Sorry, I don't have the numbers to the company safe."

My phone beeped.

Aaron: *I'm done at the bar, heading your way.*

I waved Jim over. " Can we go ahead and get our check?"

He nodded and ripped it off the pad, setting it on the middle of the table.

I didn't know how Hailey had witnessed all that with her head down, but I also hadn't known how she'd seen us come into the bar.

She looked up. "Well, that was quick. You must be going to meet Aaron if you're leaving all the beer."

"No, Aaron's coming here. Just paying the bill before he gets here because Jim usually doesn't charge him for drinks."

Sherrie had her cash out before I finished speaking. "Got anything you want to contribute, Hailey?"

Hailey looked confused. She reached out for her purse as if her arm was a fifty-pound weight. With the other hand, she put the phone down and took a drink.

Sherrie gestured for us to put away our wallets. "I got this. It's a five-dollar pitcher; I can handle it *and* the cocktail. People were paying and tipping in cash tonight, and I hate carrying around piles of singles. My treat."

"I still owe you for pizza," I said.

"But you had the Chinese, but more so, I owe you because I finished the ice cream sandwiches you bought."

"That's hurtful! Yeah, you can pay my half. I was soooo saving the last one after my next long run."

Well, now I don't feel so guilty about scheming to get her and Pete out on a date, I thought.

Sherrie grabbed the check and walked to the bar to pay.

I could generally work up a conversation with almost anyone, but I was having a hard time finding something to say to Hailey that was not condescending or accusatory. The two years between us felt like a generation gap.

"So, what are your plans for the week?" I finally asked after a few miserable seconds.

"Relax. I wanna watch the show with the guy from my school."

She seemed to assume I knew what she was talking about, and I didn't care enough to ask, so I tried a different topic. "Where are you spending

Thanksgiving? Parents? Grandpa Harold?"

Sherrie returned from paying the bill in time to hear Hailey's answer.

"Not with my dad. He's in Milwaukee with his other family."

In September, when Sherrie started working at C&C, EG had schooled us some on the family history. Some folks called it gossip, but with EG, it sounds like town history.

Hailey's father, Jonathan, had supposedly wanted to leave River Bend and have nothing to do with the company that bore his name. He'd attended Jameson College and worked for his father for a few years, and everyone had assumed he was the heir apparent. Then Jonathan and Harold had a big blowout.

Hailey's mother, Jessa, was from a struggling farming family. She'd met Jonathan at eighteen when she started working in the office for Harold. Jessa hadn't wanted to leave town, so Jonathan left without her. She wanted to be the grand dame of River Bend. She tried using her married-but-divorced name like currency in the town. Everyone was surprised Harold put up with her. She barely worked yet lived comfortably with Jonathan's alimony and child support, and Harold supposedly owned the home where they lived.

Trying to fill in the gaps in Hailey's answer and preventing her from throwing herself into my business, I tried answering for her. "So holiday dinner with your mom and grandpa."

"Every year, we go to the club for dinner with Nana," she said as if I should have known her schedule.

"Nana? Is that your mom's mom? Harold is a widower, correct?"

"Nana is my great-grandmother. Widow of the old bastard Alvin. We don't see my mom's family much these days. So we'll be at the club."

"Maybe not this year," Sherrie volunteered. "This afternoon as Harold was leaving, he asked if I could cancel the reservation but then came back and said to keep it and then left at two p.m. and did not return. Later, I saw him walking on Sixth Street and . . ."

Hailey's eyes focused on us for the first time at the table. She lowered her phone. "You mean Sixth Street, like around the corner? Near Wilson Avenue?" She gulped the rest of her cocktail down and stood, looking at Sherrie for more information.

"I guess it was just past the root beer stand. I remember thinking I need to do inventory there."

"Now? Isn't it closed for the season?" I asked.

"It closed after Labor Day but will open for the Winterfest weekend, selling coffee, hot chocolate, and stuff." Sherrie turned to Hailey. "Will you be here for Winterfest?"

Hailey adjusted her ponytail again and grabbed her purse before realizing the question was directed at her. "Winterfest, god, no. I was Snowball Queen, like, um, five years ago. I don't need to do that again. I'll see you guys later."

She was gone in a flash. I was relieved to be devoid of her company and was delighted Aaron was on his way.

Sherrie scanned the bar. "Hailey was right. There are no decent guys here." She drank some more and refilled our glasses. "I think I'm going to find that file."

My phone beeped with a message.

Kay: *In for Thanksgiving if it's Sunday.*

"What file?" Had I zoned out and missed part of Sherrie's story? I was doing Thanksgiving math in my head, the beer making my calculations foggy.

"The file Harold locked away in the desk. I am *so* curious!"

"You think it's a good idea snooping in the boss's office?"

"Hell no!" said a voice behind me, followed by a kiss on the cheek. "But I'm an open book. What do you want to know?" Aaron asked.

"Not talking about you." She lowered her voice. "I mean head honcho Harold Carlin's desk. What could Harold be hiding? It has to be something good to get him that worked up."

Aaron answered quickly. "I'm getting myself a drink and staying out of your schemes." He looked at me. "All of them."

I just smiled back.

"Do you guys need something while I'm at the bar?"

We declined his offer, and as Aaron walked to the bar, he surveyed the bar area not unlike Hailey when scoping out the place for single men.

Is he looking for someone?

He went to talk to Jim, and Sherrie and I continued drinking our beers.

"Do you think it is a good idea to snoop?" I asked again.

We never reached a conclusion to the aforementioned question that periodically popped back up into our conversation throughout the evening.

On Friday, I did conclude all that beer had been a bad idea.

Sherrie realized later it had *all* been a bad idea.

Guest Count: 12 (plus Jorge) Kay on hold for Sunday

CHAPTER SEVEN

The morning light was barely breaking in around the window shade. The quilted comforter was snug around my neck, and the only sound came from the hum of the fan and the wind whipping outside.

We hadn't stayed out late Thursday, but my head was swimming and looking for something to stabilize it. Alcohol aside, it was just too much liquid. The space next to me was empty, but I could see the outline of where Aaron had slept or where he'd tried to sleep. He had tossed and turned all night, causing my beer-induced sleep to be even more restless.

I got up and grabbed a pair of socks. I hate cold feet.

My phone beeped.

Jenna: *Leaving Saturday and won't make Thanksgiving unless it's the Friday after the holiday.*

After a stop in the bathroom, I headed downstairs. Before I reached the bottom step, I smelled coffee and practically tasted the bacon I heard frying.

Sherrie, already dressed for work, was at the stove managing bacon and eggs. Rita, Aaron's golden retriever, was lying by his feet while he sat at the kitchen island with his head in the sports section of the newspaper.

EG was the only person I knew under the age of fifty that still got the paper delivered. She preferred it to reading the news on her iPad. She also listened to the morning news on a radio with a metal antenna—the only antique in the house.

With a flick of the spatula in her hand, Sherrie directed me to the toaster and put me to work. Aaron got up and poured me coffee and brought it over to my workstation. Stirring eggs with one hand, Sherrie used the other to scroll through her music and decided we should start our day with workout jam music. I quickly objected to the volume.

"What's with the dance club music this morning?" My eyes were barely open, my tongue was like sandpaper, and my lips were cracked. I tossed several slices of toast on a plate and put two more in the toaster.

"I just wanted something playing before you start mumbling some rock ballad from the eighties," Sherrie said.

Aaron laughed and raised his hand in the air, waiting for a high five from Sherrie. "Amen."

"You know you were about to bust out some tune. I thought I would spare us," Sherrie said.

"Whatever" was the only reply I had at seven in the morning. "Can you at least turn it down?"

I grabbed dishes and silverware while Aaron made room on the island for the pan of bacon. Sherrie scooped eggs onto the plates, and we all took a seat around the island. Thankfully, she turned off the music. I let the coffee quickly recharge my batteries, and I was coming into the morning.

We ate in silence. A few minutes later, the food changed my morning beer-fogged head back to normal.

Aaron cleared his throat and looked at Sherrie. They both had shit-eating grins on their faces.

"Want to tell me what's so funny?" I asked.

"You don't even know you do it? You were singing John Denver." Sherrie got up and put her stuff in the dishwasher.

I wanted to give her the middle finger, but I

took the high road. "I'll clean up since you cooked."

"Thanks," she said. Singing, she walked out of the kitchen and up the stairs.

Aaron looked at me over his coffee mug. "What are you smiling about?"

"Did you hear her just now? She was full-on singing with me and country legend John Denver. Country music from the seventies is not in her wheelhouse, so that means she has been listening to it at work."

At this point in our relationship, Aaron could follow my train of thought. "If you are connecting this back to Pete, you are crazy. Again, all I have to say is leave me out of it and don't rock the ship at my bar."

"Aye, aye, Captain." I gave him a mock salute and walked over for a kiss.

"OMG!" Sherrie bellowed from behind us. "It is too early in the morning to watch that. The kitchen is supposed to be a safe space for single ladies like me."

"I am not apologizing for anything," I said.

Aaron was still seated, and I was standing next to him, my arms wrapped around his shoulders, his right arm around my waist. The sunlight was streaming through the window and warming my back.

"That was a quick trip upstairs. Why are you up and ready so early? You can't go anywhere yet.

Aaron parked behind you last night when he brought us back in my car. Give me a minute to throw some sweats on so I can move it," I said.

"I moved it already," Aaron said.

Again, he was one of the good guys. I gave him a squeeze to show my appreciation.

"I could use a ride since I'm assuming Morning Glory here still needs to shower," he said.

"Ugh, the ick!" Sherrie cried. "Morning Glory? Now I have to listen to pet names you guys have for each other?"

I answered quickly. "No pet name. Just a not-so-subtle hint I need to brush my teeth and probably my hair."

"Cool." One-word answers meant Sherrie had accepted what you said and was ready to move on.

Aaron stood up, stretched his good arm out, and took one more sip of coffee. "I gotta get to Peach's and help Jan. She's having trouble with one of her ovens." He kissed my cheek, then looked like he wanted to say something but changed his mind and went to put on his shoes.

"You do electric work?" Sherrie asked him.

"Hell no! That is way above my pay grade. She just wants someone to look at it before she has to call a professional in case it's something obvious. Can I catch a ride?"

"Of course. Give me a half a minute." Sherrie

slid across the kitchen in her socks and poured coffee in a to-go mug.

"Why are you leaving so early?" I asked her.

"Gotta lot to do at work today," Sherrie said with a slight squeak in her voice.

Last night, we had discussed the pros and cons of her trying to sneak a peek at that file. While we thought it would be fun to know, it was not worth the risk. She thought about telling him she had seen the contents of the file before he'd pulled it away and then get him to talk about it. She didn't know how to start that conversation. Sherrie valued her integrity and work ethic, but she always loved a good story and was curious by nature.

We—or Aaron—had concluded that whatever was in the file was probably best left between Harold and the file cabinet.

I went upstairs to shower and couldn't help wondering if Sherrie would let the file rest in peace. *RIP.*

That was funny in the moment but not so funny later.

Guest Count: 11 (plus Jorge) Kay on hold for Sunday

CHAPTER EIGHT

My plan was coming together. When I got done with work, I went for a quick run because I wanted to save my energy for the following morning. That would be my last chance for a long run outdoors. I finished my three miles two blocks short of the house. I took time to notice the last of the fall leaves tumbling across the ground.

Jorge pulled into his driveway next to EG's house, and he and his girlfriend, Addie, got out of the car. She shouted a hello, and Jorge gave me a partial wave and a mini wave under his chin and mouthed *No Thanksgiving*.

Jorge, in his midthirties, would make any woman a terrific husband. They had been dating about five months, but I thought the end might have been near. Had he been trying to tell me not to bring up Thanksgiving in front of her?

Something's not right with them.

Addie, a visiting professor at Jameson College, is leaving at the end of the spring term. I wondered if that had something to do with the gag order on Thanksgiving.

I nearly tripped on the sidewalk as I compared their relationship to mine and Aaron's.

Is that why I don't want our families spending the holiday together? Because I'm hopefully being promoted out of this town where Aaron lives and works?

I caught myself before I face-planted in front of them but not before I jammed my toe, flapping my arms to steady myself. I said a quick goodnight to them before dashing into EG's house.

"My god, woman. Do you have to slam the door?" Sherrie howled. She was half sitting and half lying on the couch with her feet up on pillows eating Hun's special number nine, watching a National Geographic special about national parks.

"What are you doing home? I thought you had another double shift." I kicked off my running shoes and went to the kitchen. I made a peanut butter and jelly sandwich.

"I had a crap morning at C&C. Then when Pete and I started at three, from the moment we walked in together, he was in a mood. When he wasn't throwing stuff around, he was mumbling *salad shit* or *shit salad*. The wording changed every twenty minutes. When I tried to lighten the mood, he just got more annoyed. When Jacob called looking for a shift, I offered the rest of mine. With my classes and working fifty hours between C&C and BAR, I figured I would take a night off instead of dealing with Pete. I did leave one-up on Pete."

"One-up? What do you mean?" I asked.

"It was my turn to buy dinner, and instead of ordering our standard Friday-night burgers from Bumbles, I ordered from Hun's. Noodles for Aaron, number nine for me, and a salad for Pete. Thankfully, Jacob showed up when the delivery did, because Pete did not find it humorous. Aaron laughed and even offered to pay, despite it being my turn. How can a salad piss off someone so badly that is all they can talk about? I understand pissing and moaning about a significant other, a boss, or even a football team, but a salad? I am happy not to be there listening to him all night."

"You do know it probably wasn't a salad that upset him," I said wisely and sat at the dining table between the kitchen and living room.

November brought darkness early. One lamp and light from the TV cast a soft light into the living room, contrasting Sherrie's mood.

"No shit, genius, but why curse the salad?" Sherrie wiped sauce off her face and slurped up some rice noodles.

"Crack the window behind you. I'd rather be

cold than smell that all week. What happened at C&C that made it a crap day for you?"

Sherrie straightened herself up and balanced the Styrofoam container on her lap while reaching for the window with the other hand.

Initially, it was fun watching this spectacle. However, fear of Hun's number nine sauce cascading down her leg into the sofa fibers made me stop her acrobatics.

"Hold your dinner and sit back down. I will get the window. Now tell me about your morning."

"Harold was in before me. In the office with the door locked. Before you ask, I had no intention of sneaking a look at the file. I was sitting at Eva's desk, completing the weekly reports and answering the phones. Because of the upcoming holiday week, some of the other offices and buildings are closed, so they transferred all the phones to Eva's line. I am pretty well versed in everything for the billboard company and some warehouses, but I guess I made a mistake."

Sherrie paused. She never paused— especially when telling a story. This was no pause for dramatic effect. She seemed a little unnerved but was still munching on her rice noodles. "I thought business is business. Now, I'm stuck working tomorrow and maybe Sunday."

"I thought you just said everything is closed for the holiday week. What do you have to do?"

"I guess not everything can close. Harold was so mad. I tried asking what I did wrong so I could learn. I don't know if I broke protocol or some type of code violation. He was practically shaking after I told him about the call. But all business is good business, right?

"He pushed me out of his office. Five minutes later, he comes out and tells me I have to work tomorrow and Sunday and that I have to meet him in hour so I can fix what I just did. I hate making mistakes at work like most everyone, but I am not sure what I did was wrong. I just have to do some . . ." She paused and, again, seemed lost for words. "Some work shit."

"But at least it's not salad shit." I got a fragment of a smile from her and took that as my opportunity to invite her to the pancake breakfast and got an easy yes, but she threw a twist at me.

"Leather Jacket Woman showed up looking for Harold, but he and nearly everyone else was gone. I was in no mood to answer her questions. Neither was One-Way-Talkie when she showed up at the bar. They are equally matched on the annoying scale, and he even seemed annoyed by her presence. Back at C&C, she tried getting all up in my business but was not in the mood to chitchat. When I was getting in my car a half hour later, she pulled back into the empty parking lot and got out with a bag of treats from Peach's and a coffee. She held them out for me and said, 'Peace offering.' "

"You take them?"

"Absolutely not."

"The woman might be crazy, but those treats were from Peach's."

"That woman did not have a speck of powdered sugar on her. Can't trust her or what's in that bag if she comes out of that café clean."

"Amen to that." I left Sherrie to her Hun's and showered. I fed Wilbur a fresh supply of clothes and a new mascara. I rethought my wardrobe and threw in my hundred-thirty-seven-dollar sweatshirt that matched my eyes.

Aaron would be at the bar until around two in the morning, but I didn't want to be home for Sherrie to start asking questions about the pancake breakfast so I headed to the loft and kept Rita company. I was good at coming up with schemes, but sometimes, I had trouble pulling them off because I usually confessed everything.

Saturday morning, my hands were wrapped around a hot cup of coffee, and I was perched on the window seat. Aaron lay on the sofa where he'd slept. He had tossed and turned so much, he eventually moved to the sofa so I could get some rest.

He was refusing to get up because he believed if he was up, he would be named an accomplice to my matchmaking scheme.

That was the most I had gotten out of him between last night and this morning. He'd said few words last night and fewer this morning. He had even let his phone go to voicemail when his brother called earlier.

Chuck was working somewhere in the Middle East and was to return in a month or two. They usually talked weekly even while he was on assignment, but Aaron avoided the call this morning.

I asked if I should answer it for him, and he shook his head and rambled something about it being too early and that Chuck was just calling to wake us up. My reply of "But we are up" went unanswered.

The loft had giant windows overlooking Main Street, with a narrow view of the river, the edge of the Jameson campus, and most importantly, the sidewalk below. I finished some oatmeal and my running shoes were on, so I was ready to go after conducting the last step of my plan.

Another morning of gray skies and fierce winds. The wind rattled the old rooftop antennas.

At seven thirty, I texted Pete that it would be Sherrie instead of me. At seven fifty-five, he was five minutes early and stood waiting on the sidewalk below the window. That was impressive since he'd worked until 2 a.m.

Right at eight, Sherrie rounded the corner. Her head moved to the music in her earphones, her hands in her pockets. I nearly spilled my coffee because I was so giddy to be so close to pulling this off.

As soon as I saw her, I pushed send on the pretyped text explaining Pete was going to breakfast with her. It was too late for her to back out.

She pulled out her earphones, glanced at her phone, and looked up at the loft windows. I didn't know if she could see me or not, but she put a big smile on her face as she walked up to Pete.

They turned back in the direction Sherrie had come to head to the church, quickly falling into step together. Sherrie raised her hand behind Pete's back and gave me the finger. I expected nothing less from her. Only from Sherrie did I not find it offensive. It was confirmation she had fallen for my plan and was irritated she hadn't seen it coming.

It was cold, only forty-five degrees out, but I needed to smooth out my nervous energy from setting up Sherrie and Pete and stay on track with my marathon training schedule. The ground was clear of ice, but the wind whipped my face, regardless of the direction I ran. The first mile, every raw degree tingled down my body.

Running in the cold gave me the sniffles, and my nose produced more snot than the average cold.

At some point, I had to use my shirt as a tissue. *Classy* was never a word I used when I thought about me running.

Only one other person passed me while I ran, looking like a cover model for a fitness magazine. Sweat glistened on her face. The long brown ponytail bounced in sync with her steps.

All I wanted to do was trip her, but before I could contemplate doing it, she stopped in the parking lot to stretch. When I circled back, she was getting into a rather mundane-looking car for someone who had color-coordinated tennis shoes, running pants, windbreaker, and headband. Granted, it was all black and white, but it was too coordinated for a morning run in crappy weather.

My morning run eventually became enjoyable, and I found my rhythm as I deleted thoughts of others. I was on mile eight of ten when my phone went crazy with messages. The phone beeped over the music in my earphones, but I did not want to stop. I had my groove going and couldn't risk stopping short of my goal.

Right on cue, I finished my ten miles three blocks from the house. I used the three blocks to cool off and read the seven messages from the Thanksgiving group about the shift in the weather hitting sooner rather than later.

Dinner would have to be moved to tomorrow, and I hoped everyone could make it in.

My head swirled with the guest count and my sudden to-do list. I had to recalculate who could make the Sunday Thanksgiving meal, and in order to stop a headache from forming, I counted everyone. It would be like an open house with people coming and going all day.

I sent the text declaring Sunday to be the day, and I was so caught up in the sudden shift of date, I accidentally included the neighbors behind EG — the O'Brien's — in the group text. We would be fine on food but short on space if they showed, but that would be a problem for tomorrow.

I was enjoying the cooldown from a great run, navigating the sidewalk with my head in my phone, coordinating the holiday feast while still giddy about my scheme working. The day was starting out great.

I stepped into the screened-in porch and was immediately shielded from the wind. I thought about collapsing on the couch but realized the cold would hit me after the runner's high left my body.

Our days of sleeping on the porch were officially over for the season. I made a mental note to put the storm windows on and covers on the furniture.

I pulled open the front door and walked into the living room. A throw pillow grazed my nose as it went flying past.

Without looking at Sherrie, I bent down to

pick up the pillow. "How long have you been sitting here waiting for me?"

"Not long. After the pancake breakfast, I stopped at the grocery store for my contribution to Thanksgiving dinner. I got home a few minutes ago, and I saw you with your head in your phone as I pulled in the driveway. Just so you know, I'll say nothing more about the stunt you just pulled."

"Good to hear that. Did Pete think it was a setup?" I threw the pillow on the couch, pulled off my running shoes, tossed them back on the porch before I walked into the kitchen.

Sherrie followed behind me and unpacked the groceries, ignoring the Pete question. While I brewed coffee for us, I pulled out some leftover cheesy potatoes. Some call them funeral potatoes because people always bring them after a funeral. The gooey warm dish is the best thing after a long run in the damp, cold air.

"Are you seriously going to have that for breakfast?" Sherrie asked.

"I had oatmeal earlier. Running makes me hungry. I earned these cheesy potatoes; every bite is a mile I ran." My mouth watered as the potatoes spun around in the microwave. "So, how was the breakfast?"

"All right, I guess. Although the more I think about it, it was a kinda bizarre world." She took the mug of coffee I passed her and leaned back. "First,

Pete was still in the same sour mood as last night. He was his usual polite self at first as we walked there, but then he was sort of a lump. But at least I only heard 'salad shit' once. When I asked what his problem was, he just kept saying, 'All we made was a salad. A *salad*. A *fucking salad*, I waited for a salad.' Like I'm supposed to know what that means. Same shit as last night.

"Anyway, that's the Pete saga from this morning. Then, there is the Holton portion of the story. He was there, surprisingly not in his cop uniform, and got all weird when he noticed I was there with Pete. Before we got in line for food, we went over to say hello. Pete actually stepped up at this moment and told him we were there representing the bar, then he went to get us some coffee.

"Most guys don't catch on to stuff like that, so kudos to him for being aware that I could still be interested in Holton. It would have probably looked tacky for Pete and me to walk into breakfast together like that if Holton and I had been dating. Hailey Carlin was there, giving us a strange look. I asked Holton what's up with her, but he talked in circles. From what I could gather, he brought her to the pancake social. For a cop, the dude lost all ability to remain steady under pressure. Normally, I would have let him squirm, but I was not in the mood, especially after dealing with Pete. I told him we were never really dating, and he could be with whoever. I have a feeling he's going to audition all the single ladies of River Bend until he finds one to fit his predesigned wife prototype."

I shoveled potatoes into my mouth. "I hope, for his sake, he gets better at juggling all his dates. This is a pretty small town. If you had any genuine interest in the guy, I could not imagine how it would have gone done between you and Hailey."

"No problems there; if I'm at the beginning of a relationship with a guy I'm dating, and we have no commitment to each other, he is free to do what he wants. That's the point of dating. If we're in a relationship and I find out he's cheating, I think I could make a clean break. I would be mad at not having seen the guy as the fool he is, but also I'd feel lucky to catch it in time, hopefully if I'm not too deep in the relationship. Isn't that the point of dating—learning?"

"Fair point. How was Hailey when you left? I don't think she has such a mature look on things as you do."

"Fine—she avoided Pete and me the whole time. We grabbed our pancakes and sausage and sat with Richard and Emma. They were going back and forth about what's safest for you to run on at campus next week—trails or pavement. To be honest, I kinda tuned them out when I realized I couldn't take my bike on any of the routes.

Anyway, I overheard all the old ladies talking about some guy that died. I tuned them out too until they started taking bets on whether the old guy would come home to be buried, and I got in on the action."

"You're betting on the dead?" I asked but not in complete disbelief.

"I've got five dollars in the pot. You pick a side—does Pigeon come back home to be buried, or does he stay away? If you're in for the guy coming back and he does, your name will be put in a bowl with the others, and Sangria Sara will draw names after the burial in the town square. There is a three-week deadline for the burial. All those that bet against Pigeon returning will meet three weeks from now in the town square for their drawing with Singing Cynthia. By the way, Kay was there with Sangria and Sing from Chambray. She wanted to make sure you knew her availability for Thanksgiving. I hope you know when she can make it; I sorta tuned her out too. You know she doesn't gamble. She wouldn't throw money on the Pigeon bet."

"That's kind of an unfortunate name. You know nothing about the man—why did you side with him coming back to River Bend? How big is the pot?"

"Pigeon is a nickname. I guess the old man was small, not too many people liked him, almost seemed scared of him when they spoke about him, like he could be listening, so they whispered the whole conversation. I bet for him returning because of the nickname Pigeon. Homing pigeons always return no matter how long they've been gone. Last count was eighty-five dollars. I walked away when One-Way-Talkie started schmoozing with the ladies."

I pulled the turkey from the refrigerator and put it in the sink, hoping it thawed by tomorrow morning. I couldn't help thinking if I would rather be a turkey or a pigeon. As a turkey, you know your destiny. Pigeons live longer; however, nobody likes them, and few people understand them.

Sherrie was still talking when I bounced back in to the conversation. She'd have to forgive me since she'd tuned out so many people this morning.

"You wear jeans, sweats, or polyester pants if you are over seventy-five like most people there. You do not wear cute workout clothes. At least she didn't have on the bomber jacket and left fairly quickly."

I didn't think I needed to reply so I let her ramble.

OMG, she is really rambling. She spent the morning with Pete and now, talking nonstop. My plan, my plan, my plan is working.

A few minutes later, we headed to our

rooms to get ready for the day. We were halfway up the stairs when I started stomping twice on each step.

"What are you doing?" Sherrie asked.

"It used to drive me nuts hearing the creaking or having to tiptoe up those two squeaky stairs at night so I wouldn't wake you. Now with the new boards in place, I kinda miss it," I said, referring to the stairs being fixed after the small electrical fire we had in August.

Sherrie bounced with me on each step as she went up. "I know what you mean. It was a little bit of security—like no one could sneak up here."

"It was our alarm system. Now, we may have to start locking doors."

We stood in the hallway. I looked into Sherrie's room, which she had painted just before the fire and again as soon as the repairs were done. I walked into my room, which had new drywall on one wall and rock posters on the other three, making me feel I was in a time warp. My mother and EG had hung them to reflect my childhood room in St. Paul.

I took down the posters and moved the furniture around, deciding to paint and organize my clothes when I had some time off. I had been in River Bend for five months with plans for another ten.

It's time to get rid of the suitcase on the floor.

Maybe I'll even shop for some new bedding I can take with me when I leave, start investing in things for my next apartment.

Texts about our holiday dinner kept rolling in.

Jenna: *What should I bring? You are not allowed to say nothing. I will bring something anyway, so you might as well choose something you'll hopefully enjoy.*

Me: *Bring a hot date or someone that will make us laugh.*

Jenna: *Not funny. I will bring spicy smoked sausages.*

Connor: *Do we have to do it on Sunday? Why not stick with Tuesday?*

He was angling to boycott but struggling to come up with a valid reason to keep our celebration on Tuesday. Not surprisingly, school was not his top priority.

Dad: *Sunday's great. Football will be on!*

Mom: *I'm still concerned about my gravy and your dad's cranberry sauce.*

Guest Count: 11-12 (plus Jorge), maybe the O'Briens. Don't know if Kay's schedule changed because Sherrie tuned her out.

Body Count: Soon to be one

CHAPTER NINE

It was not the ice on the roads that I should have been worried about, but the snowball I created. I had rocked out the last six hours and forty minutes at work. That evening would be crazy, as the meteorologist had predicted, and foul weather was in the forecast too.

Maddie and I were at work behind the front desk of the hotel. At seventeen, she had big brown eyes that lit up her face. She was about my height, five foot five, naturally skinny, and had the demeanor of a giddy child reading *Harry Potter*.

Nearing victory, I was giddy. We usually played a game where we bet on random stuff—

anything, really—to keep ourselves entertained and not bored. Would Roy from Maintenance radio the front desk and complain that Ronnie in Housekeeping was blocking the loading dock with the laundry delivery, or would we smell Karen's dinner first?

Karen was set to relieve me in twenty minutes. No doubt she would bring the same thing she'd been bringing for a while: Hun's number fourteen in to-go boxes that did nothing to contain the smell. Hun's food was amazing, but the leftovers could leave a smell that hung around for days.

I had earned two points by correctly guessing the mileage between the hotel's front entrance to the town square gazebo within two-tenths of a mile. I had nailed it—at least according to Maddie's phone map. I got one point for correctly guessing Allison in Housekeeping would lose her keys before noon. My last two points Maddie gave me for shoveling and throwing salt down on the front entrance. Maddie earned most of her points guessing numbers—like the final balance of someone's room bill within five dollars.

I felt good about my chances of winning. I had twenty minutes before my shift ended, and I was up six to five.

One last point and I could secure my win with a two-point lead and leave with the phone charging cord from lost and found. We didn't make a habit of taking things from lost and found—usually after three months, we donated it—but this cord was nearly ten feet long!

My money was on Roy complaining. I figured Karen would be late because of the weather, and each day her car started was a miracle.

Maddie was ready to dock my points when she heard me radio Roy to check the dumpster and to make sure the plows had full access to the parking lot. She claimed I was setting up Roy to see the backlog of trucks on the loading dock and stacking the deck. She was right on the money.

"Stop reading the newspaper. It does not look good when guests walk in," I said.

"I get that, but I'm obsessed with this story. I was hoping the local paper would have more information. The *County Gazette* has a crap online presence unless you want to know when the next pancake breakfast benefit is. It was this morning if you're interested. I couldn't find much from the Chicago online news. Aren't you curious about River Bend's mob connection?"

"Here? In this town? What, some mob guy got off the highway, got gas, and gave someone a dirty look, then kept going to someplace more interesting?"

"You haven't been in River Bend long

enough to know about this, I guess. There is a connection to the big families in Chicago, and tradition has it, he would be buried in the crypt with his family here in River Bend. Didn't you see the news about Anthony 'the Pigeon' Coletti, who died a few days ago in Chicago? He was said to be one of the old bosses." Maddie used air quotes around *bosses* and waited for me to acknowledge I knew what she was talking about.

"I haven't seen the news lately," I said.

Seventeen-year-old Maddie rolled her big brown eyes at me. Instead of her usual giddy, happy-go-lucky self, she was thoroughly ensconced in the dark underworld of the mob.

Maddie filled in the gaps of my missing River Bend history and current events. "My grandmother told me stories about the Coletti family being part of the logging industry here and then one day just shutting down the logging operation and some of the factories in town and taking off. My grandmother was bitter because her father had lost his job because of it.

"Coletti was originally from River Bend, and rumor has it, he left after a bad family argument. I'm not sure if one or two people were killed. There is very little information to be found. Supposedly, the police stayed away from the Coletti family out of both respect and fear. The rest of his family left quietly or just disappeared from the records. He disappeared from the scene in Chicago but still held some power with the new bosses running the area.

"The funeral has to be soon, but I can't find any information. One reporter said they might be keeping it a secret because some of the old family members want to pay their respects and want to keep a low profile and remain out of public life. Another theory says mob families may still be feuding and someone has a hit out on the Colettis." Maddie giggled with delight. "Can you imagine being a fly on the wall at that funeral? Maybe I should check incoming arrivals for any names associated with the Colettis."

My turn for an eye roll. "Look at you, little miss Agatha Christie, you have the who, what, where, and why all figured out. The research will have to wait—we have a guest walking in."

The front door thirty feet to our left slid open. A gentleman of about sixty stepped into the entryway, removing his cap and shaking off the snow and ice. He pushed his hair back and pounded his boots on the carpet. He came through the second set of doors and into the lobby, bringing the early winter storm with him, despite the entranceway having two sets of doors.

"Brrrr," I said, wanting to be back at the house getting ready for everyone to arrive.

The gentleman struggled to unzip his black

coat. "Hi, ladies, I am hoping you got a room for me."

Always eager to please, Maddie tossed the newspaper quickly aside and answered first. "Of course, sir. Does that mean you don't have a reservation?"

He was still grappling with his coat, but the problem seemed to be his fingers, not the zipper.

Arthritis, or something else?

"Nah, wasn't expecting to stay, but the roads are horrible. I promised Ron, my son, I would take it easy with the load. Being his business and all. I'm just helping while they escape to Florida for the holiday. Just gonna make my delivery, rest up, and hope the roads are . . . Excuse me." His right hand reached for his left arm. "I must—I must be more tired than I thought. The bad roads got me stressed."

"Well, you're here now. So you can take it easy," I said.

"Aye, not done yet. I still have to make my delivery. Just wanted to know if there was a room at the ol' inn." He put his hand on the desk, his face tightening.

Maddie and I looked at each other, and when she raised an eyebrow, I knew we were thinking the same thing but too scared to say it.

"Sir, we have room for you, but unfortunately, semitrucks are not allowed in our lot. We don't have much parking. I may have to send you across the street. I know they have rooms available. Would you like me to call and have them hold one?"

"Mighty sweet. I ain't got no big rig, just a special delivery. My son or his associate usually takes care of it, but sometimes, I help . . ." His breath was short. "Sorry, don't know what's wrong with me." He grabbed his left arm again.

"Maybe you should sit." Maddie walked around the long front desk, and her face went from a look of concern to a slight smile and back to concern.

"What is it?" I asked.

Maddie quietly said, "Wait for it." Turning towards him, she reached out and touched his arm. "Sir, come sit."

"Now listen, I have to make my delivery." His breathing was labored.

"It'll have to wait. I think you're having a heart attack."

My heart was pounding and palms sweating. I was cool with staff-scheduling crises, food delivery issues, and I could even reboot the computer system, but medical shit made me nervous.

I walked from behind the desk and stood on the other side of the man. "Listen to Maddie, sir. I'm sure the delivery can wait. I'm going to call an ambulance."

"No. I'm fine. I *have* to make the delivery. You don't understand. This can't wait."

We gently guided him to the bench near the lounge area. Over the lobby music, I heard the irregular beats of his breath.

"Girls, you are so kind, watching over an old bugger like me, but I have to do this for my son. It could jeopardize his license." The old man's eyes pleaded with me.

"It's going to have to wait. I'm going to call."

He held both his hands around my hand. "It's for my son. You are too young to have children. Even at my age, I can't help it, but it is still possible for me to let my son down."

Maddie and I smiled. Such a tender moment. *But is it going to be his last?*

I left Maddie and the man on the bench and called for an ambulance. Working as the middleman between the man and the 9-1-1 operator, I learned his name was Norm Hauge, and he was sixty-eight years old, single, and the only medicine he took each day was a multivitamin with a shot of whiskey. When I put down the phone, I finally figured out why Maddie had smiled moments before. I could smell Karen's dinner. She must have come in at some point and put her dinner in the fridge in the back office.

Maddie saw my face and knew what

happened. She mouthed, *We tied!* She went back to chatting with Norm, trying to get him to understand he was not going to make his delivery.

The man had tears in his eyes and held his left arm with the right. "Listen, please someone, please. The address is in my pocket. Promise you will make the delivery. You will see the vehicle out front." He pressed the keys into my hand.

Norm was very fortunate. The ambulance arrived less than three minutes later, and the paramedics came flying in.

"Where are you guys parked? Why are you not up front?" I asked as they were putting Norm on the gurney.

"Someone's got it blocked," one of them barked.

"That's me," Norm gasped.

They were trying to lay him down, but he was fighting it. One paramedic opened Norm's jacket, and the other paramedic tried to put an oxygen tube around his head.

Norm grasped my hand. "Promise me you'll do the delivery today."

"Of course," Maddie and I said together.

He could barely pull the paper from his pocket before the paramedic took complete control over his failing body. The paper slipped to the floor, and Maddie picked it up as they wheeled Norm out.

"I will give you two points and the win if you make the delivery," Maddie said.

"Me?" I wanted that phone cord, but I had no desire to drive in that weather. "How can we debate this? Aren't you freaked out?"

Maddie looked a little shaken and seemed to be trying to gain control. "Nah, Norm will be fine," she said, assuring me.

I wasn't sure she believed her own words.

She didn't stop there. "We got him help in time. The paramedics will do their job. C'mon, make the delivery and the victory will be yours."

"We *both* promised the old man. Let's play rock, paper, scissors to see who finishes Norm's delivery." I stuck out my fist, getting ready for the duel.

Maddie didn't raise her arm. "You took his keys and shook his hand; you have to make the delivery."

My arm still stretched out, I bounced back. "*You* made the same promise. You have seniority."

"Only by two weeks. Four months on the job for both of us, so seniority means nothing. I could say you're older, six years is a lot, especially to a seventeen-year-old like me. You have management aspirations." Maddie seemed proud of her last conclusion. She opened the folded paper that had fallen from Norm's hands as the paramedics rolled him away. Her eyes grew wide with delight. She'd found the nail in the coffin to make me the driver. "The address is 605 Wilson Avenue."

"So? I think that's a couple blocks off the town square, but I don't know it. Why does that make me the driver?" I asked, my arm still hanging in air, ready to settle this the way most arguments should be decided. "Let's do this—rock, paper, scissors."

"That address might not be yours, but . . ." Maddie approached and gave me a victorious smile.

I wanted to punch it off her face with my still-outstretched arm. Maybe not really punch her, but I wanted her confidence to go away.

Maddie open the folded paper, her eyes were wide with delight and her smile grew bigger. "You have to make the delivery. Your roommate is listed as the recipient."

"Sherrie?" I was frozen in place with my fist out.

"Yup!" Maddie stepped towards me and set the paper on my fist. "Paper covers rock!"

Sherrie? She had said they shut the warehouses down for the holiday week. Maybe that had been the problem when she answered the phone on Friday. She had agreed to the delivery, so Harold had made Sherrie be the one to sign for it.

I quickly did my shift paperwork and turned over the front desk communication radio to Karen after I made her wipe Hun's number fourteen off her hands.

At the end of each shift, I changed clothes because no matter how much I earned, skills I learned, or connections I made, nothing would ever justify that hideous uniform outside the building. At some point that summer, my sole focus at the company had become my goal of getting the uniforms changed.

I wrapped a scarf around my neck, grabbed my coat and Wilbur, and walked out of the locker room, saying a quick prayer for Norm. I was almost out the front door with Norm's keys in my hand when I realized I had forgotten my prize, the extra-long phone cord.

I went to the back office, threw Wilbur on the counter because I had to spend an extra minute washing Hun's number fourteen off the cord. Maddie yelled at me to hurry because Norm's car was causing a traffic jam on the front drive.

I was not sure what I expected to deliver to Sherrie, but it would have never occurred to me it would in Norm's minivan with a body in it.

Guest Count: 12 (plus Jorge), maybe the O'Briens
Body Count: One

CHAPTER TEN

Norm said it wasn't a semitruck, but I hadn't known what to expect. I was pleasantly surprised to see it was smaller than a cargo van yet larger than a minivan and looked like a combination of both.

Nervous energy shot through me when I looked in the rear window. I did not want to unload a ton of boxes. Dead energy flooded my body when I focused on the single item. The nearby highway noise evaporated, as did the air I was breathing.

I stumbled to the side. A lady rushing past nearly knocked me down when her rolling suitcase took out my right knee. My body felt nothing but shock standing there looking at the funny-shaped van, which I could now call a hearse.

Do I need a special license to drive this thing? What about the thing in back? What am I supposed to do?

What would Sherrie do with the delivery? Sherrie! That was my answer. I grabbed my phone from Wilbur, but my fingers were so cold, I could barely tap the number out.

When she answered, I had trouble hearing her.

"Why are you whispering?" I asked.

"I didn't realize I was." Her voice was only slightly louder.

A car beeped behind me, prompting me to step along the side of the hearse.

Sherrie continued, "What's up?"

"You need to tell me why I have your name on a Post-it with an address I don't recognize, and why the hell I am driving a damn hearse to you!"

With the deadpan voice of a PSA announcement, Sherrie said, "If you're driving, you should not be talking to me. Pull over. It's not safe."

"Stop messing with me. I am not even in the damn thing. Tell me what's going on?" I bellowed, my feet frozen in place, clutching Wilbur for warmth.

"I don't know why you have the hearse. That you have to explain. Remember when I told you I screwed up yesterday at work? Well, um that put me here at C&C Funeral Home today to receive, um, oh, you know, what's in the back of the hearse and to answer phone calls and inquiries. What is the hearse like? Is it like driving a fully loaded old-fashioned station wagon?"

"It's boring, more of a cargo van than a car." I tried taking a step forward but ended up down on the ground in a heap. "Aghhhh!" My ankle was twisted under my butt and my arm on top of Wilbur.

If it hadn't been for Wilbur, I probably would have broken my wrist. My ankle was not so lucky. Shivering, clutching my phone and the long phone cord, I rolled over and gathered everything that I'd pushed out of Wilbur when I landed on it. I couldn't figure out why everything was not fitting inside. Underneath my uniform were three newspapers. I must have grabbed Maddie's papers when I'd put down my stuff to clean the long cord. I struggled to stand up.

"Are you ok? What happened?" Sherrie whisper-shouted. "Helloooo?"

"Ice! Give me a damn minute," I shouted, brushing the ice and sleet off me as I shimmied and limped back into the hotel, clutching Wilbur. I lost politeness when I shouted for Maddie to come out from the back room.

The rolling-suitcase lady looked me up and down, rolled her eyes at my appearance, and turned her attention to Karen to proceed with her check in.

"Maddie, listen up. Get Roy out front

immediately. The weather has landed. The front drive is ice again. Have him salt and shovel up here and at the employee entrance. Both areas need constant care. I want someone out here every twenty minutes. Write all this down, ready? Call Ken from third shift, have him come in early and to be prepared to stay late if the morning crew can't make it.

"Then call Monica and get a plan together for breakfast. Figure out if we will have a full staff in the kitchen. I want a modified menu ready or a buffet-only menu based on what we have on hand. No Sunday deliveries are expected, so we should already have everything, but the staff might be limited. Look at Housekeeping staff for tomorrow. Have Josie come in early and tell the housekeepers we expect them and they better show up. Stagger the schedules if we need too to make sure there are no excuses or call-offs because of the weather. We should be fine on linen inventory, but call and double up on Monday's delivery. Catherine from Housekeeping might need help from Roy moving slip mats around. Got all that?"

Maddie put down the pen and nodded.

"No need to call Gloria. She will probably be in within the hour checking on everything. Present the list of things you're doing. You can call me with questions." I pivoted back towards Norm's vehicle, not waiting for a reply.

Gloria's pep talk a few months ago had sparked all that confidence in me.

Damn, if I can orchestrate keeping a hotel together, I should be ready to take on the next challenge.

"Hellooo" came a muffled voice from my phone.

I almost forgot Sherrie was listening. "Hiya, ok, then. I am about to get in this thing."

"Can you see it? Sherrie's voice was a mix of nerves and hushed excitement."

"Yes, I can see the van."

"No shit, I mean the body. Can you see the body? By the way, I can't make it Sunday for the feast. I gotta stay here at the funeral home all day."

"Now you're a funeral director? How many jobs can you handle?" I flipped through the six keys on the key chain and got lucky with the first one. My hands were shaking from the cold, and my legs were shaking from the unknown.

After swinging open the door, I threw Wilbur across to the passenger seat and hoisted myself up without turning around.

Sherrie whispered again, "I am only at the funeral home hopefully until Monday. Now, tell me what you see."

"The narrative will have to wait. Just be ready when I get there. I have to figure out this van."

Sherrie protested, but still in a whisper, she

said, "Don't hang up. Talk to me."

"Have you been at the funeral home since I left you this morning? Are you by yourself?" A little giggle came out of me. "Are you scared?" I turned the ignition switch, and the gray beast roared to life. Through the rubber on my tennis shoes, every mile this van had made over the last decade vibrated up my leg.

I pulled up the bottom of my jeans. My ankle had swelled, the pain slowly growing.

"Not scared!" Sherrie protested. "Maybe just a little weirded out. It's all the quiet."

"Let me call you back. Aaron is beeping in."
"I'll hold!"

"Whatever. I never seen you like this. Hang on."

I flipped the call to Aaron. "Hey, I can't talk long, but I got a story for you."

"Can't wait to hear it. Just checking that you're done with work. Did your car start ok?"

Talk about work ethic. My old red Ford Escort, named Debby, had several hundred thousand miles and hadn't failed me yet. The odometer and radio were nonfunctioning, but I didn't have a worry about it starting. "Oh, Debby started fine, but I will need a lift if you can get away from the bar in about twenty."

"I actually closed the bar for the weekend about an hour ago. The weather is forcing everyone around the town square to rethink their hours. Between the sleet, ice, and snow, there's no point in staying open. We are just about finished with cleaning and locking down the place."

"I'll text you the address. Oh—maybe I can get a ride with Sherrie. But I'm not sure how long she has to be there. Don't come unless I call."

"I have to head to the house to get food for Rita. I've got nothing at the loft for her. After I'm done with Molly, I'm out of here."

Even in an ice storm, Aaron was willing to help his neighbor.

"What's wrong with her? Can I help?"

"No," Aaron snapped.

"Well, that was harsh," I said.

"It's nothing. I'll explain later," Aaron said.

"Oh, ok. My parents are on their way, so no slumber party for us tonight. They are taking my room; Connor is on the couch; and I'm bunking on the couch in Sherrie's room. EG will be here late. Probably ordering pizza for dinner. Can you bring pie?"

"Are you sure they're coming? The storm is coming from the north."

"As far as I know, they're on their way. Let me take care of this delivery, and then I'll worry about the three of them."

We said our goodbyes, and I agreed to call later if he needed to pick me up.

Thirty minutes ago, my mind had been counting bodies for our Thanksgiving feast, and now I had just one body to be worried about.

Guest Count: 11 (plus Jorge), maybe the O'Briens

Body Count: One too many

CHAPTER ELEVEN

The old van had to warm up. There was no way my ankle would allow me to walk around scraping ice off the windows. The defroster was going to do all the work. I didn't want to look behind me, but I couldn't not look. I knew I would have to look before I started driving. I wanted to anticipate any noises coming from the back.

I wanted it to just be a normal ride. Dead is dead. Dead people can't do any harm. I thought about all those strange stories of dead bodies having muscle spasms or air puffing out of them. I didn't know if those were just urban legends or something to be worried about. I had been around death before at several funerals—and I had killed someone—yet I have never hung out with death before.

Dead is dead. There is nothing to be afraid of. Dead is dead.

I put my hands in front of the air vents to catch the heat. The feeling in my fingers came back quickly. I rubbed my hands on my thighs and let the jeans absorb the nervous sweat. I grabbed the steering wheel and, steeling myself in the driver's seat, slowly turned around.

As I had seen before when I'd looked in the rear window, one gurney sat in the back with what appeared to be a heavy quilted blanket. Not a grandma quilt, but something movers used to wrap furniture. I couldn't actually see the body, but my mama raised no dummy. It did not take a genius to figure out what was under that blanket. The rest of the cargo space was as plain as any new van sitting on any dealership parking lot.

A vacant space was behind the driver's seat for a second gurney. I said a silent hallelujah because that space was empty. There did not appear to be anything else of interest back there.

A black curtain behind the passenger seat was tied back. At this point, I didn't see the need in drawing the curtain closed. The dashboard was flat with a no-frills radio in the center. A double cupholder stuck out below the radio, holding a large cup with a straw and two empty candy bar wrappers. The only smell came from the food bag sitting on the floor between the seats. Minus the bag, there was nothing else between the two front seats. Actually, the entire van was clean. I just wished it were empty.

Aaron and Sherrie had always made fun of my constant singing, and I was ok with that because, most days, I'd find them singing along. I got my love of '70s, '80s, and '90s rock music from my dad. Any bar trivia night, I conquer the music category and anything to do with kid actors. I guessed my current song choice came from the band's name and not so much the song title but was still on-point for the current situation. The Grateful Dead's song "Truckin' " kept me grounded at that moment.

Sticking out from underneath Wilbur on the passenger seat was a large manila envelope with a string wrapped in a figure eight around two tabs, sealing in what I assumed were documents belonging to my passenger. None of Norm's personal items were in the van. Then again, he had not anticipated having to stay in River Bend. He had provided us his address when I called the paramedics, but the only thing I remembered was the town of Kenosha, WI, which was about a four-hour drive from here. He could have made the delivery in one day.

I didn't know what my responsibilities were here, but we'd promised Norm we would complete his delivery. But then what? I guess I would just leave the hearse at the funeral home and call the number on the envelope.

The warm air pushing through the vents was making it overly stuffy. I switched off the heat.

That can't be good for the body.

I heard a noise that I couldn't figure out, then laughed at myself. My phone was on my lap. After I'd hung up with Aaron, Sherrie was still on the line.

"Hey, can I have the heat on in the van? What is it going to do to the body in the back?" I asked her.

"How am I supposed to know that?" Sherrie whispered. "They didn't train me for any of this stuff. I'm sure it will be fine. Let me think." She was seriously taking her time thinking it over. "It's covered up, right? Or in a box? I mean, it's not just a *body*," she said, drawling the last word.

"Yes, its covered! I can't even really see the body."

"Are you sure it's a body?"

"Oh my god, I am not going to poke it!"

"Is it embalmed, like you see at a funeral, or is it . . . fresh?"

"Fresh?" I asked in disbelief. "If I had to guess, it's embalmed. I can't see Norm picking a fresh one from the side of the road or a hospital letting a *fresh* one go for a four-hour drive!"

"Don't yell at me. I had enough of Harold

yelling at me yesterday. I would think it's embalmed, so you're fine with the heat, plus you are five minutes away. Just get here!"

"Ok, don't rush me. I will see you in five."

"Wait, don't hang up! I have to ask . . ." She was almost giddy in her whispers. "Is it *wanted dead or alive*?"

"What? I don't have time for your humor. I am trying to keep my shit together, and I'm about to drive this thing."

"Just tell me, are you singing Bon Jovi's 'Wanted Dead or Alive?' "

"Not even close by a decade." I hung up and tossed my phone on Wilbur.

Seconds later, the phone beeped with an incoming text message. If there was someone around to bet with, my money would have guessed Sherrie was texting with another song title, but instead, it was Kay.

Kay: *Opting back in for Sunday Thanksgiving dinner*

A car honked behind me. I looked in the side mirror. Three cars were lined behind the van, and one other car was blocking the drive. I had no choice at this point other than to forge ahead.

Guest Count: 12 (plus Jorge), maybe the O'Briens

Body Count: One

CHAPTER TWELVE

I told myself it was like driving any other vehicle and turned the ignition key. I was comfortable enough to turn up the radio. Norm had been listening to college football. I didn't know the names of the teams, but it was comforting to hear the voices of two men talking, filling the void in the van.

It was early evening, but the storm clouds and the short daylight hours made it look like it was the middle of the night. Artificial light from the streetlamps and neon restaurant signs lit the parking lot and road.

When I turned out of the hotel parking lot, I saw Roy with a bucket of salt and assisting a guest with their luggage. If I could supervise the ice storm at the hotel, I could drive 2.33 miles to the funeral home.

My right ankle was tender but could manage the gas pedal.

Main Street from the freeway into town had been salted, and enough drivers were out there to keep the roads smooth. It was easy driving since no one was going over twenty-five miles an hour.

I drove past Aaron's bar in time to see him lock the front door. I honked, but he wouldn't have recognized the van and I doubted he could see me in the driver's seat, so he gave the courtesy wave one might give a neighbor.

Like a slow-motion movie, I witnessed Bomber-Jacket Brunette standing unnaturally close to Aaron. She seemed to be doing all the talking. She had exchanged the knee-high boots for something more practical—combat boots.

No one else was crazy enough to be out in this weather so why was Bomber-Jacket Brunette out? Out with Aaron? Was she helping Molly too? The Douglas clan was large in numbers and each one nicer then the next, so if one of them needed help many in this town would be there for them.

Need to focus and tackle one situation at a time.

I had gotten the hotel staff on track to prepare for the storm; I was fulfilling my commitment to Norm; and then I would connect with Aaron and figure out the mystery lady.

For those brief seconds, my attention had

drifted away from my cargo.

Did I just call this person cargo?

I laughed out loud when I thought that if Sherrie had been driving, she would have been having a conversation with the cargo—sorry—with the deceased.

I turned off Main onto Sixth Ave., distracted and overconfident in my driving, not anticipating how slick the side streets were.

The van fishtailed, and pain shot up from my ankle, making me slam on the brake. Fear and pain radiated through me, sweat pouring from my pits.

The van slowed. I gained control and righted the van, easing to the curb and putting it in park. I needed to make sure nothing had shifted in the rear of the van. Although I didn't know what I would have done if my passenger had moved.

In the darkness, someone on the sidewalk applauded my efforts. I didn't know if I should be flattered or give the person the middle finger. It was crazy to be driving in this weather. I couldn't figure out why someone would walk in the ice storm.

My phone beeped. I couldn't care less about who was coming to Thanksgiving and who was bringing the green bean casserole.

I pressed the brake pedal so I could shift the van back into drive, but my ankle twitched in pain.

The van and I were idle until I jumped out of my seat.

Someone knocked on the passenger window, startling me. It surprised me to see Pete standing there. He was the person on the sidewalk moments ago, appraising my driving skills.

I hadn't realized my death grip on the steering wheel until I went to roll down the passenger-side window and found my fingers molded in a curl. I was so flustered, I couldn't figure out how to open the windows or unlock the door. I propelled myself over Wilbur, stretching as far as I could until I finally reached the handle and opened the door.

"Hey, Claudia, whatya doing out here? Are you a valet driver for the hotel now?"

"Hop in, Pete. Can I drive you somewhere?" I reached for Wilbur and the paperwork when Pete was halfway in, but he took the stuff and held it on his lap.

"You think you're actually driving this van, or is the van driving you?"

"I guess the side streets haven't seen the salt trucks yet. Plus, my ankle is tender to the touch."

"How far do you have to go?" he asked.

"Just a few blocks. I can drop you off at home first," I said. "You can put that stuff behind you."

"I don't mind holding it. Are you sure you

can give me a ride? I don't want you late or get you in trouble with the hotel."

"No trouble at all. Actually, this is not the hotel van, but I am making a delivery." I left a lot of information out, but it wasn't like Pete was the most-observant guy in the van. "Where do you live?"

"About a half a mile up the road. I wasn't expecting the sleet."

"You and me both. This sucks." I pressed the brake and tried shifting the van into drive. I winced in pain and let up on the pedal too soon, and the van jerked in place. "Sorry, I slipped and hurt my ankle, and each minute it seems to get worse."

Sometimes, one plan rolled into another, and things turned fun. *My plan, my plan, my Pete-and-Sherrie plan is up and running again.*

"Are you in a hurry to get home?" I asked.

"No, do you need help with something?" Pete offered.

"What if you help me with something, and then I'll drive you home?" I tried to conceal my smile.

"You already offered the ride." He looked at me, but I gave no reply so he kept going. "Of course I will help my boss's girlfriend during an ice storm."

"I would like to think you're doing it because you're a good guy, and I have never done anything to piss you off."

"Fair enough, but you'll have to put in a kind word for me."

The ice continued to peck at the windshield, but Pete turned the vents away from himself. I turned the heat down in consideration of Pete—but also for the body in the back. It seemed silly to think the heat was going to undead the dead, but how could I have known the proper way to care for a corpse?

"Does it have to do anything with your sour mood yesterday?" I asked.

"He told you that?" Pete asked.

I shook my head.

"So he told you about the case of broken pint glasses?" Pete asked.

I shook my head again.

"He told you about—"

"We could do this all day, but I'm tired of sitting here and worried someone is going to crash into us. Sherrie just said you were in a pissy mood."

"Oh. I guess I have to apologize to her too." Pete looked away from me and out his window.

"If we're going to get out of here, how about you drive so we won't have to listen to me curse like a sailor as we approach each stop sign?"

"Are you sure I can drive the hotel vehicle?" he asked.

I laughed and swung my legs to the center,

kicking Norm's fast food bag. I scooted in back, staying behind the driver's seat and away from the gurney. Pete handed me Wilbur and the folder. He tried pushing his legs between the center console and seat, but his enormous frame made it difficult. He pushed the seat back as far as it could go and got one leg over the console, and with his body half-turned, he looked in back.

"What the hell?" Pete recoiled his leg and pushed himself up against the dashboard and door, trying to put as much space between him and the surprise in the back of the van.

"Don't tell me you're scared?" I said with a measure of control meant to convey I was cool standing where I was. By standing, I meant I was half-bent over, gripping the driver's seat for support.

"Just not what I expected to see."

He waited for an explanation, but I waved my arm at him, telling him to move over to the driver's side. He opened the passenger door, slid out, and walked around the front of the van. He hopped in the driver's seat and waited for me to get settled.

"Where to, miss?"

I pointed ahead.

Pete continued, "Sit back and enjoy the ride."

"Thanks."

"I wasn't talking to you. I was talking to our passenger." Pete pointed to our cargo, relaxed as if he did this every day.

I rolled my eyes and told him to turn right in a few blocks on Wilson.

I looked at my messages.

Mom: *We're stuck, can't make it tonight. Tomorrow is questionable. Call me after your shift.*

My mom would have to wait.

I texted Sherrie, asking her where we should park. She called seconds later, and I put her on speakerphone, my finger to my mouth, telling Pete to be quiet.

"We?" she asked. "You said, 'Where should *we* park.' Are you counting the body in this conversation? Is it talking back? Don't answer that. You need help, girl. Anyway, don't turn on Wilson. The funeral home sits on the corner. There is a small parking lot off Sixth. Far corner of the building, you will see my car and a ramp that leads down. I'll be at the door."

"Ten-four," I said.

"Trucker lingo. One delivery, and you got yourself a new vocabulary. Hey, do you have the words to tell someone he was acting like an adolescent twat—"

"Can that wait? Let me concentrate."

That was close, I thought.

We passed Wilson Ave., and Pete slowed

down, approaching the lot, the right blinker ticking away. We were at a crawling pace, looking for a break in the barriers blocking the entrance to the lot.

I shrugged. "What are we supposed to do, Sherrie? There are cement barriers blocking both driveways."

"They weren't there when I arrived this afternoon."

"Cool! So does that mean we drive through them?" I asked.

"Don't give me that tone. Let me think." The sound of her shoes squeaking came from the speaker.

Without seeing her, I knew she had one knee locked straight and the other leg swinging front to back like a broken wooden nutcracker.

She bounced on her toes when she was giddy and flirty; rotated like a wobbly ballerina when conspiring; looked like a frozen statue while doing mental math and puzzle-solving; and stood like a nutcracker when pondering high-stake situations.

"Swing back around to the front drive. We'll have to move fast," she said.

"Well, we're not lollygagging around in this weather."

"No shit, I just mean the car cannot be seen. Stop saying *we*. It's freaking me out." Her voice was still a whisper.

"Over and out." I giggled and hung up.

Pete circled the van around the block, driving slower than a grandpa on a Sunday drive.

"I know the roads are bad, but can you do over four miles an hour?"

"Sorry, every time I go by, I can't help but look at these big historical stone houses. The different styles fascinate me, and each time I walk by, I see something new. In this six- or eight-block area, some were built of old money made from logging before River Bend was incorporated. The single-story, early modern–looking homes are by Frank Lloyd Wright. It's usually too dark to see much on the way home after the bar closes."

"Not to mention it would be two a.m.? Do you always walk?" I asked.

"Whenever I can. It clears my head when I'm stressed." He stopped the van. "Look over at that house."

The windshield wipers removed the sleet from the front windows. Across the street was a beige ranch-style brick house with a flat roof and long windows. The shades were drawn.

"Now that you said Frank Lloyd Wright, I can see the style in the long lines. The house looks a little dreary with the curtains closed."

"It's unfortunate for them that it's probably a Wright house because that puts them on the official list of historic houses. It comes with lots of restrictions on what they can do to the house. Those could be original windows, which means they are old, and the weather is beating through them. That family probably has not seen sunlight in the living room in years."

We sat in comfortable silence, listening to the rain pelt the van.

Pete put the car into drive. "Sorry if I was rambling."

"Don't worry about it. The longer I live here, the more I realize I know very little about this town, which I am really growing to like."

"City girl are you?" Pete asked.

"I thought I was."

He didn't press for details.

I took a moment and looked around. "I like the big front porches and the garages hidden in back. Like that one over there." I pointed.

"These days no big porches—instead, patios hidden in the back and garages that must be attached to the house. My father was an architect and passed on all sorts of information to us kids."

"I might take you up on a tour on a day when the wind won't blow us into the river. We should probably speed it up; otherwise, Sherrie will send out the national guard to find us."

Pete made two more right turns, and the funeral home came up on our right. It was a beautiful large two-story red-stone home. The large circular drive encompassed a grassy area and a koi pond. The only thing that retained any color in November were stunted evergreen bushes on either side of a beige wood sign with large black letters outlined in gold that read C&C Funeral Home with Serving River Bend Families for Over Fifty Years in smaller letters below.

The top of the drive was under a canopy that stretched from the grassy area over the driveway to the porch and the large double doors to the funeral home. To the right of the stairs was an ADA ramp that must have been added some time in the last two decades as its function did not match the style and age of the old historic home. I didn't care how it looked, I was happy I would not have to lift the gurney up the stairs.

Sherrie was nowhere to be seen.

"Where is she?" Pete asked.

I rolled down the window and hoisted myself on the armrest to look for her. Still no sight of her. Pounding noises were coming from somewhere from or close to the building.

I retreated quickly back inside and, opening the heat vents, called her. "Where are you?"

"Claud, help. I am f'ing locked inside. I can't get the front door open. The knobs are turning and I hear clicking, but the damn door won't open." There was no panic, just anger in her whispered grunts.

"There's a chain and padlock on the door," Pete said.

Sherrie's voice rose above a whisper, seemingly taking her out of her agitated state. "Who's that?"

"I picked up a hitchhiker." I smiled and held a finger to my lips.

"Really? You're throwing out jokes when I am locked inside a funeral home?"

I didn't know why I found that funny.

"I am currently stuck in a closet of a van with the body, so let's not play who has it worse!"

"Whatever. You still didn't tell me who's with you. I thought the driver, what's his name, Norm, went to the hospital."

"A hitchhiker, I told you. Now let's figure out how to get the body to you, ok?"

"How about we figure out how to get the front doors open and that van out of here? I have strict rules from Harold: Receive the body. Tell no one. Put up signs on all doors and make sure that van is not seen on the property. Any inquires for—"

"I don't care about the rules. Can we just get this over with? I made a promise to a potentially dying man that, at the time, I did not know involved a body. If you keep talking, there will be a second body." I rubbed my hands together in front of the vents, then pounded my fists on the dashboard. I forced myself back into the get-shit-done mode from the hotel. "Go out the door you went in when you got here—I'm assuming by the ramp. We will pull the gurney out and roll it across the lawn on the right and around the building. If we can't bring the van to you, we'll just bring the body. Be at the open door so we're not out here longer than we need to be."

"If you could see me right now, I would salute you," Sherrie said.

"Respecting the boss," Pete commented.

Before Sherrie could respond, I said, "Not at all. When I give Sherrie directions, she gives me a mix of a traditional salute and a one-finger wave."

My phone started ringing, and it was Sherrie trying to turn the call into a FaceTime call. I declined.

"We don't need a demo of the Sherrie-gives-Claudia-the-middle-finger salute. I'm hanging up now. See you in a few."

Pete opened the driver's-side door and looked at me. "Let's do this, boss."

I opened the passenger-side door but stayed seated. "Boss? I don't need you mocking me. We got Sherrie for that."

Pete had opened his door and had one leg out. I could tell he stopped moving, so I turned back and looked him in the eye as he spoke.

"That was *respect*. All respect. You are driving a body around in a storm because of a handshake, with a bum foot, and the fact you are steady under pressure and not freaking out about your friend being locked inside a funeral home—it was all respect for you."

"Oh." I recoiled in my seat. "Sorry for the snap. I guess I'm on edge a bit, but if you are calling me boss, I say let's do this shit and get it over with." I grabbed the envelope Norm had left behind and slid out of the van seat too quickly. My right foot hit the payment, and my yelp reached the sky.

"You ok over there?" Pete slammed the door and walked around the front of the van to my side.

"I should be fine. Just need to put some ice on it, and it'll be as good as new." I used the side of the van for support as I went to the back of the van.

Smiling, Pete walked slowly next to me, ready to catch me if I should go down again.

"Why are you smiling?" I said.

"I thought you made a joke."

I stopped wobbling and stood there, the sleet pelting my face.

Pete understood he had to explain. "Ice. Just need ice on your foot? Ice caused the problem, and currently, you have your foot on an inch of ice, and if we keep standing here, we will both be covered in ice. I guess I'm the only one with a sense of humor, boss."

I could see why Sherrie was falling for Pete. He put his right arm out for me to hang on to. I held onto the envelope and Pete with my left hand and kept my right hand on the van. We made our way to the back.

"Maybe you should stay in the van, and I will take the gurney around back," he said.

There was no way I was going to miss seeing Sherrie's face when she saw Pete on the other end of the dead body. "I'll come with you. It will be too hard to navigate this thing by yourself on the icy driveway and the grass. Plus, I can use the gurney as a cane."

Pete didn't put up a fight. He opened the rear double doors, and we stepped as close to the bumper as we could. We used the doors as protection from the wind while we figured out how to release the gurney.

We stood with our hands on our hips, surveying the van. It was dark out, and the only light was coming from a single bulb near the front. I was looking for a big red sign with an arrow that read Gurney Release, but no such luck. Pete touched the blue quilted blanket and the bed of the gurney, and I gasped.

"Be cool, would you!" He shook it a little. "I'm trying to figure out the release points. Let's just figure this out, and get on with it."

I nodded and leaned in. "Look, there's a

metal lever. Shift it and see if it releases the wheel lock."

Pete didn't move.

"Seriously, now you're hesitating when your left hand is resting on a body, but you won't touch a metal handle. The body is not going to be ejected."

"Whatever, were you so cool when you first realized you were driving around with a body."

"Of course I was."

There was no need for him to know otherwise.

Pete released the metal lever, and the wheel locks collapsed into the floor of the van. He also released the brakes on the gurney's rear wheels. He gently pulled the gurney towards the middle, and we shifted ourselves to either side of it. We looked at each other and could tell we were thinking the same thing.

I spoke first. "So the legs to this gurney just open up on their own?"

Pete took off his knit hat, ran his fingers through his hair, and wiped the rain off his face. He looked straight at me. "Well, when I did this last week, it was all automated. We hit a button, and it rolled itself off the end of the van right into the funeral parlor. I was in the salon getting my nails done within seconds of hitting the magic button."

My hands were on the quilted blanket, and I

grasped the metal frame underneath to steel myself. "Wow, sarcasm. Is that Plan A? If I didn't have to hang on to this for support, I would probably give you Sherrie's one-finger salute."

"I got nothing else. You? Got anything? Maybe we should stand here longer in this weather while you conduct Plan B of googling how to take a gurney out of a hearse?"

"Plan C," I said.

"Plan C?"

"Slowly pull and hope for the best. If nothing releases, we just push it back in."

We were lucky when Plan C worked smoothly. The legs dropped, and we rolled it a few feet without incident so we could shut the doors. We took positions on either side and slowly sidestepped towards the grassy area, quickly developing a system of me stepping, Pete stepping, sliding the gurney—and repeat.

The ice on the driveway was thin, but it still controlled our situation. The gurney slid by itself. We barely maintained the proper direction. Fifteen feet felt like fifteen hundred. We managed the driveway's slight hill with our methodical approach. Whenever one of us stepped, the other was the anchor holding our little operation in place.

We hit the grass and had to change our approach. We didn't have the fear of sliding down the driveway but lost the ability to glide. I put the envelope down on the body so I could wipe the mascara running down my cheeks and push my matted hair out of the way.

Pete nodded toward the envelope. "Can't you put that in your coat so you have a better grip?"

"I didn't want to bend it. I don't know what's in it."

Pete grabbed it and, lifting the quilt, slid the manila envelope underneath.

"What are you doing?" I asked.

"Let's keep moving. It's fine," Pete said, as if he had done this before.

Rolling on the grass was easier than we expected, but we kept our same approach of each of walking one at a time, so I could use the gurney as a cane.

Brown frozen grass broke under our shoes with each step. Quiet in our endeavor, we listened to the wind howling around us and the sleet pelting the windows on the large house.

Step, step, glide, repeat.

We came to the first corner of the funeral home and easily made the turn. The tall stone house blocked the wind to our left. The right-hand side was lined with giant pine trees and an eight-foot wooden fence beyond the trees. We felt like we'd won the lottery when we got a break from the wind and face-slapping sleet.

I couldn't help but ask, "So, which end do

you think is the head? At first, I thought he would have gone into the van headfirst, but this could be his feet. What do you think?"

Step, step, glide, repeat.

"He? You know who this is?"

"Not a clue. I don't know why I said he. Maybe because the original driver was a male. I wonder how Norm is doing and if it freaked him out that some twenty-three-year-old has possession of a body that was in his charge."

Step, step, glide, repeat

"Want me to look? I'd like to know who I'm dealing with."

I did not step. "No!"

Step, step, glide, repeat.

Pete seemed to be second-guessing his decision to call me boss and cool under pressure. "I would open the *envelope*! Not the damn bag."

Step, step, glide, repeat.

"Oh." I couldn't help but laugh at myself. "Do you think we should?" I was kinda curious who this person was.

We turned again. The parking lot was laid out before us. Sherrie's VW Bug was the only car there and was covered a thick coat of ice. The motion-sensor lights snapped on, and the cement barricades blocking the exits to the street became visible.

It was my turn to step when I heard Pete say,

"Oh, shit."

I could hardly bear to look at what was causing his distress.

We were still protected from the wind by the tunnel created between the funeral home and the trees, but the cold had penetrated down my spine, my shoes were wet, and the water was slowly creeping into my wool socks. Pete hadn't taken his step, and when I went to push the gurney, he held it still, so I had no choice but to turn and look.

The door where Sherrie stood waiting for us was probably only thirty feet away. There were large metal double doors on the other side of the sloping driveway. If it was anywhere else but a funeral home, I would have called it a loading dock, but that seemed too industrial for this situation. It wasn't much of a slope under normal conditions, but now, it looked like the downhill slalom event at the Olympics. It was mostly covered by a second-story porch, but the first fifteen feet had a thin layer of ice.

"Claud, hurry up. I need to . . ." Sherrie's voice was barely audible. She stood with her back holding open one door, her hands cupped at her mouth, and then she rubbed them together as if rubbing sticks together to start a fire. It annoyed me she was worried about keeping her hands warm when I was trying to find one warm spot on my body.

Seeing her face when she realized Pete was my hitchhiker was priceless. She was as stiff as the body we were moving but regained her composure somewhat quickly. "How? What? Pete, what are you doing here?"

"I picked him up on the way. Come help us."

"I put the keys down inside, and I don't know if the door will lock behind me."

"Pete, why don't you google what to do if a door might lock behind you? Why—"

"Sarcasm? I got chastised for it. Let's just go slow," Pete said and yanked the gurney forward.

Sherrie disappeared inside and came back seconds later with a shovel and a broom, which she laid between the doors. She quickly ran up, pushing the shovel and scooping the sleet away. She went back down and up again. I was busy watching her work and didn't notice Pete pull the envelope out and open it.

Sherrie dropped the shovel in the corner, clapped her hands, and went into boss mode. "Ok, you two, we're clear. Bring that, that thing, that person down here. Hurry. We got to move that van."

I hit my breaking point. While she had been warm and cozy inside with two good feet, I had ice cutting through my face and socks so wet and heavy we could have used them as an anchor. "I know why I'm rushing, but what's your rush?"

"I'm under strict orders. Get this inside, lock doors, and get rid of that van." Sherrie walked up to the front of the gurney and started pulling it towards the double doors. She didn't seem to anticipate how fast it would slide on the wet ground, and fought for control.

I leaped forward to catch the end, but my sore ankle stopped me a foot short. Pete was slow to catch on to the commotion because his head was buried the papers. He caught the end of the gurney in time before it sandwiched Sherrie into the metal doors.

The metal frame of the gurney jiggled from side to side but, thankfully, remained upright. We breathed a sigh of momentary relief.

Pete took half a step and, finding a patch of ice, lost his footing. Down he went, and the envelope went flying. The papers were somehow miraculously still in his hand.

"Hells bells," Sherrie and I said together and waited for some sign from Pete that he was ok. I was still at the top, and Sherrie was blocked by the gurney.

She squeezed past the body and extended a hand to Pete, but he didn't take it. He was focused on the documents.

"I will not stand here all day," Sherrie said. "I got strict rules to—"

"We know! Trust me, I don't want to be here

any longer than needed either. Let's just get this thing inside." I hobbled to the side of the house, using the stone wall as support, and made it halfway down before I realized Sherrie didn't snap back at me. That made me nervous.

We had been friends since freshman year of college. One of us could snap at the other, and the other could snap back, and there were no hard feelings. Sherrie didn't walk away from a good argument—she *cherished* a good debate.

She walked quietly around the gurney and picked up the envelope that had gone flying from Pete's hand. She extended her arm again, but he sat there holding his wrist. The papers he was reading were on his lap, and he was muttering something between *shit*, *holy shit*, and *damn*.

"At least you stopped swearing about a salad," Sherrie said. "Now are we going to bitch and moan about your arm?"

"I don't think it's broken but . . ." Pete said nothing more and got himself up.

"But nothing. We gotta get movin'," Sherrie hissed.

"I know. Believe me, I know." Pete had the papers under his right arm, rubbing his right wrist.

Sherrie stood with her arms on her hips ready for a fight. "Are you going to complain that I have been rushing you and—"

"If you let me finish, I was going to agree

with you. We have to get going."

Sherrie squared off to him. "Now that we have to take you to the hospital, you're suddenly in a rush. My job is on the line here."

"I'd almost rather be eating a damn salad right now than standing here. My wrist is sore. Not broken, but now I understand what the rush is," Pete said.

I had to chime in before Sherrie challenged him to a who-knows-better debate although I wasn't any more kind than Sherrie had been. "So falling on your ass suddenly gave you grand insight."

"Wow, I see two people talking, but I hear only one attitude," Pete balked.

Without looking back, Sherrie stretched her left arm back over the gurney, and with my right hand reaching out, we slapped hands and in unison sang, "Yup, to-get-her!"

I would have kept talking, but I was shivering and wanted inside.

Pete rolled his eyes and motioned Sherrie towards the door as he calmly said, "Let's get this thing inside. Then we'll get the van out of here. I'll sit in back, and you both can take the front seats."

"I can't leave for a couple more hours." Sherrie reached for the metal door, but it wouldn't open because the gurney was blocking the right-hand-side door. I shimmied my way forward and adjusted the gurney, and Sherrie pulled the door open.

Pete let out a sigh of relief, but when I turned to look, his face was all business, eyes forward, left hand at the back of the gurney, right hand holding down the paperwork on top of the body. Sherrie reached around the closed door and released the lock. Pete and I pulled the gurney back so the second door could open.

It probably took thirty seconds to maneuver the gurney inside, but each movement felt heavy and slow. Our shoes made squeaking noises, and my socks spat out water with each step. The only other sound was the metal undercarriage clanging as it went over the threshold of the doorway. I hoped for warm air to rush by my body, but I was met with stale, cool, metal-like basement vapors.

The metal doors slammed behind us. My heart jumped into my throat. Once the three of us, actually four of us, were inside, I felt a huge sense of accomplishment, but little did I know, it was just beginning.

Guest Count: What was I counting
Body Count: Still One

CHAPTER THIRTEEN

My eyes scanned the hallway. Beige-and-gold-specked linoleum covered the floor, and a long fluorescent light hung over head. About thirty feet ahead was another set of double doors, but this time, the doors were a warm, dark wood with a brass handle.

Sherrie was back to speaking in whispers. "That door on the right is a janitors closet. We need to take this through there on the left." She stepped forward towards a large gray metal door with a single window. She had her back to us as she spoke. "After that, you guys can get going."

I took a half step forward and slid the gurney, ready to resume our earlier method of walking, but I was on my own. Pete hadn't moved from the entryway, but now I could move the fifteen feet on my own. I rolled up to Sherrie as she held the large double-size door open. The hallway was wide enough for us to turn the gurney without a problem. She reached inside and flicked the light switch, and the room glowed behind her.

Pete still hadn't moved.

"I guess it's you and me," I mumbled to Sherrie.

We held out our hands, this time tapping our fingertips, and softly repeated, "Yup, to-get-her."

In a slightly louder whisper, Sherrie said, "Claud, once we get this in there, you can drive Mr. I-Am-Too-Scared-To-Move home, and I will meet you at EG's later."

"No," Pete said, but he still hadn't moved.

Sherrie rolled her eyes. "He is—"

"You two can banter all you want, but we are not leaving." The sleet on Pete's jacket had melted and was collecting in a puddle at his feet. He stood at the back door like a sentry, holding the papers identifying our passenger. "I would prefer we all leave, but, Sherrie, I know you will not leave your post, and if I had to guess, Claudia, you will not abandon her. So we are all stuck here together."

Sherrie and I stopped moving and looked at each other for answers, searching the other's eyes. Clearly, we had nothing, so we turned our attention back to him.

"What were your instructions? From Harold, what are you supposed to do here? Did he explain anything?" Pete demanded.

Sherrie stumbled with her words. "Just receive and secure the delivery. Tell no one of the delivery. Make sure no one comes in, post signs referring any potential walk-in clients to the funeral home in Kirkasaw. Make sure the answering service is set with the same message."

"You two stay here. I'll move the van and be back in a minute."

"Where? How are you going to get back here?" I asked.

"I'll drive it a few blocks and look for a discreet spot. There's no signage identifying what type of cargo it holds."

Sherrie said, "Just move it across the street to the root beer stand. There are four or five parking spots on the other side of the shack. People from the neighborhood park there all the time when it's closed. Harold told me to park there but it was too icy out so I parked right here."

He was gone before we could say anything else.

"I am not even going to ask how you got him involved, but it's nice having more company."

We stood under the fluorescent light and took in our surroundings. Without realizing it, we crept closer to each other.

In the far-left corner stood a gray metal desk with a lamp and a single plastic tray with nothing on it. Behind it, along the left side wall, were three tall filing cabinets. Along the interior wall to the right of the doorway were two tall cabinets. Next to that was a metal shelving unit with various boxes. Everything neatly stacked and labeled. The center of the room had two metal rolling tables with hoses attached. The wall on the right had four square metal doors side by side. An educated guess led me to believe they were refrigerated drawers. One of them would be the final stop for my passenger.

The far exterior wall was cinder block painted dull yellow, with only a row of windows maybe eight feet long near the ceiling. I figured if I was tall enough to see through the windows, I would see the side of the house Pete and I just came from only minutes ago.

The exterior door slammed shut. Seconds later, Pete walked in. Dangling from his hand was Wilbur. Water dripped from his hat. His breathing was heavy, yet underneath the ruby complexion from the cold, he was ghostly white.

"That was fast. So I'm assuming there were parking spots by the root beer stand," Sherrie said.

He handed me Wilbur, and a trail of water followed on the floor. "Did you fall? Why is Wilbur so wet?"

Pete remained quiet. He looked between

Sherrie, me, and the body. It began an uncomfortable silence. The hum of the four-drawer cooling unit was the only noise.

Sherrie leaned over the gurney and spoke to the body. "I'm surprised this makes you uncomfortable. You haven't spoken a word since you've been here."

"Speaking to the dead? Is that your superpower?" I asked.

"I just thought I would—"

"Can we just move the man where he belongs?" Pete asked.

Sherrie met my eyes, and I shrugged. I didn't know what had gotten into Pete.

We pushed the gurney around the first table, and Sherrie pulled the end to the front of a drawer. I held onto the metal table for support as I made my way down to the drawers.

Sherrie adjusted the gurney just off-center from the door. "A table will slide out, and we will lift and transfer the . . . a . . .that . . ."

"Man," Pete said.

"How do you know it's a man?" Sherrie asked.

"I read the file. Remember when I landed on my ass out there?"

"Yes, on your ass, but gracefully, I must add." Sherrie was still doing what she could to lighten the mood. She grabbed the shining metal handle and clicked open the door to the drawer.

Her snarky presence turned to stone. Her eyes popped from their sockets, and her arm swung ninety miles an hour slamming the door shut.

"What the hell?" I screamed.

"There is a body in there!" Sherrie whispered.

"We are at a funeral home!" I shifted my feet, and water sloshed around in my shoes.

"It wasn't there yesterday," Sherrie gritted through her teeth. "No one else has been here. Harold sent the regular funeral director on vacation."

I thought it was a bad joke. Pete took the information in stride, processing it all.

I was waiting for the punchline. "Stop messing with us."

Pete was now at the head of the gurney with the two metal tables on either side, trapping him in on three sides. The body was between Sherrie and me with the cooler drawers on one side, metal tables on the other side.

Since Pete had been on his ass ten minutes ago, his whole demeanor had changed and become systematic. "Claudia, help me move this table over two feet."

We pushed the table, and he came forward and opened a different door, pulled the metal table out, and stepped back. He motioned for Sherrie to push the gurney over to the sliding table drawer. She did it without moving her legs, using her arms like a robot.

Pete continued to guide the operation. "I don't know how much I can lift with my wrist, but we should be able to pull the man over. Sherrie step here to the top and left when Claudia and I pull."

I stepped up to the drawer table and reached over to the quilted blanket, feeling the vinyl bag below it. Pete had shifted the blanket, so he was only holding the bag with one hand. Sherrie had not moved. We looked at her and waited for acknowledgment that she had heard Pete's instructions.

She stood with her arms straight, statue-like. She was puzzle-solving. "You don't understand. There was no body here yesterday. No body and no one in the building. Harold showed me where to keep him. This unit was empty. All the staff is gone. I don't understand this."

"I don't know what to say. But I'm tired. I'm wet. My ankle hurts, and I am getting a little freaked out. Can we just move him into this unit and get the hell out of here?" I said.

"No can do," Pete said.

"You can stay here. I appreciate the gentlemanly approach of not wanting to leave Sherrie here by herself, but I just want out and I am sure it's late enough for you to go home for the day,

Sherrie."

For the first time since getting here, Sherrie raised her voice above a whisper. "I am telling you that body was not here. The staff is gone, and I know I locked the doors yesterday when I left. Let's just move this body and leave. I don't care if I lose my job."

Pete shook his head. "We can't leave."

"It's fine. I was only supposed to stay another hour," Sherrie said.

Pete looked at both of us before he spoke. "You don't understand. We can't leave because someone stole the van."

Guest Count: Can't remember
Body Count: One too many
Van: Minus one

CHAPTER FOURTEEN

Dead silence engulfed Sherrie and me.

I dropped my hands from the blue quilt. I understood Pete's words, but I could not comprehend the situation. "So . . . what, how?"

Pete's hand still rested on the body bag. "One situation at a time. Let's move him inside the fridge and then we can worry about the van."

Silently, we resumed our positions. Sherrie lifted the end while Pete and I pulled. With some effort and with as much grace as we could muster, we heaved the man to the table. Pete lifted the papers identifying the man, pushed the drawer in, and Sherrie quietly shut the door, making the sign of the cross.

"What was that for? You're not even Catholic."

"I felt like we should do something," Sherrie whispered.

We turned our focus to Pete, who once again was reading the contents of the envelope as he spoke to us. "I understand why Harold did not want this delivery. That man we just escorted here is Anthony Coletti."

"Coletti. I know that name," I said.

"You should, but I'm kinda surprised since you're not from here."

"The name rings a bell." Sherrie was resting on her heels with her fists clinched. I didn't know what that meant, so I prepared for anything when she spoke. "Can we go somewhere else and discuss this?"

"Well, we have no van, your car is trapped in the lot, and it's not the best weather for a hike," I answered.

"No shit. I mean let's move to a different room and figure this out."

"You're the host. Where do you recommend? Got a nice empty viewing room?"

"Actually, that's not a bad idea. Follow me, you two." She headed out of the embalming room.

Pete followed, and they waited at the door as I hobbled towards them. Sherrie told me to wait and went to the janitors closet, and Pete followed her. I heard some talking, something breaking, and some unidentified noises. Those two emerged looking triumphant. Pete walked over and handed me a former broom handle turned cane. It had rubber feet from the bottom of a metal chair duct-taped to each end. "It's the best we could do. Hope it helps."

"Ok, let's march forward. Sherrie you lead." She took Wilbur from me and walked to the double wood doors.

We quietly followed. The doors opened to a softly lit hallway. Beige wallpaper and carpet erased the sterile feel of the workroom. However, the dry tones of the walls and carpet did not kindle any warm feelings. Sherrie waited for us and gently closed the door behind her.

Not for one second since arriving at the funeral home did I forget where I was, but I gasped when I saw several coffins in the room at the end of the hallway.

Sherrie was back to her softer whispery tone. "Get a grip, lady! Those are empty. That is the sales display room, before that a bathroom and the elevator. The stairs here on our left will take us to the main floor."

"Elevator?" I held up my cane.

"It's shut down. Can you make it up the stairs?"

"If we go slow, I'll be fine. Lead the way."

Pete and I followed, making several turns before landing in the grand foyer. Sherrie stopped on the main level. One turn and the staircase continued with a grand wooden banister and plush carpet so thick anyone in high heels would sink a foot. Pink tones and Victorian architecture captured the home's original style.

We stood in front of the door Sherrie had previously tried to open. The center of the foyer held a large mahogany round table with a lace doily absent of a floral centerpiece. Gilded gold frames held oil paintings of flowers and pastures. A high-backed rose-colored velvet-covered sofa sat beyond the staircase, flanked by two small tables holding plastic flowers. Sherrie's coat lay over the arm of the sofa.

She continued her tour. "On the right is a small sitting room for families, restrooms, and beyond that, a kitchenette, a smaller viewing room, and the entrance from the parking lot. The main viewing room is on the left. Upstairs, I think, is the old living area. Harold told me not to worry about it."

She pushed the lace curtains aside and looked out to the front drive.

"Are you looking for the van? Thinking maybe I couldn't find it?" Pete asked.

"It's not that I don't believe you. I just find the whole thing . . . odd, unbelievable, or surreal. You guys were only here a few minutes. I did not mean to question your ability to lose a vehicle."

Pete let out a big chuckle that filled the house. He flinched when he realized his own volume, and that made Sherrie laugh. Their eyes met, and I would have given anything to disappear and leave those two alone, but it was not the time or place for that.

Not so tactfully, I broke up the moment. I sat down on the top step and removed my shoes and socks.

"What are you doing?" Sherrie asked. "This is a funeral home, not my Aunt Rosa's house where you have to take your shoes off."

"You know I hate cold feet. My shoes and socks are soaking wet."

Sherrie rolled her eyes and walked to the larger viewing room, adjusted the overhead lights to a low ambient glow—romantic in some places but clearly not here in a funeral home.

We followed her in. I carried my shoes with one hand and used the cane with the other hand.

Coletti? Coletti? How do I know that name?

About a hundred chairs sat facing a small lectern on the wall opposite us. There was about ten feet of space between two empty brass flower stands. On our right was a couch against a closed accordion door. The smell of Pine-Sol filled the air.

Pete walked to the front window, adjusting the heavy tapestry curtains, making sure no one could see in. "You can see they made this room up from three smaller rooms." He pointed to the wooden archway in the middle of the room and to the one holding the accordion door. "Up front here is the original parlor. This place is the family's original home. I'm not sure when they converted it to a funeral home, but you can see the additions every ten years or so, from the wheelchair ramp outside and the second-story porch over the it. I'm guessing, at some point, they upgraded that workspace downstairs when they put in that covered loading area."

Sherrie took over. "They did that twelve years ago. Eva told me the story. I guess there was a horrible car accident, and a family was killed. The town did not have a funeral home large enough to accommodate the work that needed to be done. Harold was so upset that he lost all that business, so he expanded the workroom, added that covered ramp, made the viewing rooms larger, and added the retractable doors for multiple smaller viewing rooms."

"I remember that." Pete's eyes dropped to the floor. He removed his hat and balled it up in his hand.

"Was your dad part of the construction design company?" I asked.

"No, I mean, I remember the funeral. It was Coach Woodikin and his family. They bussed us schoolkids to the funeral."

Sherrie spoke first. "I am so sorry. That must have been awful."

"Not really. We didn't know the kids because they went to a private school south of here. Coach was kinda a dick, and at that age, we loved getting the afternoon off from school. It was in some auditorium and lacked any emotion. I think my class got in trouble for our behavior while sitting on the bleachers."

"Huh, I don't know what to say about all that," Sherrie said.

"I have been in this room too, many times," he said.

We let that hang in the air. Pete walked back over to us and motioned to the couch against the faux wall. I dropped my shoes and sank so deep into the sofa I didn't know if I'd be able to get out. Sherrie leaned on the arm of the sofa with her legs extended in front of her.

"Damn." Pete winced when he grabbed a chair from the viewing section. He used his foot to angle it towards us.

Sherrie immediately stood up and left.

"Where are you going?" Pete demanded.

"I'll only be a second."

Pete stood up. "Where are you going? We need to figure this out."

"Give me a break. Just going across the hall."

"Let it go, Pete." I took off my coat and tried to get comfy. I dissected Wilbur looking for a pair of dry socks but came up empty.

Pete kicked another chair around for me to put up my foot. Sherrie returned two minutes later with two plastic bags full of ice. She gently placed one on my foot and pitched the second one at Pete. He pushed up the sleeve of his jacket and laid the ice packet on his wrist.

"I was playing nurse. Not running out the door and leaving you two here," she barked, barely audible, while she paced between the couch and doorway. "What's got you so uptight? I am about to lose my job. All I had to do was keep everything and everyone out, but I wound up with an extra body downstairs and the three of us stuck here."

"Have a seat. We have to figure this out," Pete said.

"No shit, genius! Next, you are going to start bitching about salad again."

Pete's eyes got big. "Sorry about that. I was in a foul mood. I . . . sorry. I didn't handle that well."

"Ok." Just one word of acceptance from her, and they were good. "One day, you will have to tell me what Caesar or romaine ever did to you. Right now, can we focus on what the hell is happening?"

My phone continued to beep with messages I left unread.

Pete took the lead. "Sherrie, how did you come to be here today? I thought you were covering for Eva at the main office."

"Next week, because of the holiday, most everything is shut down and phone lines are transferred to the main number. Earlier in the week, Harold went all crazy and decided to shut down everything early, giving employees holiday pay starting this week. I thought the funeral home would still be open for business. I just assumed that portion of C&C did not apply to the holiday closure. When a man called saying there would be a delivery, I just said ok. I went back and forth with the man on the phone because I was not understanding what he was implying. I thought he was trying to be delicate about the death and funeral business. I told him I understood the nature of his delivery. When I asked Harold how to contact the funeral director, he said I would be receiving the body. Then he made some comment about there probably being only one person at this funeral."

"I know why Harold did not want this funeral. The man down there . . ."

Sherrie said, "The original body."

"Christ, I almost forgot about the second body," I said.

Pete continued, "That is Anthony 'the Pigeon' Coletti from Chicago."

"Mob!" I shouted when I made the connection between the name and newspaper story Maddie had told me about.

"Do you know anything about the mob?" Pete asked.

"Only what Hollywood tells me. So not much."

"My eighty-five dollars, I can still win the bet from the pancake breakfast," Sherrie said almost gleefully.

"From my understanding, Anthony was a big deal in Chicago. Actually, he was a big deal here before making a name for himself in a big town. Ironically, small in size—I think under five feet four—but vicious as hell. His main thing was running numbers and giving out loans that people had a hard time paying back. The details are fuzzy on his disappearance from public life. Some say once when he went to collect a payment, he accidentally took out the wrong person, and there were too many witnesses. Others say he started doing business where he didn't belong. The different families have their territories, and it worked well for everyone not to cross those boundaries, but Anthony may have gotten greedy. Regardless, something sent him into hiding, but he still had control over his territory. This funeral could attract some unwanted attention. Some people like to pay their respects, some like to spit on the deceased, and other people, the feds for instance, like to watch all those who show up."

"Harold is money-hungry and would love the attention," Sherrie said. "So why is he freaked out?"

"Like I said, all the attention. Maybe he needs to keep his distance from the Coletti family."

"Why River Bend? We are hours away from Chicago," I said.

"You always go home. Home to your final resting spot, I guess," Pete said.

"So, what's with the van? Why would someone take the van?" I asked. "Or was it random?"

"Did someone hot-wire it?" Sherrie snickered.

My phone beeped several times, and they looked at me questioningly but I didn't answer it.

Pete shifted the ice on his wrist. "They didn't have to. I left the keys in it." He looked at me. "I'm sorry. I know that puts you in a real bind."

"How did you end up with Wilbur?" I asked.

"Wilbur?"

"My bag, Wilbur."

Pete shook his head. "I found it on the grass where I parked the van."

My fists sunk into the old cushions as I tried to sit up. I braced my elbows against the armrest and the back of the sofa. "I don't think the van being stolen was random. No one is out in this weather. If someone was looking to steal a vehicle, why not keep my bag?"

Beep, beep.

"You're right," Sherrie said. "It wasn't random, but who would do it? It was only sitting there a few minutes. They must have been watching you."

"Watching?" I mumbled.

Ignoring me, Sherrie continued. "Can we talk about the bigger issue?"

"Bigger than the missing van?" I asked.

"The body!" Sherrie let out a sigh. "The second body. I am telling you guys. That body was not here yesterday."

Pete leaned back in the chair and crossed his right leg over his left. "You were serious about that?"

"Yeah!"

"I thought you were just screwing with me."

Beep, beep.

"OMG! Answer your phone, sister." Sherrie kicked over Wilbur to me.

I dug out my phone. My night had just gotten worse.

Did I put them on the road at the wrong time?

Did I make a hasty decision without thinking it through for everyone?

Guest Count: Still can't remember
Family Members Stranded: Three.

CHAPTER FIFTEEN

I scrolled through the seventeen photos my brother had sent, and finally read the message from my mother.

Mom: *We are ok but stranded eighty miles north. We skidded into a ditch to avoid a semitruck and an eight-car pileup on the freeway. We're not hurt from ditch encounter, but I slipped on the icy road and hurt my wrist. Connor fell helping the police get people out of the wrecked cars. He can walk but not very well. I haven't seen your dad in twenty minutes. I'm assuming he's still helping the accident victims.*

"All that was via text?" Sherrie asked after I read it out to them.

"She thinks I'm working and doesn't want to disturb me. She said they're waiting on a tow truck and for their neighbor to come and get them. My

151

brother sent me the photos of their car and the accident that filled in the missing gaps from my mother's story."

Pete chuckled to himself. "Tell her to put ice on it."

I rolled my eyes. "Are you sympathizing or just trying to be the funny guy?"

"Anything to avoid believing there's a second body downstairs that shouldn't be."

"Are you sure no staff from the funeral home was here last night to receive a body?" I asked.

"I highly doubt it."

"*Doubt?*" I said.

"Look, I know this sounds funny, but I'm serious." She stood up and walked the length of the room from the doorway to the front, passing between Pete and me. "I can't prove no one was here last night, but Harold told me the staff was gone and the place was closed. I remember thinking it was odd because I thought someone was always on duty here. Harold must have read my mind because he told me I was the only one working here the next few days. The regular funeral director and his assistant are on vacation at the same time. I thought that was odd but Harold was not in the mood to answer many of my questions."

"The body downstairs looked different from

the other one you brought in," Sherrie said.

Pete and I exchanged looks. I was about to speak when he held up his hand and mouthed, *I got this*. "Different?" he asked Sherrie, and the two of us sniggered.

She did not acknowledge our doubt. "The body you brought in was in a bag and covered with a quilt. This one was dressed, not lying straight. He . . ."

I held my hand up to Pete and asked Sherrie, "He?"

She walked between us, this time turning left to circle the viewing chairs. "It had a man's suit, trousers, and shoes. I didn't see much more."

Pete regained his composure. "So what do you think happened? Who would have put the body there? Are you *sure* it wasn't there before?"

Sherrie was on her second lap and had developed an even pace. "Harold could see I was nervous. He thought it was about the whole funeral home and dead bodies atmosphere, but I was a wreck about disappointing him, Eva, and maybe losing my job. I have never been fired from a job before."

I raised my hand like a schoolgirl waiting to spell the answer out for the class. "What about that job—"

"I was not fired. Technically. Can we forget about that? Harold opened each drawer to show me they were empty. He told me to make sure the temp gauge was right and how to lock up."

Pete took the next question. "So how do you suppose it got here, and shouldn't we call someone?"

Sherrie's voice almost reached normal speaking levels. "OHMYGOD. We have to report the body!"

From her whispering to nearly yelling, her sudden melodrama made us laugh.

I asked, "Are you sure it's dead?"

Pete said, "Do you want me to call—"

Sherrie stopped walking in front of us and pulled out her phone. She swiped the screen, and it lit up. We couldn't see the screen, but she opened what I assumed was the phone app, and her finger tapped three times on the screen.

I was sure the horror on Pete's face was a reflection of mine. I had thought she would call Eva for advice, or maybe Harold. I wasn't sure who Pete wanted her to call, but 9-1-1 was not our first choice. We instinctively knew how this call would go. I reached up to stop her, knowing it was too late. She batted my hand down and moved to the end of the sofa.

Deep breath, steady voice but still barely loud enough for the 9-1-1 operator to hear her, she said, "I am at 608 6th Street, and there is a body here."

. . .

"Business."

. . .

"Funeral home."

. . .

"But I'm serious."

. . .

"Hello, hello, hello?"

I was shaking, tears streaming down my cheeks, and Pete had his head in his hand.

"Can you believe they hung up on me?" Sherrie stood with her hands on her hips, looking down at us. "What's with you guys?"

I managed to get out. "Do you know what you just did? The operator thinks that was a prank phone call."

"Oh, agh. Oh." Sherrie threw herself on the couch next to me. Her face was flushed as she replayed the phone conversation to herself. "Did I really call 9-1-1 to tell them there was a body at a funeral home? Why didn't you stop me?"

"Why don't you call back and tell them the story that it magically appeared?" Pete asked.

"I'm glad you find this funny. The operator said they were busy with actual emergencies." She slid down lower and extended her leg, playfully kicking Pete. "But she told me where to find a good salad."

"Touché."

"Shhh. Quiet." I swung my leg off the chair and moved to the edge of the couch cushion. "Somebody's here."

"What did you hear?" Sherrie asked.

"I don't really know. Something banged together, some loud noise. I just know it wasn't us."

Pete shook his head. "I thought you were with me on the right side of crazy." He kicked Sherrie's foot back. "This house is over a hundred years old. It's going to make noises."

"I thought I heard it before. This was a more deliberate sound. Sharp. Not a creaking." I looked at Sherrie. "All the doors locked?"

She nodded. "You saw that front door was padlocked from the outside. The parking lot entrance is locked. Where did the noise come from? Down or up?"

"I really don't know. Up, maybe."

"Wait here." Pete left the viewing room and headed to the rear of the house. He flushed a toilet, banged on a counter, and we guessed he pushed on the back door before returning to the doorway. "Was any of that the noise?"

I shook my head, and Pete moved towards the stairs. His foot hovered over the first step.

"Are you scared?" Sherrie asked.

"Scared of what? I was just listening for sounds." He took two steps down and looked back at Sherrie. "You know you have not spoken in anything but a whisper since we got here."

"He's right," I said.

"Whatever." She stood and watched him go down the steps. "I am not scared but just—"

"Uncomfortable. I get that. I'm sitting here with no socks and shoes, on a couch that is ready to suck me in, with a missing van."

"At least you kept your promise to the old guy at the hotel and got the body delivered here. Now follow me." She handed me the cane, reached out her hand, and helped me stand up. "Let's go." She was out of the viewing room and was waiting for me on the first step going up.

I took our ice bags and dropped them on a potted plant that looked artificial, but I would worry about that later. I hobbled as fast as I could. "Where are you going?"

"If Pete is checking out downstairs"— Sherrie cleared her throat and tried speaking in a normal tone —"if Pete." She coughed again, and this time, she almost got it. "If Pete can check downstairs, we can check up here."

"You're scared *and* competitive. I love it. Let's go!"

"Harold said not to worry about anything upstairs, but he failed to mention that he added barricades, padlocks on the front door, and the possible addition of an extra body," Sherrie said.

I used my cane to clunk past her and went up. The grand staircase was wide enough for the two of us to walk up together, and she easily caught up. Midway up was a landing four feet deep, and we paused.

She leaned in. "Are you a little scared?"

I whispered, "Not really scared, but I feel like I'm spying or stealing or breaking into someplace."

"I work for the company. I have a right to be here."

"Then why are you not moving?"

We locked arms and stepped up to the landing. The hallway began at the stairs. On the right, a half-moon table sat with a vase of dried flowers. Dark wood paneling covered the wide hallway. The floor looked to be original hardwood with several carpet runners outside two closed doors on the left. The light sconces beside each door barely gave off any light. Two tall windows stood opposing each door. The end of the hallway opened to what I guessed to be a kitchen area with black-and-white-checkered flooring. A single light came from that area.

A creaking sound came from the kitchen, and our eyes could not translate what we saw. We crumbled like the dead flowers as a white shadow floated across the kitchen.

Guest Count: Is there a Thanksgiving feast?
Body Count: Two
Ghost Count: One too many

CHAPTER SIXTEEN

I wobbled, my knees quivering, and I held on to my cane as if it was a life source. Sherrie was completely frozen, unable to move. "Hells bells," we uttered softly.

Before I registered my own thoughts, a metal clanking noise came from the kitchen, like a spoon dropping into the sink. We were fixed in place—not retreating yet but not moving forward either.

Without moving her lips, Sherrie asked, "What the hell was that?"

We didn't yell, but I came close to peeing in my pants when a hand touched my shoulder. Sherrie spun around and cocked her arm back to swing.

Pete's laugh was cut short when his eyes

shot past us. I assumed he saw the same image we had. He seemed steady and not bothered and broke the tension. "I guess we know what made the noise."

We turned to see our ghost figure walk across the opening with a mug in one hand and the other sweeping hair from her face. After having a moment to realize it was an actual person, Sherrie and I let out a nervous laugh.

Pete solved the mystery. "I guess Maribel lives here. Didn't Harold tell you? Let's let her be before we disturb her."

Sherrie and I needed a minute to reorganize our thoughts and settle our heart rate before we shuffled back down and sat on the velvet sofa at the foot of the stairs. Pete leaned against the doorframe leading to the viewing room.

Still in her whispered tone, she demanded, "Why did you sneak up on us?"

"Sneak? I walked up the stairs. There is so much carpeting on the steps, you wouldn't hear a freight train. I couldn't hear anything downstairs besides the furnace. You didn't know someone was up there?"

"Harold told me not to worry about upstairs. I really had no need or want to explore any more of this place. I just sat here on the bench or down there and waited for someone to knock on the ramp doors. Wait, who is Maribel?"

"Maribel Carlin, grand ol' dame of the town. She was married to Alvin. She'd be Hailey's grandmother—no wait, her great-grandmother."

"That's it. I'm done with this place. I'm going to call Aaron to come get us. Sherrie, call Holton and explain the situation, slowly so he understands what is going on and that it is not another 9-1-1 type call."

Pete looked away and walked into the viewing room.

"I can't call Holton," Sherrie said. "I deleted his number. No use having it in my phone."

"What? Speak up. Stop whispering. Whoever is upstairs obviously is hard of hearing."

"I deleted his number," she said louder.

I made the mistake of smiling when I said, "What was that again?"

Sherrie punched me in the arm after she realized I was trying to get Pete to hear that she had deleted Holton's number.

Pete came back dragging a chair and put it down in the doorway. I called Aaron, but it went to voice mail. I sent a text telling him to come get us.

"What do we do in the meantime?" I asked.

"I think I should call Harold and tell him what's going on."

"It's a good idea," Pete said. "I think maybe we should look at the body, maybe get some answers. You will have all the facts lined up when

163

Harold demands some answers."

I sounded like Sherrie when I whispered back to Pete, "Answers?"

"I'm not doubting that there's an extra body down there, but I think we should take a closer look. Is there paperwork? Toe tag? Maybe the regular funeral director received the body sometime during the night. Maybe Mrs. Carlin upstairs received the body."

"That lady could barely hold a cup. You think she could move a body? You think she worked a day in the last forty years?" I asked and didn't wait for response before I continued, "I'm assuming when there's a proper delivery, someone more experienced and less mobility-impaired and too scared to speak in a normal voice than the two of us, it might be less complicated."

Trying the best she could, Sherrie raised her tone, but it was still a whisper. "Why can't we just leave? That body isn't going anywhere."

"Footprints," Pete answered. "When I went downstairs to check for noises, I looked out the ramp doors. There were fresh footprints in the snow."

"Snow!" I shouted.

Sherrie jumped up to the front door. She pushed away the lace curtains and hopped with joy. We loved fresh snow. A white blanket of cheer. One jump before she saw the intrusion and then she fled back to me.

She looked at Pete and nodded. "Footprints."

Pete shook his head. "Someone took time to walk around the building but never bothered to knock. Maybe they were not watching us, but why see the padlock, walk around, not bang on any door?"

Sherrie jumped up again. "I'm in. Let's figure out what has us imprisoned in this place." She was already down the first step.

Pete helped me up, and we followed. She waited for us at the double doors leading to the hallway and the embalming room. She held open the door, and Pete took the lead.

Sherrie ran into me when I abruptly stopped on the linoleum floor. "What's your problem? Terrified?" she asked.

"I forgot I don't have shoes or socks on. I hate cold feet."

"Do you want me to go get them?" Sherrie opened the door, ready to run back up.

I grabbed her arm. "I'm sure they're still wet. Maybe you guys can go back into the janitors closet and make me some shoes." I couldn't help but chuckle. "Come on, let's get this over with."

Sherrie stepped back onto the linoleum and held the door so it wouldn't make noise as it shut. She wouldn't talk above a whisper and could not let a door close on its own.

Before the latch clicked, we flinched. There was no doubt about the noise coming from above us. It definitely could not be Maribel. The voices were sharp, and I seriously doubted I wanted to confront it.

Guest Count: I forgot what I was counting
Body Count: Two
Uninvited Guest Count: TBD

CHAPTER SEVENTEEN

Sherrie waved Pete away from the entrance to the embalming room and motioned upstairs. He quickly retreated back to us. I held the door in her place when she and Pete bounded back up the stairs, and I wobble-hobbled up behind them. I caught up to them standing next to the front door.

There was the source of my angst. I did not want to explain why the three of us were stuck here to anyone, much less Hailey Carlin.

Walking down the hall with Hailey was a man in his late twenties wearing khaki pants, a black wool peacoat, and tennis shoes, carrying a backpack. They had come from the parking lot door. Hailey handed a grocery bag to the man and pulled off a wool hat with a pink pom-pom. She adjusted her ponytail, looking fresh despite the winter storm.

Hailey seemed to have hooked another guy, but she didn't act flirty towards him. Instead, she was eagerly listening to him until she spotted us. I realized it was One-Way-Talkie when he put his black glasses on after drying them off. Maybe he would be a better fit than Holton.

"What are you guys doing here?" Hailey asked.

Sherrie jumped in first. "Us? What about you? Your father is not here. I am working."

"So you invited friends to jam with you. You didn't bother Nana?" Hailey moved swiftly to the staircase and was on the second step before she spoke again. "She's fine, right?"

We had whiplash watching her move.

Sherrie answered for us. "If you're talking about the lady upstairs, we did not disturb her. Are you supposed to be here? Who is he?"

Hailey, caught between wanting to check on her great-grandmother and claiming responsibility for One-Way-Talkie, said, "Anderson is writing a story about Nana and the family business and our history in the region."

"You're a reporter?" I didn't hide my doubt in my tone.

"I'm a freelance writer, doing a series about families that date back to the colonies," Anderson replied. "Wait a minute, you're the bar people."

"Bar people?" I snapped.

"Sorry, I mean nothing by that. I categorize people by where I meet them. I listen to stories. There are coffee place people, library moms, powder-sugared locals, and bar people here in this town. It helps me get a feel for the place. You can hear the same story told three different ways."

"You're doing a lot of talking for someone who should be listening." Sherrie's voice was sharp.

Pete and I looked at each other. It was the first time we'd heard Sherrie talk above a whisper. "Hailey, when were you here last?"

"Yesterday morning. We sat with Nana for an hour. I'm only here for her. I am not working a shift for you."

"What time yesterday, and was anybody else here?" Sherrie moved closer to the stairs and seemed ready to pull Hailey down.

"Anderson and I met at nine at Peach's, and then we were here by nine thirty for an hour." She clearly didn't like the questions. "Can I go see Nana now?"

"Was there anyone else here? Downstairs?" Sherrie was three feet away from Hailey, ready to pull her ponytail to get her talking, but when she tried getting closer to Hailey, Sherrie got snagged on the brass hook attached to the wall holding a velvet cord. Dangling from the cord was a small sign that read Private Residence, Do Not Enter. If we would have seen that sign earlier, I'm guessing, we wouldn't have been so surprised to find someone upstairs.

"Was anyone here?" Sherrie asked again.

"I have no clue. I came in the parking lot door and went upstairs. I don't get involved in what happens down there." Hailey took two steps up before she turned to Sherrie. "Is this about your screwup? Something happen here? You lose a body or something?" Hailey didn't wait for a reply and was up the stairs in seconds.

Pete stepped back and let Anderson pass. The three of us didn't notice that Anderson did not follow Hailey all the way upstairs.

Pete said, "The timing is not right. You were here later with Harold. Let's go back and look."

Nobody saw, but I nodded in agreement. "She's in her own world. Let Hailey be upstairs, and let's get on with what we were doing so we can get out of here."

I led the way downstairs, pushed open and held the heavy wood door for Sherrie and Pete, and was surprised to see Anderson following along.

"What do you think you are doing?" I asked.

Anderson's hands clutched the straps of his backpack like a child heading to grade school. "Letting Hailey be upstairs. Let's get on with this, you want to get out of here." He wasn't smiling, but the corners of his mouth turned up in such a way I wanted to wipe the smirk off his face with my fist. He recited my words as if they were a secret handshake in our little club. "I want Hailey to have time with Nana before I sit with her." No one replied, and Anderson finally confessed. "Whatever this is down here seems a ton more interesting."

Pete shrugged.

Sherrie crumbled. "Whatever, dude. I'm too tired to figure out if you should be here or not."

Chuckling, Pete leaned in to Sherrie. "At least this guy didn't hang up on you like the 9-1-1 operator."

She gave a small laugh. "Not yet, remember he hasn't seen the body."

"Bodies," Pete corrected.

Anderson looked at me. "Bodies?"

"You wanted in. So here you are. *Bodies.* You can leave now or shut up and come for the ride with us." I closed the heavy door behind him and hobbled down the cold floor to the embalming room. He took two steps forward before I threw something else at him. "All the ghosts are upstairs."

Guest Count: When is Thanksgiving
Body Count: Hopefully just two
Ghost Count: Let Anderson think there is one

CHAPTER EIGHTEEN

The four of us stood inside the embalming room. Anderson was near the door, taking in everything in the room. Sherrie, Pete, and I were not any more comfortable here than we'd been on the first visit.

Sherrie and I stood in the center between the metal tables. Anderson moved towards the desk.

Pete shifted the empty gurney under the windows on the far wall. He turned to the wall of drawers and started on the left. "I just want to make sure we're only dealing with two bodies." He opened the first door, and his chest relaxed.

Anderson craned his neck, getting a glimpse of the empty drawer.

Pete moved to the second drawer and again found it empty. He skipped the third door and went to the end that held my passenger from

Norm's van.

Damn the van! I forgot about that. I will have to deal with it eventually.

Pete opened the door, and it was comforting to see the body at rest.

"Do you hear that?" Sherrie asked.

No one moved, and the three of us looked at her for some reference.

"There is no noise now—there's usually a motor thing running," she said.

"Motor thing? Is that the technical term?" I asked.

"Yes! The motor thing is not making noise," Sherrie repeated.

Pete pulled the steel table all the way out and reached in. "You're right. It's cooler deep inside. I don't feel any fans."

"How long have you guys been here?" Anderson asked.

We ignored him.

"Does it kick on at some point?" I was hoping for a logical answer.

Anderson spoke again. "The reason I asked was to know if you lost power or if the lights flickered? A circuit breaker could have tripped. That is a nasty storm out there."

"I spent most of the afternoon upstairs on a bench or sitting by that ramp door. I didn't notice any lights blink, and trust me, I was on high alert sitting in this place."

Pete was running logic for us. "This room could be on its own power supply since the upgrade and renovation. Something could have happened while we were upstairs, and we would never have known. I'll look for the circuit breaker box." He struggled for a second, easing the metal drawer back in. He used his one good hand and gently maneuvered his bulky frame for leverage.

We collectively let out our breath with the fourth successful wiggle/push. The paperwork that Norm had had in the van and Pete had set on the body during the delivery fell to the ground, but relief swept over us when the table drawer retreated.

Anderson came forward and picked up the fallen papers identifying the man. "Who's the guest of honor?"

Something strange happened to the three of us. Since Hailey and Anderson's arrival, we had taken a collective stance on answering questions as a team. I looked at both of them and shrugged.

"He will find out sooner or later anyway," Pete said to Sherrie and me.

Sherrie shook her head. "I don't want to wrestle the paperwork away from him."

Pete answered for the group. "Anthony Coletti."

Without missing a beat, Anderson replied,

"No, it's not."

"Well, it was until a few days ago. But I believe we can still call him by his given name," I retorted.

"That body is too big to be him."

"What are you talking about?" Sherrie asked. "Did you know him?"

"I know *of* him. That table is eight feet long and a couple of feet wide. That body underneath the blanket is covering most of the space. You could fit six Colettis in there. I'm telling you that body is not Coletti."

We had no reason to believe or doubt him. He certainly held our attention.

I spoke for the group this time. "Nobody has seen the man in years. Decades."

"True, but the guy was maybe five feet four and rail thin. He was called Pigeon because he was small and shit on people. There is no way he transformed into someone that size."

"How do you know so much about him?"

"I'm from Chicago. You just know stuff about the families. It was part of the news growing up—oil prices, weather, did the Cubs win, Coletti and Tarduchi families, and the Bears."

From the corner of my eye, I watched Sherrie raise her hand to Pete. He met the high five, and they whispered, "Da Bears suck."

Sherrie addressed Anderson this time.

"Why do you care?"

Fast and almost as if it had been rehearsed, Anderson replied, "I'm a reporter. Curious. This is better than listening to an old lady ramble about the way life used to be."

I nodded in agreement. "Honesty. Nice."

"I gave you honesty. Now, your turn. Why did you guys come down here?"

We didn't answer. It wasn't because we didn't want to share; it was because we didn't want to know the answer.

Anderson stepped closer to the four drawers. "Let me guess. It's lucky drawer number three that you guys have avoided." No one moved. "You already mentioned bodies."

Pete stepped forward, grabbed the metal handle, and pulled open a shit of trouble.

Number of People in the Funeral Home: Too many
Body Count: Is there ever a good number

CHAPTER NINETEEN

Before Pete opened door number three, I realized we had a question hanging out there.

"Wait." That had come out louder than I'd expected, but I had everyone's attention. "Before we move on, we need to know who I drove here."

"Drove?" Anderson asked.

I held up my hand to him. "Long story."

He seemed to understand that was all he was getting from me.

"Let's put a face to the paperwork that came with it. Back to body one please," I said.

"Why?" Sherrie asked. "Why does it matter?"

Pete answered. "The same reason we came down here to begin with. We need to have our information right when we call the police this time."

"This time?" Anderson laughed. "How long has this Scooby-Doo gang been getting into messes like this?"

"Shut up, Anderson. You are still doing too much talking," Sherrie said.

Unfortunately, Pete and I did not have Sherrie's back and started giggling.

After I'd almost composed myself, I said, "Someone had a misunderstanding with a 9-1-1 operator."

"What do we gain by looking?" I could not tell by the tone if Sherrie was whining or really wanted to know.

Pete regained composure and laid it all out. "We, or Claudia, will have to answer for the missing van. If it turns out the paperwork and body number one don't match, *we* could have a problem. We will also have to answer for the second body, especially since there is no real chain of custody for it. The police are going to have a lot of questions for us." There was no disagreement from anyone. "Plus, at this point, I'm kinda curious about body one and body two."

"Ditto," I confessed.

"Copy that, I guess." Sherrie sighed.

"Doubling down. Scooby-Doo would be proud," Anderson said.

Body Count: Too nervous to count anything.

CHAPTER TWENTY

Now that we had a plan with a motive laid out, I was nervous. There would be no good answers to whatever or whoever we found. "Who do we start with?"

"Let's finish with One," Sherrie said, unofficially naming the bodies.

Pete opened the door wide. Sherrie stepped alongside Pete with me and Anderson facing them, leaving a gap for the steel table. Sherrie softly placed her hand on Pete's arm as he reached for the table. It was a small gesture of a kindness from both of them, Sherrie again recognizing the injury and him accepting the help.

Anderson watched as Sherrie and I slid the table out. We turned back the blue quilt a third of the way. The fluorescent overhead light emitted a bright glow and provided the only noise. The black vinyl bag's zipper waited for one of us to open it. Sherrie touched the metal clip, paused—maybe saying a silent prayer—before she slid the zipper down.

We pulled back the opening of the bag. Everyone stepped closer together.

Nobody had to say a word. The weight of the situation fell on us.

The man looked peaceful with his eyes closed, but his closed mouth seemed unnatural despite us never having met him. The deep eyes and large facial features were characteristic of a person born with some type of disability. I was in no position to diagnose or label this person, but I recognized similarities to people I have known.

We zipped the bag back up and replaced the quilted blanket before sliding in the drawer. Sherrie, Pete, and I exchanged looks, knowing we were sinking into something we did not understand. The two of them backed up, and Anderson and I took two steps forward, repeating our positions around drawer number three/Body Number Two.

I pulled the door handle, slowly swinging it wide. Sherrie guided it all the way open, reaching across Pete's chest.

It wasn't the shoes we noticed first, but that they were not pointed up. The body lay on its side.

Before we could consider what that meant, an odor swept over us. Pete pulled his hat over his nose, and Sherrie cupped her hands over hers.

My impulse was to reach for the door handle, but Anderson blocked me.

"You came to look. Let's look." He pulled the table halfway out.

Before us lay an expired elderly man. The wrinkled, pockmarked white hand and style of clothing concluded that Two was a man. The legs were bent and turned sideways, body twisted at the waist, allowing both shoulders to touch the table. He was dressed in black dress pants with matching suit jacket, shined black shoes, a white Oxford button-down shirt with a large red stain. A rug the size of a car floor mat covered the origin of the stain and the man's head.

Anderson reached in for the floor mat. I grabbed his arm. Sherrie projected something like *no* or *don't* from her mouth, but it came out sounding like *nodontno*.

We all understood her command. Anderson chose to ignore her. His arm was still moving forward when I pulled the sleeve of his wool coat. He shook my arm away and reached in with his other hand. I gave him a small jab, but he could only grab a tiny corner of the rug because he was holding his phone. The small rug shifted ever so slightly, partially exposing the man's face. Maybe,

I should say, exposing what was left of his face.

Anderson's arm jerked when I bumped him, and his hand dropped into the dead man's bloodied body. Sherrie abruptly propelled the table back into the drawer. Pete closed the door, narrowly avoiding trapping Anderson's arm inside. He moved so close to Sherrie he only had to dip his head a few inches to whisper something in her ear. She nodded. Pete looked up and caught me staring, and his faced became flushed before he mouthed, *You good?* I nodded, but I wasn't sure anyone could be good after seeing Two on the table.

The three of us silently herded together next to the desk. Alone, Anderson turned his back to us, poking around the metal shelves.

Rarely at a loss for words, Sherrie snapped us out of our daydreamlike state. "Looting the place now?"

"I'm looking for something to clean my phone. I'm sure you noticed where it has been." Anderson lifted a few bottles and found nothing of interest.

"Pete, check behind the file and storage cabinets. I'll check the janitors closet for the circuit breaker. I can't imagine it's good for them sitting in a heat locker."

I walked out of the embalming room, trying to find a reason never to have to go back in there. Death or the dead do not scare me. I actually love a good mystery until I'm one of the players. Is One connected to Two? Is Two connected to the missing van? I'm connected with the van, so did that make me connected to Two? This was like that fourth-grade math problem. Train A leaves a hotel in River Bend, travels several miles when Train B shows up and this all equals . . . trouble for Claudia.

Can I take myself out of the equation?

Train A and B had already collided, but could Sherrie, Pete and I escape the wreckage?

Bodies: Coletti (maybe) and Two

CHAPTER TWENTY-ONE

Anderson followed me to the janitors closet, holding his phone by a corner like it might bite him. "I wasn't sure I should use those chemicals to clean my phone. I figure there's something here I might recognize." He popped the phone out of the case, slipped it into his coat pocket, and delicately placed the case on a shelf. "I guess we should look for the circuit breaker first."

We spotted the gray panel door, and I nearly toppled over when he cut me off, trying to reach it before me.

"What was that for?" I barked.

"Do you know anything about circuit breakers?" Anderson asked.

"Why? Because I'm a girl? I can't figure out what I should flip?"

"I don't want to argue. Since I'm here, why don't you go stand in the doorway and listen for a 'motor thing' to pop on."

I didn't want to laugh at Sherrie's expense, but with Anderson's use of air quotes, I couldn't help myself. Plus, the janitors closet had a clammy cement floor that was colder than the linoleum.

I opened the embalming room door and was met with a pair of flying socks I caught before they hit my face. "I found these for you. Don't worry, they're new. Came from a fresh pack." No comical tone in Sherrie's voice, she was all business. She and Pete were about to slide the metal cabinet aside, but I told them we'd found the panel.

Seconds later, a hum grew louder, and a "motor thing" kicked on. I remained in the doorway as we listened to Anderson root around in the janitors closet looking for something to clean his phone.

I made my way to the desk chair and slipped on the men's black dress socks. "Where did these come from?"

"When we moved the first file cabinet, the bottom drawer slid open. I also got you covered if you need some boxers or granny panties."

"No thick cozy socks?"

Sherrie rolled her eyes. "Just some nylons. I

could try other drawers for you. Who knows what else we could find."

"That's probably it." Anderson walked back into the embalming room. "Funeral homes have that stuff because family members often forget it when picking out an outfit for the deceased. They think about it later and hate for dear ol' grandma to be going bare-ass when they drop her into the ground. Most places carry a stock of supplies, but I wouldn't open any more drawers." We waited for a longer explanation. "I thought we all concluded that second body is a—"

"Tunnel of trouble. Yeah, I don't think Two needs a fresh pair of socks." Sherrie squared her body towards Anderson. "We don't need a replay of what we just saw."

"I think he was going to tell us not to get our fingerprints on anything else in the room," Pete said, interjecting some common sense. "We need to call the police and reexplain our situation in a manner that doesn't cause them to hang up on us. Tell them about Two and the van."

Sherrie nodded in agreement. "That makes sense. Pete, let's go upstairs; the signal is better up there."

"I have a full signal." Anderson held up his caseless phone, then dialed a number.

We listened as he explained the situation and gave the funeral home's address, with only minor clarifications of the situation. Sherrie and I laughed when he said there were six of us at the funeral home.

Pete whispered, "He wasn't counting One and Two—he meant Hailey and her nana."

Anderson stepped out of the room when we laughed and returned a minute later. "I couldn't hear well with you talking. I guess my signal isn't so great down here after all. Bad news, we're stuck here until they can get to us."

"No shit. I figured we could do some ice fishing and wrap up the night with hot chocolate. The freezing rain will do wonders for the skin," Sherrie said.

Anderson let that roll right off him. "I meant to say it might be a while until they get here. The 9-1-1 operator would not tell me much but implied the only two ambulances and two cops in this town are attending a different situation. Unfortunately, we are not top priority since we're in a county with Barney, Andy, and Opie, and the full cast of characters from Mayberry."

"I guess our guests of honor are not going anywhere soon," I added.

"Speaking of which, we need to make sure Ms. Carlin doesn't leave," Anderson said, taking control.

"That lady is not going anywhere," I replied.

"He means Hailey," Pete explained. "Let's head upstairs."

People in the Funeral Home: Six, One and Two

CHAPTER TWENTY-TWO

PETE
SEVERAL HOURS AGO

Fuck Shania Twain. How do I have that song in my head for the last seven hours—"Forever and for Always"? How can one person be that cheery about being bound with someone forever?

But that music brought me to Sherrie. She's the reason the song's in my head; she had control of the music at the bar.

There is no way I have a shot with her, not with my mood lately.

Her ordering the salad for my dinner last night was pretty funny, but I couldn't tell her that. I was too busy plotting something funny to strike back with, but Jacob came in begging for a shift.

I had a can of tuna, a questionable loaf of bread, and two beers to live on until the grocery stores open tomorrow. I was hoping for bar pizza tonight, but that got nixed when we closed early.

The only decent thing I've done today was wear this jacket. The collar's top button could chok me to death, but it's better than getting the bar's flannel uniform shirt wet. It's one of the last new shirts, and the color isn't washed out yet. If it gets wet, I'll be painted pink and turquoise for days. These shirts are ridiculous but, at the same time, pretty funny.

Jacob started a mosaic at the bar, hanging in Aaron's office where, every time a shirt button pops off or a sleeve unravels he adds it to his masterpiece.

It's pretty amazing how Sherrie got Aaron to order the shirts. He is so frugal, it's incredible he spent money on a uniform shirt that nobody beside Sherrie thought we needed. She has a way with men.

Speaking of which, isn't she dating Holton? What's the point of trying to date her? Aaron probably wouldn't like his employees dating anyway.

I've barely just broken up with Anna, so if I make a move on Sherrie, she'll probably think I bounce from woman to woman. I knew I should have skipped that damn cooking class and broken up with Anna weeks ago.

Whatever my problems are in this moment pale in comparison to being run over by a van swerving all over the road.

I better pay attention before it knocks me off my

feet. I should have gotten a ride instead of walking.

Wait, is that Claudia driving?

These days, I'm not surprised to find her and Sherrie at the forefront of chaos—controlled chaos. Like, it was seeing Sherrie at the pancake breakfast until Holton showed up—that went from nice to chaotic.

Sherrie taking ownership for whatever she did at C&C to end up working in a funeral home over the weekend—controlled chaos.

Why am I thinking about Sherrie when Claudia is about to run me over?

PETE
PRESENT TIME

"Did you hear that? Hey, Pete, are you still with us?" Sherrie asked.

I snapped back to the present as we were walking down the hallway towards the doors that led upstairs.

"What? Sorry my mind wondered back a few hours. I was thinking about walking from the bar when Claudia almost ran me over and roped me into this mess," I said. "Did you hear something?"

"You didn't hear Claudia's stomach

197

rumbling?" Sherrie asked.

"I thought it was mine. We found socks, so do you think we can find something in the kitchen area?" I said.

"When I got the ice, the only thing I saw were some butter cookies that look like they've been sitting around since the last viewing." Sherrie held open one of the double doors.

Anderson turned right towards the showroom.

Sherrie didn't like the change of direction. "Up the stairs on the left."

I couldn't see him, but apparently, he had ignored her. Claudia and I knew this was not good. She motioned for me to go ahead and help defuse the situation. I left her hobbling down the hall and opened the door.

Sherrie stood at the opening of the casket showroom, hands on her hips. She had returned to whisper-shouting. "What are you doing?"

"Just making sure we're alone. I want to know what's going on." Anderson walked around the room and opened a closet. Satisfied no one was in there, he closed the door and joined us back in the hallway.

A metal bar clanked, then something thumped on the door to the hallway. Claudia's voice echoed a chorus of damns. We raced back, pushed open the door to find her against the wall, one hand braced against the closed door and the other hand holding the cane like a fishing rod trying to scoop up Wilbur.

"You ok?" I asked.

Sherrie didn't say a word. She just went to Claudia's aid, scooping up the contents that had fallen out of Wilbur.

"I'm almost too embarrassed to tell you. I tried pulling open the door. It needed an extra yank, but with the silky dress socks, I lost my footing and tried to catch myself without much luck. Now that the show is over, can we go up?"

"Why are you laughing?" Sherrie asked me.

"The two of you can't walk down a hallway without something happening. I'm not surprised I'm spending my evening here in a funeral home."

"Like you had better plans. A big date planned with Anna?" Sherrie said.

"I was supposed to be working," I answered.

Anderson cut me off before I could tell her Anna and I were done. *Damn.*

"Should we take the elevator?" he said, gesturing to Claudia.

I shook my head. "No can do. It's off."

"Well then, shall we?" Anderson said. "Up we go, get a move on."

We marched up the stairs slowly behind Claudia, letting her set the pace of something below slow.

Three of us turned on the main level to continue up, but Anderson kept walking straight.

He poked his head into the main viewing room, walked to the kitchenette, and towards the back door. "Just checking we're still alone."

While he checked the rest of the main floor, Claudia tried to have a conversation on speakerphone with Aaron. It circled between picking us up at the funeral home and him saying he was with Molly Douglas. The connection was so bad neither one fully understood the other person. Sherrie finally took the phone away from her and disconnected the call with no protest from Claudia.

I knew it wasn't Molly Douglas but Mallory Douglas he was with, but I didn't want explain what that meant. I was torn if I should say something.

Back in August, I had been working that night. "That night" is how I referred to it. I didn't have other words for it, and I didn't want to use a cute name either.

That night, Aaron had been shot in the shoulder and pushed into the walk-in cooler. I was hardly conscious when I watched Claudia kill a man. She did not want to leave me or Aaron that night; she stayed to help us.

Some people and experiences stick to your soul, and no matter how much time passes you are bonded together for life.

My loyalties were split between Aaron and Claudia. Right now, however, I felt like the ladies at the pancake breakfast this morning sorting out the town gossip. Would I betray Aaron, my boss and friend, by telling his girlfriend that he was stuck in a storm with his ex Dougie? Just because those two were together at his loft or wherever, didn't mean they were together.

"Do you think we're having more fun here than Aaron is having with Molly fixing whatever needs his attention on the farm right now?" Sherrie asked, seemingly looking for a distraction more than wanting a real answer while we waited for Anderson to complete his walkabout. "Living next to a pot farmer can have its disadvantages."

"I wouldn't call her a farmer. For that, you need real acreage. Molly is not that ambitious," I said.

Claudia's face squinted like she was smelling something she couldn't identify. "How long have we been here?"

"Not long, why?" I said.

"I'm just trying to piece together what Aaron said—or, really, what I could understand. I don't think he's at the farm," Claudia said.

"I think he's with Mallory, not Molly. Mallory is a niece or second cousin or something. The Douglas family gets a bit confusing with the large numbers of the brothers and sisters, marriages, divorces, and more marriages." Just being honest, not selling out Aaron.

"I haven't heard that name before," Claudia said.

I turned towards Sherrie. "You've met her or at least served her a drink. She was the tall brunette giving Anderson a hard time at the bar the other day. She goes by Mallory or Dougie."

"I saw them leaving the bar when he was locking up, right before I almost hit you. Are they at his loft?" Claudia said.

Shit, how do I get out of this?

"I don't know where they are. I just know it sounded more like Aaron was saying Mallory than Molly, but you were the one holding the phone. Mallory was in the bar when I left, so that makes more sense than Molly. I don't think he could get out to Molly's this fast."

"I'm assuming she's another River Bend native returning home for the holiday," Claudia said but seemed unsure whether she had answered any of her own questions.

It was clear Aaron never mentioned his ex's name. To be fair to him, how many of us brought up our exes when dating someone new, especially someone like Mallory—for whom he had bought a ring. They'd split before he could propose.

Anderson returned from his scouting

expedition satisfied no one else was there, and the four of us continued to the top floor of the house. At the top level of the staircase, we marched like a band in a parade. Claudia and Anderson led with Sherrie and me lined up behind them.

I didn't know what to expect, and I don't think anyone else did either. The doors on our left were closed. The windows reflected the night's black sky, and frozen rain clung to the glass. Sherrie had Wilbur slung around her chest and was nervously drumming her fingers, otherwise maintaining calm.

A chorus of beeps rang out from our phones. We finally all had a decent signal.

Hailey entered from the opening at the end of the hall. She must've heard our phones, because we had not made a sound otherwise. "Quiet," she said, bringing a finger to her lips and motioning us in and to the right, to a kitchen table.

Anderson turned left, but Hailey pulled his arm.

"She's sleeping. Don't wake her," she said.

He pulled loose, walked beyond the kitchen cabinets, and looked through the archway. He seemed satisfied with whatever he saw.

We were in a galley-style kitchen with everything lined up on the outside wall. Floral wallpaper covered the opposing walls. The kitchen table anchored the right side, and beyond, there was a deck area that I assumed covered the ramp where all this shit started.

There seemed to be a twenty-degree-temperature swing from the hallway to the kitchen area. Harold spent zero money heating the main level when there was no business. Maribel was probably like my grandmother who could have been wearing her nightgown, sweater, and a robe and still insist on turning on the heat. I was impressed there was no burnt toast smell like my grandma's. The place had a smell, but I couldn't put my finger on what it was. I was searching for any smell to erase the odor we'd caught from our brief look at Two.

Hailey took the chair on the right at the kitchen table, Claudia took the one on the left, and Sherrie pulled the table away to make more room for everyone.

I leaned on the counter. "It's ok. You can leave it where it is. I'll stand, and he probably wants to keep checking how many people are here so he can file a good report."

Anderson was between me and the hallway, his eyes constantly scanning the room. I wanted to toss him and his backpack out the window. I undid the top four buttons of my coat, but I couldn't take it off because I had sweated through my shirt six times over.

Hailey asked, "What are you guys still doing

here?"

"How is your nana?" Claudia asked, ignoring the question.

"Sleeping. Finally. I don't know what has gotten into her lately. So, what are you guys still doing here?" She turned to Anderson. "I don't think she's up for an interview tonight. I'm not sure how she'll feel tomorrow. You should leave and maybe make something of your Saturday night."

Claudia's stomach rumbled, making everyone laugh.

"We're all stuck here for a while. Would you happen to have any food?" Sherrie asked.

"You can't eat Nana's food. I brought her some stuff to hold her over until her nurse returns on Monday."

Sherrie got up from the table and gingerly started opening cabinets, much to Hailey's dismay.

"Stop going through Nana's stuff."

"These cabinets have no system. Coffee cups with cereal bowls. Plates in a cabinet with spices. Is your great-grandma ok?"

"Stop going through her stuff." Hailey's voice started strong but lowered when she looked down the length of the kitchen.

We all turned, expecting to see Nana. Hailey stood up, but Claudia gently placed her hand on Hailey's arm and spoke as if Hailey were a toddler. "Hailey, it's ok. We will be here for a while. We're all starving. We'll replace everything we eat. Is Nana in that other room? Is that her bedroom?"

Hailey relented and collapsed back into the dining chair. "This floor is all set up for her. She was raised in this house, moved out when she married PaPaw, and moved back in when he died. None of the layout makes sense, but she knows where everything is. I once put a clean spoon away with the other spoons, and she talked about it for months. Apparently, that is the spoon she uses to mix sugar into her tea, and it belongs with the china cups. The layout of this floor is as disorganized as the cabinets, but it's how she likes it."

"Is she in her room or in the living room?" Claudia asked.

"Sleeping on the sofa. She's very hard of hearing if her hearing aid isn't turned on, so we're fine sitting here unless we make too much noise."

"Are you sure it's off? We can move downstairs," I said.

"We ain't going anywhere. I'm hungry," Sherrie said and opened the refrigerator.

"We can still go downstairs. I don't want to upset Maribel," I said.

"You really do know her?" Sherrie asked.

"I know of her. That guy knows Chicago"—I gestured to Anderson—"and I know the old ladies of River Bend. Got a problem with that?" I shot back at Sherrie. "What do you have in that fridge?"

Sherrie laughed. She grinned a sweet smile at me. "I don't have a problem with you and old ladies, but we have a problem in here."

"There has to be something we can munch on. I'll take a carrot stick at this point. Why are you laughing? You holding out on us? Do you need us to turn our backs so you can eat Nana's cottage cheese?" Claudia said.

"Since when is cottage cheese old folks' food?" Sherrie shot back.

"Can you just find us something to eat!" Claudia begged.

Without another word, a one-sided food fight started when Sherrie launched something from the refrigerator. It went slicing through the air. Anderson's arm went up so fast you would have thought he was deflecting a bag of dog shit. His fist punctured the bag of lettuce, causing it to bust open and rain down two pounds of Italian spring mix around him and me, and a packet of dressing hit Sherrie in the face.

"That was my dinner! The only thing that was not for Nana," Hailey said, but did not move to clean up.

Claudia was bent over at the waist laughing, nearly knocking her head on the table. Anderson went to check on Sherrie, but she brushed him away. I picked lettuce out of the collar of my flannel shirt. I reached for a piece, pulled the collar back, and a button went flying off.

Not salad. Not a fucking salad.

Sherrie barricaded herself behind the open fridge door. I picked out lettuce leaves and tossed them at her, kicking the button across the floor. When she realized I was out of ammunition, she went to look for a broom.

"Hailey, is there anything besides Nana's food to eat?" Claudia asked.

"Not here, but across the street, the root beer stand might have something."

"You were supposed to have cleared all that out at the end of summer." Sherrie was sweeping her way down the galley. "What are we going to find there? Got keys?"

Hailey dug in her purse and tossed me a ring of keys.

Sherrie threw the broom over to Anderson. "You need anything, One-Good-Foot Claudia?" When Claudia shook her head, Sherrie turned to me and said, "Let's go."

Anderson made a half attempt to block the hallway. "I don't think you should leave."

"We're going across the street for food; we're not abandoning our post," Sherrie snapped.

Sherrie and I went downstairs. She grabbed her coat from the bench, and we went out the parking lot door. I walked behind her as close to the house as we could get and stayed on the frozen grass when we turned the corner. There was not a car in sight. Two distant streetlights and a couple of houses with living room lights were the only signs of life in the neighborhood.

We had not spoken since we'd left the kitchen. I was spending all my energy trying not to land on my ass again and deciding if I should tell Sherrie that Aaron was with Dougie. Telling her would put her in the position of telling her friend that her boyfriend was currently riding out this storm with his ex. The ex of all exes.

We circled to the other side of the root beer stand, looking for the door, and a motion light snapped on. Sherrie fiddled with several keys before she found success.

I flipped on the light switch, and the single bulb flickered before it popped off. Something scampered away when we turned on our phone flashlights. The front side of the shack had two large windows covered by wood and a register covered with a blanket. Overhead, shelves held cups, napkins, and boxes. The right side had a soda dispenser, fryer, ice cream machine, and a grill.

Sherrie mumbled some swear words.

"What—you found more salad?" I asked.

"Mice are not my favorite. I have a feeling if Hailey had cleared this place out at the end of summer like Harold instructed her to do, this would not be a problem."

"We should probably avoid any dry goods. That box of old ice cream cones may house a family of mice. I don't think we need a gallon jug of maraschino cherries."

"I'm supposed to come back next week and take inventory, but now, I'll have to schedule an exterminator. Why can't Hailey do shit, and what's with her friend the reporter?" She turned and sat on top of the white ice chest.

I didn't know if I should tell her my theory or not.

She flashed her light in my face. "Well?"

I guess my expression said it all.

"Spill it?"

"I don't know what Anderson is, but I don't think he's a reporter or a historian. I don't think he's doing a story on the Carlin's settlement in Eastern Wisconsin like it is some *Little House on the Prairie* crap. My money is on him looking for Coletti or whoever was in Claudia's van. He was way too calm and not surprised by One or Two." I turned my phone light so I could better see her face without blinding either of us.

Her expression changed from a smile to angst to a smile when she replied. "When I said 'Spill it,' I was asking for the whole salad story and the anger that came with it."

"Oh." *I am such a dumbass.*

What she said next surprised me.

"I think you're right. Something is not right with the guy. Do you think we're in danger?"

"Danger? Doubt it." I didn't know if I was trying to convince her or me. "The police are on their way."

Sherrie hesitated before she spoke. "Are they? Did he really call the police, or did he just pretend? You tell 9-1-1 there's a dead body, and the police find their way here."

"But what could his motive be? Steal One or Two? Thinking about it now, where is his car? Did he come with Hailey?" Neither one of us had an answer. "Let's get some food and get back."

I looked into her dark eyes and lost myself. I think she had to repeat something she'd said.

"I said I think we struck out on food. Stale ice cream cones will not hold us over."

"Not ignoring you; just looking around. You're sitting on the freezer, and it appears to have a 'motor thing' running."

"I guess it is my turn to say oh." She smiled a smile that was so damn hot.

I wanted to kiss her in that strange moment, and for half a second, I thought she wanted me to. She reached out for me, but I hesitated. I didn't know why.

I stepped towards her, and her hand touched my chest as she pulled a piece of arugula lettuce off my shirt. I wanted to grab her right there on the freezer but flinched when her fingers touched where I had sweated through my shirt.

She tossed the lettuce on the floor. "Let the mouse have some fresh greens before I snap its head off in a few days." She inhaled deeply, hopping off the freezer, and flipped up the lid. "Bingo! It has some freezer burn, but at least it's something. We have ice cream bars and wings."

She grabbed a bag of wings and a box of ice cream bars in the shape of bears and tossed them into a plastic garbage bag. Moving past me towards the door, she asked, "Are you coming?"

"Hold on a sec. I think I see something. I hope they have my size."

"What are you talking about?"

I moved over an empty milk crate, stepped up, and reached the shelf above the soda dispenser.

"Pete, what are you doing? I thought we agreed to stick to the frozen stuff."

My face was flushed, and I was happy for the darkness. "I need a fresh shirt. I can't take my jacket off because I sweated through the flannel one," I said, unable to look at her.

I pulled the box down, and we found all sorts of shirts and sweatshirts of various colors from neon to pastel, in sizes from toddler to adult. All of them had a dancing bear holding a root beer, the C&C root beer stand logo.

"There's no good choice for a guy my size."

Sherrie sifted through the box and then carried her phone light over the counter. She opened several drawers and came up with a pair of scissors. I couldn't see her work, but she tossed me a sweatshirt and told me to put it on.

"Wait, I gave you the wrong one. Toss it back." She took off her coat, and I did mine. It was dark and we could only see shadows, but we still turned our backs to each other. She cut the sleeves three-quarters of the way and slit the collar in the middle, channeling the Bill Belichick look.

"I think the size will be good around your shoulders. You have long arms, so I had to cut the cuffs off. Thank god you found that box. I didn't know how to dress for work this morning. Nothing in my . . . my, uh, education taught me what to wear when working at a funeral home. I'm surprised Claudia hasn't called me out for wearing her blouse. I think I pitted out the sleeves beyond any washing. Turn your puffy jacket inside out— the rain has dropped off it, and it is probably drier than the inside." She reached for her coat and started to put it on.

I did as I was told and held a hand out to her. "Wait a sec." I grabbed another large plastic garbage bag, made one cut, and slipped it over her head. "You should be able to move your arms enough for balance; we're only going across the street, but you can't flip your wool coat inside out.

This will keep you surprisingly warm and dry, and you won't have to put your sweaty coat back on either. The plastic bag jacket trick my grandfather taught me. You don't look cool but you will be dry."

"Cool, we used to do this while cleaning up after soccer practice." She grabbed yet another bag, slipped her coat and the remnants of our sweatshirts in it. She put the scissors back and double-checked that the space was how we'd found it, minus our shirts and dinner.

Sherrie locked the door and walked into shit.

Literally — shit.

CHAPTER TWENTY–THREE

SHERRIE
THREE MINUTES AGO

"I think the size will be good around your shoulders. You have long arms, so I had to cut the cuffs off. Thank god you found that box. I didn't know how to dress for work this morning. Nothing in my . . . my, uh"—*Don't turn around, don't do it. Claudia can't be right. I just want a look. Oh, his back is lean, and his shoulders could carry me anywhere*—"education taught me what to wear when working at a funeral home. I'm surprised Claudia hasn't called me out for wearing her blouse. I think I pitted out the sleeves beyond any washing."

Pitted. Did I just say I pitted and confessed I too sweated through a shirt to a cute guy? I've already started to sweat again in my fresh shirt.

"Turn your jacket inside out."

He's so close. God, his breath on my neck . . . give me more.

"You should be able to move your arms enough for balance; we're only going across the street."

I gotta do something . . . need something in my hands before I grab him! He's dating Anna! Just grab our stuff and prepare to tell Claudia off for filling my head with thoughts about a guy who is already taken.

I turned the lock and pounded on the door twice, once to make sure it was locked and once because Claudia was right.

Then things got worse when I literally and figuratively stepped in shit.

CHAPTER TWENTY-FOUR

Claudia

"What happened to your forehead? What are you wearing!" I put down my teacup, pulled open the freezer, and grabbed a tray of ice cubes. It took me three cabinets before I found a plastic bag between the toaster and some light bulbs. We exchanged the ice bag for the bag of frozen chicken wings she'd been holding against her forehead.

"I tried avoiding stepping in old bird crap, Pete tried to catch me, but the bag of wings he was holding came flying forward instead. I didn't land on my butt but got nicked in the temple with frozen wings. I'm not hurt that badly. It's probably more dirt and dust than bruises."

Pete placed a box on the counter, took a

garbage bag from Sherrie's hand and lifted another one off her, tossing it in the sink because logic could not tell him where the garbage can was located, before guiding her to the table. He returned to the box on the counter and passed out ice cream teddy bear bars to Hailey, me, Sherrie, and took one for himself. He resumed his position, leaning against the counter, and I joined Sherrie and Hailey back at the table.

"I made tea. It may not pair well with ice cream, but it will warm you up. It's on the stove behind you, Pete," I said.

He poured two cups for Sherrie and Hailey, but Hailey declined.

I blew on the hot tea and said over the cup, "Did Anderson come back with you, or is he checking if anyone else is here again?"

"Come back?" Pete asked.

"He left a minute after you. He said it wasn't good for you to leave the house and was going to have you wait until the police get here. You didn't see him?"

Pete and Sherrie exchanged looks. I thought Pete's face flushed, but he turned and took off his coat.

Is his coat on inside out?

Hailey finally joined the conversation. "What are you wearing?"

Pete had on a pea-soup-colored sweatshirt,

and part of his neck was painted turquoise. Sherrie had on a neon-yellow shirt with a blue dancing bear on it.

She answered Hailey's question without looking at me. "We had trouble with our clothes."

"Ooooohhh, la la," Hailey said, giggling.

"Nothing like that," Sherrie said, still not looking at me.

"You're going to have to pay for them. Don't be stealing from Harold."

"Just think of it as payment for services rendered for this overtime of a shitshow I'm working for Harold right now. Why do you call him Harold and not Grandpa or Papa?"

"I think I used to call him Grandad, then years ago, my father started calling him Harold instead of Dad so I just followed what he did, and no one stopped me."

Pete held up a hand. "Wait. So Anderson is not up here, and we didn't see him. Does that mean he left?"

Nobody answered, so with a frustrated grunt, he looked for a garage can for about five seconds, then tossed his ice cream stick on top of Sherrie's discarded garbage bag jacket.

"I'm going to look for Anderson," he said.

"He is not with Nana," Hailey said. "We didn't see him go past the hallway opening."

"Could he have gone through the doors in

the hallway? You guys don't have a view from the table."

"I got up soon after you left to make the tea, and I would have noticed if he opened a hallway door."

"The first door down opens to the sitting area where Nana is resting." Hailey leaned forward in her seat. "Its hinges are really squeaky. The only time that door's open is if Nana is having her friends over to play mahjong. We would have heard the door even if we couldn't see him go in. The second door, the one closest to stairs, is a faux door. It's part of the original layout of the house. Behind it is either Nana's bathroom or her bedroom. I'm not sure how it lines up on the other side. Her bedroom is up-front with windows overlooking the front drive and 6th Street. The bathroom is between her bedroom and living room."

"I am gonna see if your friend is still here," Pete said.

"Don't go alone. Take Hailey with you," I barked, wanting time with Sherrie alone to find out what had happened in the root beer stand.

"I'll go. Hailey, stay here in case Maribel gets up and freaks out 'cause we're sitting in her kitchen," Sherrie said.

When they left, I wiggled back up to the stove for more hot tea.

Why is Aaron not responding to my texts?

I walked back to the table, nearly tripping on Wilbur and its contents. I bent down and picked up Maddie's newspapers I had taken from the hotel and started reading.

And there it was—the local *River Bend Gazette* told me everything I was missing. A guest columnist by the name of Mallory Douglas had posed a question in the editorial column: how should the town of River Bend welcome back one of its own? Mallory was back to write a story about Anthony Coletti and was now peppering Aaron with questions.

That's all *she is doing, right?*

Again, Aaron was one of the good guys, so I had nothing to worry about. I was sure they were old high school friends. She was the one bothering me, not him.

I sent a quick text asking when he could get here. Three dots appeared, but he didn't reply so I turned my focus back to her editorial.

. . . Anthony Coletti helped establish River Bend and developed most of the manufacturing plants. Does his reputation in Chicago preclude him from returning home? Harold Carlin has not been available for comment. Why won't Carlin answer questions about his father's former partner and company's namesake. Is Coletti officially out of the business, or did Carlin just drop the name?

I leaned back in my chair and looked at Hailey who had her head in her phone. "C&C—Carlin and Cole—is actually Carlin and Col—"

Hailey looked up after tossing her phone down again. "Sorry, just my dad texting for the hundredth time. What did you say?"

Sherrie and Pete walked back in as I made the connection.

"Carlin and Cole is really Carlin and *Coletti*. Harold is not worried about some mob family coming home to River Bend. He's worried about Coletti returning to this home, *his* home."

Sherrie stopped in her tracks. "I work for the mob?"

Bodies in a funeral home: The Scooby-Doo Trio, plus Hailey, minus Anderson, plus One, Two, and Nana

CHAPTER TWENTY-FIVE

"My family is not in the mob!" Hailey yelled, then backpedaled. "Not really."

"Mob or mob-adjacent, or do you care to elaborate?" Sherrie asked. With one shake of her hand, she motioned for Hailey to get up.

Together, they pulled the table away from the wall, and Sherrie forced Hailey to the back chair. She summoned Pete to the now-vacant seat. The four of us sat around the oval wooden table that was probably older than the four of us combined. The four high-back chairs with burgundy seat cushions provided support with minimal comfort. The tabletop held two woven floral place mats, bread crumbs from that morning's—or last week's toast—a smear of butter, and several coffee stain rings.

The three of us stared at Hailey, waiting for her to explain. Sherrie literally had her pinned against the wall. The four of us were sitting around this oval wooden table, and waited for Hailey to help it make sense to us.

"Yes, it is true Coletti used to be part of C&C. I really don't know much."

Sherrie looked at me as if Hailey wasn't in the room. "It's like talking to a kindergartener."

Pete tried a different approach. "Hailey, do you think Maribel would give us more details?"

"I don't know. She has been a wreck. I've only been back from college a few days, but the nurse said she's been erratic all week. She might not be the most reliable."

"What about your mom?" I asked.

"All she does is talk crap about the Carlin family since the divorce. I don't think we'll get a straight answer from her."

"What about your dad? Don't give us that whole he-abandoned-me-for-another-family routine. You said he's been trying to call or text you numerous times tonight," I said.

Hailey didn't move a muscle to react or respond.

I gestured towards the stairs. "Do I need to tell you about the bodies down there? *This is important.*"

"Bodies?" Hailey looked at each of us.

The three of us looked at each other as it dawned on us that Hailey hadn't been part of the escapade in the embalming room. She didn't understand our urgency.

"Can you just call your dad?" I said.

Sherrie jumped in. "Wait, before you call him, can you call Holton and ask him when someone will get here?"

"What do you mean? You had a date with him, but you want me to call him?" Hailey said.

"I am not dating the dude. We went to two community events together that I confused as a date. I have no romantic interest in the guy. We just have to make sure the police are on their way."

Sherrie had looked directly at Hailey while she'd spoken, but I thought she had been talking to someone else in the room, or maybe it was just my hopeful imagination.

"Why? How badly did you screw up? You want me to call Harold or the police?"

Sherrie kept her temperament in check, knowing we needed Hailey to be an ally. "The police, please."

"Why?" Hailey swiveled her head back and forth between all of us, seemingly waiting for the punchline. "What's going on? Is Nana safe?"

"Why do you ask about Nana?" Sherrie said.

"You guys are freaking me out. Why are the three of you here, and why do the police need to come?"

Pete deflected, not answering her direct questions. "Tell us about Anderson. How do you know him?"

As Hailey spoke, I looked around the kitchen, which was more of an afterthought than an actual kitchen with one overhead light in the center of the room casting shadows on everyone's faces.

"I met Anderson in Chicago. One night, my roommates and I went out, and we started talking to him. It was crazy when he mentioned he was writing a collection of stories about families that date back to colonial times. He was using the archives on campus to research different families in the area. One of my roommates tried to convince him to do a story about her family, but he said his editor had given him a list of twenty families in the Midwest to research and contact. It turned out Papaw and Nana were on the list."

"Coincidence," I said.

Hailey missed the sarcasm, and I kept going. "When did this happen?"

"Maybe five or six weeks ago. I told him I would set it up for him to talk with Nana."

Sherrie had her phone in her hand. "Is Anderson his first or last name?"

Hailey shrugged.

Sherrie kept at it. "Do you have an email address for him or something that proves he is who he says he is?"

"What are you getting at? Is Nana in danger?"

I leaned forward. "Why do you keep asking if Nana is in danger?"

Hailey didn't answer, so I tried Sherrie's trick and placed my hand on her arm.

"What is it you're not telling us?"

"I usually talk to Nana at least once a week when I'm at school, then last month or something changed in her." Hailey sounded like a concerned toddler. "I'm not talking old people crazy talk. She seems genuinely worried and sad about something. She wouldn't say much to me. When I got here a few days ago, I thought she was better, but her mood changes quickly between sadness, anger, and a little anxiousness." True fear resonated from Hailey's far-off gaze. "She's been carrying around this old photo of her and a baby. I asked her about it, and she just patted my back and smiled. She even seemed excited to talk to Anderson about the Carlin family story, saying she could add a lot to the story that has never been told. When I told Harold about Anderson, he freaked out and tried stopping the interview and article. Nana made me promise to let Anderson tell the family story, and she would deal with Harold."

Pete chimed in. "How did you get here today? I didn't see a car in the lot when we went across the street, plus it's blocked off."

"I'm across 6th Street in the small lot by the pond. Probably can't see it from here. I nearly drove into that cement barrier you had them put here— why are they here by the way?"

Sherrie answered quickly. "That wasn't me. How did Anderson find you today? Did he have a time set up with Maribel this evening? Did you drive him here?"

"I bumped into him at the grocery store. He wanted to try and get Nana to open up more this evening, thinking she might be more relaxed later in the day."

"So he drove here on his own, or you gave him a lift?" Pete asked.

"He followed me, and before you ask, I don't know what kind of car. It was something boring. Why are you guys asking all this stuff?"

Sherrie answered for the group. "We just need you to call Holton. I deleted his number."

She did as she was told and, getting his voicemail, left the most nondescript message asking him to call her back. Sherrie grabbed Hailey's phone and sent him a text message.

"Come here right away. Something happened and need police help," she read as she typed.

"Seriously, what is going on?" Hailey said, full-on whining.

My stomach rumbled again.

Pete got up and started searching the cabinets. "Hailey, do you know where pans are?" Using Maribel's logic, he opened the oven and found all sorts of pans and baking sheets. "Oh, never mind, found them."

"Yeah, only Nana and her nurse use the stovetop, but I'm not sure if the oven works."

Pete took the wings to the freezer, exchanging them for more ice cream bars and passing them out to everyone.

Noise came from Nana's area, and Hailey stood up. She was up, around Sherrie's chair, past Pete, and almost to the end of the kitchen, in time to greet Nana as she came into view. Maribel was wearing the same white gown we had seen her earlier in.

As much as Hailey could grate on my nerves, it was endearing to learn about her affection for Maribel.

We stood up, said hello but were unsure if she could hear us. Sherrie actually put her half eaten ice cream pop behind her back like a child hiding a stolen cookie. Nana acknowledged us with a slight head nod and hello. Hailey motioned to her ear.

I felt like an intruder. "Hailey, we'll be downstairs. We don't want to disturb you both."

"Then why don't you leave?" Hailey

retorted.

"We can't. Remember, we have to wait for Holton or whoever shows up," I said.

Hailey checked her phone. "No response from him."

Nana tapped Hailey on the arm, and Hailey motioned to her ear again.

Hailey looked at us. "Like I said, she is very hard of hearing, yet she still forgets to put in her hearing aid. Let me get her settled and heat up the soup I brought for her."

Hailey took her nana by the elbow and guided her back. When Maribel reached in the front square pocket of her nightgown for her hanky to wipe her nose, she failed to realize something dropped out.

I started to go pick it up for her. "Uh, wait, Hailey—"

"Please, just go and let me get her settled." Hailey motioned towards downstairs. "I'm going to help Nana get dressed. It embarrasses her to be seen in her nightgown." She shuffled Maribel into the next room, out of sight.

Pete stepped away from the table and pushed his chair in. He retrieved the trash bags from the sink, looking for the trash can, which he finally found in the lower cabinet next to the sink area.

Sherrie came around and picked up Wilbur

for me. I pulled out my $137 sweatshirt, and we shoved Maddie's newspapers back in. I slipped on the sweatshirt not for warmth but for a much-needed hug.

Pete and Sherrie moved to the hallway, and before I joined them, I walked over to the item that had slipped from Maribel's pocket and picked it up. It was a black-and-white photo of a beautiful woman holding a newborn.

I could never play that game where you match baby photos to the grown-up because I couldn't ever see the resemblance. I had a weird fascination with sketch artists that drew age-progression photos of missing children. However, something about the infant struck me as familiar. I thought it was the deep-set eyes.

Sherrie, yelling from the main level, drew my attention away from the photo, which I slipped into my pocket. At the top of the stairs, I heard someone pounding on the front door. Hearing Sherrie's loud voice was almost as jarring as the person on the other side of the door that she was yelling at.

People in the funeral home: Still missing Anderson but adding two more

CHAPTER TWENTY-SIX

"Move the truck! Move the truck, or I will not let you in. The other side of the root beer stand has parking. Can't you see the damn padlock." Sherrie barked and continued. "Go to the back door!"

Suddenly, I got very adept at using the cane and made good time going down the stairs. Sherrie was standing at the entrance of the viewing room, and Pete continued to the rear of the house.

She looked at me, and with a very direct but smooth voice, she warned, "Brace yourself."

A muffled pounding came from the back door. Pete slowed his steps and entered the restroom.

The pounding came again, and I took a step forward.

Sherrie pulled me back.

"Let her wait. He went to move the truck, and she didn't wait for him."

Pete exited the restroom and opened the rear door. In came bomber-jacket-wearing newspaper guest columnist Mallory Douglas walking in step with Aaron, and Pete followed behind them. Nobody was smiling, and Aaron was looking everywhere except towards me.

Sherrie nudged me into the viewing room. I stopped at a tall chair, grabbed a small decorative pillow, and tossed it at the couch where I had previously sat. The pillow acted like a booster and kept me from drowning in the old sofa.

Sherrie adjusted the lights to a comfortable midlevel, removing shadows we created as we moved around. She resumed her position on the arm of the sofa. Mallory walked in, surveyed the room, and headed towards the front windows, pushing open the drapes and looking to the front drive. Aaron walked through the large opening and paused as one might do when entering a church. He stepped aside and let Pete pass. Pete grabbed a chair from the viewing section and moved it to Sherrie's left.

Mallory walked down the center aisle to the front of the room and pulled out a chair that was about ten chairs away from us. She turned it to face us and sat down.

Aaron finally stepped into the room. Staying

in back, he placed his hands on the top of a couple of chairs almost as if using them for support when he broke the silence. "I'm not sure if everyone knows everyone. That's Mallory. Reporter and formerly of River Bend." He took a deep breath and, definitely not looking at anyone, kept talking. "Mallory, you know Pete, and maybe from the bar, you know that's Sherrie, and this is her roommate, Claudia."

ROOMMATE! SHERRIE'S ROOMMATE! Did Aaron just roommate me? What the hell happened back there at the bar?

Sherrie froze. Pete's head spun around so fast I thought it might snap off. My ears buzzed. I forced a smile and a head nod towards the woman that was not Sherrie's roommate.

I couldn't feel the air and didn't know if it was cold or warm, but the scent of eucalyptus snapped me from burning with rage. I hoisted myself up and slid the medicinal-smelling plant in a brass pot ten feet away from the couch so I didn't inhale it with each breath. I needed to do something constructive with the fury building inside me. I took my time returning to the couch, emphasizing my cane. Sherrie knew to let me be, and I thought she even motioned to Pete not to help me.

"Why are we in here? I thought I was here to pick you guys up," Aaron asked Pete.

Once again, we—the Scooby-Doo Trio—

looked at each other, and with a couple of shrugs and one volunteer, Sherrie spoke to our new guests.

"Well, we can't leave."

"What do you mean you can't leave?" Aaron asked.

He undid the zipper of his coat halfway. The puffy black coat was dry. The freezing rain must have finally stopped, but Aaron's cheeks were red and I could almost see the cold sliding off him.

Sherrie, ever faithful, resumed her Scooby-Doo Trio's spokesperson duties. "We had a few things happen and have to wait for others to arrive."

"Things?" Aaron looked at Pete again. "You got to give me more than that."

I wouldn't have ever held anything back from Aaron, even if I didn't understand that damn roommate comment. I would have shot right back at him, but the No Punchline Ice Princess held me back. She pulled off her beret and fluffed her hair. Damn, she could pull off the bomber-jacket-and-beret combo unlike any supermodel I had ever seen.

"Waiting for the police. I have to report the missing van," I said.

"Van? Someone stole it?" Aaron asked, barely looking at me. "Can't we go to the police station and fill out a report?"

Snot-ass attitude shot out of my mouth. "No,

we can't *just go* to the police station. They have to come here."

Silence filled the room. Princess Bitch or Beret Bimbo—I was so confused, mad, and unable to confer with Sherrie on the proper designation for Mallory. I had no hard evidence of why I didn't like that woman, but some people just invoked that type of response out of Sherrie and me. Maybe I felt like she had mocked my *High School Musical* sweatshirt, or she had annoyed Sherrie at work, or most likely, she had some strange hold on Aaron that was altering his usual warm demeanor.

Is this why he hasn't been sleeping well all week?

Whatever-She-Should-Be-Called finally split the pressure-filled room. "I know about Coletti being here. You don't have to talk in code."

Calmly and simply, I countered her sentiment. "Yes, we are in a funeral home with a body. There is no news there."

Aaron dipped his head to hide his reaction.

Sherrie parroted my demeanor and simply stated, "It was the prime topic at the pancake breakfast this morning."

"Can we talk about something else for a minute?" Aaron asked.

I braced myself for something else to come out of his mouth that would inspire me to launch my cane like a javelin into his neck, so I was not prepared when he turned to the dual visual of

237

neon-yellow Sherrie and split-pea-soup-colored Pete.

Aaron gestured towards them. "What the hell are you guys wearing?"

"I know, they look hideous." Hailey came up behind Aaron. "Now what are you doing here?"

Aaron nodded to her.

Suck-Up-Schmoozer Mallory said, "Hailey, it's been a while since I've seen you. You look great. I love that color of peach on you."

Sherrie had her back turned to me, but I could feel her eye roll.

"Thank you." Hailey blushed. "Nana would like you to come upstairs. I guess Aaron and Mallory should come too. I have to warn you, she's still a little fragile, and I'm not sure what she's going to say."

Pete stood up first and waited for Sherrie and me to pass before he fell into step behind us. We followed like hesitant soldiers wanting an explanation of what lay ahead.

We were near the doorway, passing Aaron, when he softly asked, "Is there something we should know before going up?"

"Ask my roommate, your employee," I said, hobbling forward.

Hailey waited at the foot of the stairs when the Eager-To-Be-Center-Of-Attention Mallory skipped ahead to be at her side.

Number of people on the stairs: One and a half too many (I still like Aaron—but I'm mad enough to count him as a half.)

CHAPTER TWENTY-SEVEN

I could not hear the chitchat between Hailey and Brunette-Twit—this is getting too exhausting and wasting too much good energy on her so I am just calling her Mallory.

At the top of the stairs, Hailey looked at her phone, and her shoulders tightened.

The dim hallway with the kitchen light at the end, the cold air coming in through the old windows, and the wind howling gave it the sensation of walking through a haunted house.

Hailey and Mallory were a few feet ahead of us. I had gotten pretty good at using the cane, and I wanted to be as far away from Aaron as I could at this moment. We shuffled into the kitchen to our left and followed Hailey into the grand parlor room. Maribel was wearing a pale cardigan and matching pants and shoes, clutching a handkerchief in one hand and the other resting on one of the two chairs that anchored the seating area opposite the fireplace.

A wave of heat steamrolled over us. We had gone from arctic to senior—I have not opened a window in twenty years—stuffy. I suddenly regretted my $137 sweatshirt and was surprised there was no rain or at least fog in the doorway. Pete collected our jackets and placed them on a chair near the doorway.

The large room was divided into distinct sections, with the seating area immediately in front of us. Two gold velvet sofas faced each other, the fireplace anchoring one side and two chairs with Hailey and Maribel fixed on the other end. There was a highly polished rectangle table with a doily and a brass bowl in the center. Behind the far sofa on the right, near an archway, four chairs surrounded a square table holding mahjong tiles. Two floor-to-ceiling windows on either side of the fireplace brought in only a faint glow of light from the streetlights. A chandelier set off-center in the room provided the only light.

The far-left corner had an old sofa with folded blankets and a pillow lying on top. It faced a small TV on an antique table. A slim television, cable box, and heavy cords contrasted everything in that corner and pretty much the entire room, which I didn't think had changed in the last few decades besides the addition of the television.

The corner to our immediate left was taken up by a closet that I thought was oddly placed and quite large for one person until I stepped around it and noticed the lights on a metal panel, realizing it was the elevator. Between the elevator and hallway door two tall bookcases flanked a reading chair with a floor lamp. The walls, wood trim, and door leading to the main hallway were painted a deep emerald green. Each vignette had a rug defining its space and purpose.

Mallory stopped in the entryway, so Sherrie and I shuffled past to the bookcases, followed by Pete and Aaron. I looked at the framed pictures on the bookcase and the walls, trying to elbow Sherrie to see if she recognized one particular person, but she was too far away.

We were held in silence as if waiting to meet some foreign dignitary. Hailey went to Nana's side.

Aaron spoke first. "Maribel, it's good to see you. Sorry if we're disturbing you."

We! What is with his we? He just got here. He is our ride out of here. He had been busy with Mallory and not part of *we.* Scooby-Doo Trio—Fred, Daphne, and Velma. We didn't need Shaggy. Shaggy always screwed up the scene.

Maribel walked forward with her arms stretched out, and Aaron stepped around the small sofa to meet the hug.

"So good to see you. How are your mom and dad? Oh, The Rhoimlys have been here almost as long as us. Maybe a ship or two later. Jan's still keeping her peach pie recipe a secret, I assume?"

Aaron gave a courtesy laugh. "No one is getting that from her."

Maribel's attention swept over to Mallory. "My goodness, darling, it is always nice to have you in River Bend. You grandmother could do with more of seeing you, and I'm sure, this one too."

Aaron tried meeting my eyes, and I looked away. When he took a step, Maribel took his arm and guided him and Mallory to the couch. Mallory sat just off-center of her cushion towards the center, and Aaron seemed to be trying to leave a space between the two of them, nearly on top of the armrest. He sat forward with his elbows on his knees and hands balled together. He looked ready to jump up at any moment.

Maribel's eyes lit up when she saw Pete. She reached out and took his hand. "You must be one of the Morris boys. You have your mother's eyes; all you boys do. It was a shame when your folks moved to Florida. I could always count on your dad's common sense at the town meetings. I remember the three of you always running around the town square during the performances in the gazebo. Your mother would drag you boys there and make you listen to the most dreadful music." She looked at Sherrie and me. "The town council would never spend money for any decent musicians." Maribel turned back to Pete. "I hope you are not the one who got caught vandalizing the streets signs or stole the Santa from the town square or . . ."

Pete released his hand from the soft grasp. "I have to stop you there, Mrs. Carlin. Those offenses belong to my brothers, but if you continue, I have a feeling you might recall some stuff I and the town would like to forget."

"Please call me Maribel. That goes for all of you. Have a seat here. You Morris boys were not that bad, not like the O'Keefes. What can you expect from the Irish though?" She directed Pete to the couch opposite of Mallory and turned her attention to us. Logical order would have her addressing Sherrie first, but her attention hopped to me. She motioned me to her side, placing her frail hands on mine. The veins on her hands were almost as big as my fingers. "You must be the one living with EG."

"Yes, I'm Claudia."

"You are the mirror image of Katie Lyn and EG with those beautiful strong features from the Graham side of the family tree and, fortunately, not your grandmother's side. We should have met sooner, but I appreciate you coming at this time."

Her voice was getting weaker, and her hand shook while she held mine. Almost under her breath but loud enough for some to hear, she said, "Maybe you did get your manners and that cane from your grandmother's side."

Maribel dabbed her nose. Her eyes had an empty look. "Next Thursday, I hope we can count on your vote at the school board meeting."

The room went still. The grandfather clock ticked, and the wind howled. Hailey touched Nana's arm, and the light appeared in her eyes again. She shifted her stance to look around the room.

Sherrie remained standing behind Aaron and Mallory. When we'd first entered the parlor, Maribel had controlled the room like a conductor. That little energy she had used getting dressed and waiting for us to come up seemed to have suddenly taken its toll, but she was clearly still orchestrating everyone in the room. She took a few steps, holding on to me, and directed me next to Pete.

I looked at Sherrie. She had a look on her face that I'd only seen a few times since I'd known her.

Her eyes were big like she was steadying herself for a fight or holding back tears. She dropped her arms straight to her sides, curled her fingers into a loose pulsing fist, yet trying to be neutral while reading the situation.

In the last seventy seconds, Maribel had zigzagged across the spectrum of social behavior. She graciously welcomed us into her world, honoring the old families of River Bend while cursing the Irish and my grandmother's side of the family, scolding me for not coming to introduce myself to her upon moving to her town, and listing the delinquent behavior of the Morris boys but praising Pete's dad.

Instead of sitting down, I made a move towards Sherrie, but with a slight shake of her head, I knew to remain where I was. As a Black woman, she had faced this more times than I ever knew possible.

Hailey and Maribel seemed to have a silent discussion with some nods and arm gesturing, ending with Hailey guiding Maribel back to her chair. I wasn't putting words or thoughts into Sherrie's mind, but I could read her expression. Sadness rippled through my body. Being ignored was sometimes just as bad as anything else.

Maribel coughed and wiped her nose. She raised her arm. "Hon, come here, please."

Sherrie walked behind Hailey's and Maribel's chairs and stood to the left side.

Maribel reached for Sherrie's hand to move Sherrie so they were facing each other. "I'm sorry I did not catch your name."

"I am Sherrie Lawrence. I attend Jamison

College and just started working for Mr. Carlin."

"That's nice, sweetie. Would you be a dear and help Hailey bring in some tea for the group? That one"—she gestured to me—"can't seem to move very well, and I don't think the other knows her way around a kitchen."

Hailey interjected, "Nana, they already had tea in the kitchen."

"Well, if you think that is good enough, so be it. Sweetie, you can pull up a chair over there."

Pete jumped up and had Sherrie take his seat. He walked back to the card table and pulled a chair between Sherrie and the fireplace.

I could not fathom what was going to happen next. What was this lady going to say to us, and why did she think we were there?

People in a funeral home: Seven, plus One and Two, still no police or Anderson (maybe he was staying away from Mallory—that would earn him a gold star for being on the anti-Mallory side)

CHAPTER TWENTY-EIGHT

The ceiling light hung over the couch Sherrie and I were sitting on. At one point, before the room had been divided up for Maribel, it had been much larger, and the light would have been correctly centered in the room and not putting the two of us under a spotlight.

Sherrie relaxed slightly but still seemed on edge with the old woman. I was overly warm but not highly uncomfortable, the cane sitting across my lap, as I forced myself to look at everyone equally. I would not give anyone the satisfaction of seeing me angry, confused, or intimidated by anyone in the room, by which I really meant anyone sitting on the couch opposite me.

Maribel cleared her throat. "It is so nice of you all to come to pay your respects for the Coletti family, our dear associates. Some people of your generation don't understand what it means to honor those that came before them and paved the way." Maribel coughed again, and her voice got weaker. "The Carlins, Colettis, and the Handleys were the first ones here. Clarence Handley started logging, but us Carlins, with the help of the Coletti clan, made it what it was. My Alvin knew how to change with the times and knew when to move on from logging and into manufacturing. Clarence tried his hand at mining, came up blank, and the family lost everything."

Maribel stopped speaking. Everybody stayed still, and I looked at Hailey watching her great-grandmother and waiting for a signal that Maribel was done talking.

Maribel turned to Hailey. "Would you get me some of my tea, dear?"

When Hailey left, Maribel continued. "Anthony left town when—" Maribel wiped her nose and also her eyes this time. "Oh, my Anthony. My poor Anthony. We had a tragedy strike our family, and when you can't count on your friend or business partner, it's a real shame. Anthony just left one day and now . . . well, as you know, he has returned home to be buried. It is so special of you to come."

Maribel's speech grew shakier and slower. She turned to me and said, "Now, miss, please let

EG and Katie Lyn know to call before they come. They should know better than to just show up."

Hailey was speedy with the tea, but when she stood between me and Maribel with the teacup waiting for Maribel to wipe her nose, I realized it wasn't tea in the cup. It could have been Scotch or brandy but not tea. Maribel took a sip and handed Hailey the teacup.

"Nana, I think that's enough. They've paid their respects. It's time for them to go," Hailey announced loudly.

It took several tries before Maribel could stand. Aaron stood and helped her up and then got a hug. He stepped back behind the couch, and Mallory came forward for a hug. That seemed to take the last of her energy. Hailey and I each took her arm and guided towards her bedroom.

Pete returned his chair to the card table. Maribel stopped and gestured to him, waiting for him to come forward.

She wagged a finger at him. "Tell your sister not to bring those kids to church until they behave themselves."

Pete looked at Hailey, confusion clear on his face.

She mouthed the words, *Just go with it*.

"Yes, ma'am," Pete said, and stepped away.

Hailey and I tried guiding Maribel closer to the doorway, but she stayed in place. "Where is the other one? I thought there was one more."

I mouthed, *Sherrie* to Hailey, who just nodded.

I called Sherrie over, and Maribel took her hand.

"Sweetie, I don't know your family, but they raised a decent child. One that comes to pay respects. If they need work, just let Harold know, and he will find something for them."

Hailey took her great-grandmother's arm and led her through the doorway. She came back ten seconds later alone. "If you guys could leave now, it would be best for Nana."

No one had moved since Maribel left the room. I assumed everyone was doing the same as me: replaying the scene that had just unfolded in front of us.

"We can't leave the house, but we will go back downstairs," I said.

"I don't want to argue, but just leave this place," Hailey spat out, then fumbled with a light switch on the wall. Two lights turned on, one illuminating the hallway to Maribel's room and the other above the TV and the corner of the sofa. Hailey's eyes lit up, and she quickly turned off the parlor room light and retreated to Maribel's side.

Sherrie and I walked around the sofa and were almost to the bookcases. Mallory and Aaron were at the entry to the kitchen. Pete stayed where he was, looking down the hallway. Hailey had just disappeared when he turned the light back on. He looked at us and then pointed to the TV stand.

"What is it?" Mallory asked.

Pete shook his head. "Ah, I just thought I saw a spider. Must be the shadows moving around."

He met my eyes. I followed his gaze to the television stand. Under it, a small dust-free rectangle, where a small rug had once lain, stood out because of the unsettled dust surrounding it. The missing rug seemed to be approximately the shape and size of a car floor mat.

Or is the car floor mat covering Two's face the same size the television rug?

If the funeral home hadn't already freaked me out, standing near the possible murder scene did.

People in a funeral home: The genuine answer? The number Maribel believes to be here? The number Hailey knows to be here? Because there seemed to be three different answers.

CHAPTER TWENTY-NINE

Pete turned off the light, and we hustled out of the room, traipsing single file through the kitchen.

Pete, taking the rear, opened a cabinet and pulled out a box of saltines. "I found these when I was looking for the trash can but thought Hailey might bite my head off. It's not much, but I need more than ice cream right now."

"I could do with some of Nana's tea," Sherrie said.

Pete rifled through two more cabinets and found a bottle of brown liquid. "Don't worry, it's not the only one. She won't miss it tonight."

"You guys having a picnic?" Aaron asked.

"It would be cool if this was only a picnic. Let's head downstairs," I said.

We made our way without incident down

the stairs and into the viewing room. Sherrie excused herself to find cups. I resumed my position on the couch, and Pete asked Aaron to help drag two living room–style armchairs over from the corner of the room.

Mallory took a seat in one of the new chairs. It became a standoff on who would not take the seat next to her.

Sherrie walked back in with a stack of Styrofoam cups. Her timing excellent, she read the room. She walked to the front window, tossed the cups on the seat of a soft, low living room chair and then she put her hands on the back getting ready to slide it over. I didn't know if it was her almost belly-flopping over or her yelp when she tumbled forward that got us laughing and broke the silence.

The pastel floral-print chair had a pleated skirt wrapped around the bottom of the chair, hiding the wheels. Pete went over to help, and Sherrie straightened herself up.

"I got this now. It's easier than it looks. How's your arm?" Sherrie asked.

"Better, just a little sore. You take the bottle and crackers. I won't be able to twist the cap but I can push a chair with wheels and remain upright."

"Really? I remember you pushing a gurney with wheels and you ending up on your butt." Sherrie smiled at him.

"Ice took me out, but half-inch-pile carpet

took you down."

Mallory and I were the only ones still seated. We waited for Sherrie to crack open the bottle. Pete handed her a cup. She poured two fingers of brown liquor and handed the first one to me and then Mallory. Aaron declined, and she poured two more and handed one to Pete before taking the vacant seat next to Mallory. Pete was standing closest to the couch, so logic had him sit next to me.

Aaron took the newly acquired chair and resumed his earlier position, sitting hunched forward, elbows on knees, and hands in the prayer position. "What has you guys drinking now? Can't you wait until we get out of here?"

One by one, we answered, each firing off our answers, raising a salute to Aaron when we spoke.

"Were you not just up there? We do have to leave before that school board meeting on Thanksgiving," I said

Pete followed with "I don't have any sisters, much less a sister with kids at church."

"That lady offered my folks work." Sherrie drew up a Southern accent. "Maybe Ma could cook, and Pa could work in the field."

"We have been waiting for the police for hours with dead bodies hanging around."

Pete answered again and nailed it when he simply said, "It's Saturday night. I'm at a funeral home."

Mallory raised her glass, took a sip, and continued. "No one is giving me a story, and according to Maribel, I need to pass on a message from her to my dead grandma."

Aaron dropped his head and let logic and reason go. He had come here to pick us up and finally realized he was stuck in here. "Oh, hell." He leaned forward to grab a cup and gestured to Sherrie for the bottle.

He raised his glass in a silent toast, drank a sip of what was now clearly brandy. "You guys have got to fill us in. There are several missing pieces," Aaron said.

I let the *us* comment slide. "There are a lot of missing pieces. Some are obvious." I just let that hang in the air.

I caught Sherrie looking at me and then to Pete, probably to see if he understood that shot I had taken at Aaron.

"Not everything is as it appears. Please fill in the gaps. I'm sure there is a good reason for everything, including why I'm drinking brandy in a funeral parlor on a Saturday night and was told I can't leave after being told to come pick you guys up."

Sherrie, Pete, and I again exchanged looks, conversing with our eyes and gestures.

Aaron was losing his patience. "Seriously, guys, what is going on here?"

"Ok, you are right, we owe you an explanation," I said. "It all started with—"

"Wait!" Sherrie turned to Mallory. "You cannot use this for anything you write. You do not get to use any of our names. If you use one name, you must get permission from the three of us, but you will never get permission from Harold, so that might be a moot point. You only get to print what is public knowledge."

"I can't agree to that."

"Then you get nothing. Agree to those terms, and you get the exclusive when we say it's ok," Sherrie said.

Mallory looked at Aaron for longer than needed but moved on to Pete and then me before agreeing to Sherrie's terms.

We took turns explaining the last few hours. I started with Norm's van, picking up Pete. He talked about rolling the gurney in and the missing van. Sherrie filled them in on why she was working there. We stopped short of telling her about Two when Sherrie had a question for Mallory.

"Tell us what you know about Anderson? You two work together?"

"Honestly, I wish I had something to tell you. I don't know him that well. I tried finding something he wrote but came up empty. It's the journalist in me. I tried digging for dirt, or really just sizing up the competition. I am embarrassed to say I don't think I even got his name correct or what he's using as a pen name."

"Maybe you should have given him some pastries from Peach's?" Sherrie said out of the corner of her mouth.

Mallory let that comment slide, and her face flushed a little. Had she tried to score with the guy and gotten turned down? Was that why she was embarrassed?

"So what do we know about him? One, he showed up in River Bend early this week," I said.

Pete raised his hand from the top of his thigh, signaling he wanted to speak, so I gave him the floor.

"I saw him before, maybe a month or so before. I never paid much attention to him. He would order a beer and do his usual routine, trying to talk to the regulars from town. I just know when he started coming this week, I had seen him before. Aaron or Sherrie might remember him from then also."

Sherrie shook her head.

"I'm with Pete. Can't nail down the timeline, but he was in maybe a month or two before," Aaron said.

Hmm, Mallory has said nothing about when she met Anderson.

"I doubt we need to pin down when he first got here. If we do, we could ask Chuck if he has the security tapes on file. Let that silent partner do some work for you. Will you text him and just have him not erase the old tapes or film?" Sherrie said to Aaron.

At the mention of Chuck, Aaron and Mallory simultaneously froze, and Pete's head swiveled between the two of them while avoiding me.

Oh my god!

An icicle ran down my spine. I took a gulp of brandy to warm my thoughts.

Is Mallory the one who almost ended the relationship between Aaron and his brother?

I had never been given a name, much less the story. I only knew a woman had almost torn them apart. Now, she was back, and Aaron had been acting strange. He hadn't been sleeping well and hadn't been very talkative for the last few days. I'd thought little of it until now.

I didn't know if I wanted to talk to Aaron or freeze him out more for not talking to me. A little heads-up would have been nice. Something like "Hey, that woman I was just talking to is my ex. Almost everybody in the bar knows that but you." But I had gotten zero from him.

Sherrie stopped talking, and I was worried that I had missed something until she tossed a sleeve of saltine crackers at me. I took a few and passed them to Pete.

Aaron had the next question we couldn't answer. "So Anderson just left?"

"Yup," Sherrie said. "Pete and I went to the root beer stand for food. Hailey wouldn't let us touch Maribel's food. Claudia, Hailey, and Anderson were in the kitchen. He told them he was going to keep us from leaving the building."

"Why?" Mallory asked.

"He thought we should be here in case the police came," Sherrie said.

"Why?" Mallory repeated. "You are in a funeral home with a body. What's the big deal?"

She may have been wreaking havoc with my emotions for Aaron, but the chick was not dumb.

Pete, Sherrie, and I looked at each other again, and all conceded quickly with a head nod, but I had a question before I told her about Two and One not matching the paperwork.

"We will tell you, but first, you need to tell us why you're here. What is this story to you?"

She looked at me and then at Sherrie, seemingly avoiding Aaron and Pete. "I take it you two are not from the area. I mean, Maribel didn't mention if your families came over on the Mayflower or not."

Damn, she's kinda funny.

"That woman was crossing history with reality so fast up there, I couldn't keep up." Mallory turned to Sherrie. "I didn't know what she was going to say to you. Mostly, I was cringing when she spoke to you. It's not my position to judge or speak for you, but you handled that with grace that woman did not deserve."

Damn, she's kinda empathic. Even if she scores more points in the plus column of humanity, I will probably never like her.

Mallory kept going. "Carlin and Cole, C&C, was originally Carlin and Coletti."

"We figured that much out," Sherrie said.

"Coletti is and always has been a legend in Chicago. Word got out a few months ago that he was sick, terminally ill. The feds have been after him for years. They were hoping he would seek medical treatment or possibly want to make peace or settle unfinished business. Everybody has been looking for the man. It has played in every angle in the press. Every corner of Chicago has been written about. I was hoping for a fresh take with the River Bend angle. Not much has ever been written about his early years before he moved to Chicago. It's probably true the interesting stuff didn't happen here, but something caused the man to flee and never come back. Why leave or why cut off ties to a very successful business venture?"

"That's fair," Sherrie said, clearly giving Mallory a passing grade. "And you don't know Anderson?"

Mallory shook her head. "Not much more

than any of you guys."

Sherrie continued. "We know nothing about the early years of Coletti, but here is what is keeping us here. There are two bodies down there, and neither one was here yesterday."

Aaron looked at me for confirmation, and I just nodded in agreement, letting Sherrie continue.

"Norm was bringing the first body we have been referring to as One. The paperwork said he is Anthony Coletti, but the body does not match any recent or vintage photos. We don't know who Two is partly because his face is missing, the smell was too retched for us to examine it any more than we did, and mostly because we knew this was serious and shouldn't touch the body."

"So you guys called the police and have been waiting here for them to show up."

"Yup, just like it's eight p.m. at the Sizzler, and we're waiting for a table. We are just sitting and waiting. Just give me a sec so I can take a picture of the brandy and crackers and post it on Instagram."

Mallory recoiled slightly in her seat. She had not expected Sherrie to fire back like that.

"We tried calling 9-1-1, but when they were told a body was at a funeral home, they hung up on us," Pete said.

I started giggling, as did Pete, when we recalled the conversation. Sherrie tried pouting, but she even laughed at the absurdity. Mallory just looked confused.

Aaron got it immediately and laughed. "So, let me get this straight; you called to say there was a body at the funeral home, expecting someone to rush over."

"All right, the joke's been told one too many times. Let's move on." Sherrie navigated the conversation back on track. "No, we knew no one was coming, so we went to investigate Two. After that, Anderson supposedly called the police, yet no one showed. Hailey tried calling Holton, but it went to voicemail so I texted him from her phone, and that pretty much sums up everything."

Sherrie looked at me and Pete. We nodded in agreement to keep the part about Two possibly being killed upstairs to ourselves.

Before Mallory interrupted to say something meaningful, I threw out, "We don't think Hailey knows much, at least not about Two. She has been too worried about Maribel."

Mallory stood and paced around the room.

It took Pete three tries before he could expel himself from the old couch. "I have to stretch my back out. The sofa could be the death of me."

Sherrie excused herself to the bathroom, and Pete monitored her down the hallway. Just a glance, making sure no one was jumping out of the hidden corner. I almost tested the theory to see if

Aaron would do the same for me, but instead, he moved over to the couch.

He leaned in with a low voice. "What are you not telling us?"

There he was again with the *us*. I willed my body to remain nonchalant, but my grip on the cane was ready to snap it in half. "I'm not sure I know what you're talking about."

"I see the looks the three of you keep exchanging. There is more to the story."

With the help of the extra pillow I was sitting on and my cane, I sprung up pretty fast. "Right back at you." I headed out of the viewing room to join Sherrie in the bathroom, not daring to look back and see no one looking after me.

She came out of the bathroom, and I headed in without a word. She waited for me, and before I could ask her anything, we heard the back parking lot door creaking open. A wave of relief washed over me until I saw it was not the police.

People in the funeral home: Still not the police

CHAPTER THIRTY

"Who are you?" Sherrie demanded.

"Who are *you*?" the stranger barked. "What are you doing here?"

"I'm Sherrie Lawrence. I work for Harold Carlin."

The man wore an untucked flannel button-down shirt under a navy sweater with jeans and ankle-high leather boots. His green waxed field jacket completed the look. He was straight off the cover of J.Crew; he had missed the Abercrombie & Finch cover only by a few years. Despite his aggression for us, he was striking.

It wasn't until he ran his fingers through his blond hair that I saw his blue eyes matched Hailey's. I knew this must be her father. I would have said older brother, but I was learning the

Carlin family tree quite fast, and I recalled seeing an old family photo upstairs.

"Sorry. I was not expecting to see anyone. I'm Jonathan Carlin, and I'm looking for Hailey. I'm her father."

Nailed it—the family tree.

"She's upstairs with Maribel," I answered.

He looked at me for the first time. "Harold has two of you working tonight?"

"Actually, there are several of us here. I'm Claudia Middleton."

Shuffling came from the other room, and Pete walked up behind us. Mallory followed, but Aaron was nowhere to be found.

"Is everything ok?" Something seemed to click for Jonathan. "Ms. Lawrence, I'm sorry if I'm disturbing you and the others. I'm going to check on Hailey and Maribel. Sorry for your loss." He shot past us and fled up the stairs.

"I don't get it," Sherrie said.

"He thinks we're here planning a funeral, and you're the funeral director," Pete said.

"Just add that to the list of jobs Sherrie's held in River Bend. That never-ending list keeps getting longer," I said.

The four of us walked back into the viewing room and found Aaron on the phone.

He ended the call. "That was Wyatt. I tried my best to relay the information to him, but our connection was crap," Aaron said.

"He's at the cabin in Black River Falls hunting," Pete said.

"Why are you calling Wyatt?" Mallory asked.

"If Holton isn't coming, then maybe Wyatt can help us. He's one of the few on the force that knows what he's doing. I forgot he said he was going hunting."

Mallory's jaw dropped. "Are you telling me Mad Dog Wyatt Baumann is a River Bend police officer? The last time I saw that kid was at some house party in high school, trying to do a keg stand with his football jersey falling over his face."

"That was more than a few years ago. Keg stand days are over, but he still likes his beer and hunting and is a damn good cop," Pete said.

"Are you going to tell me his pot-smoking sister is a nun?" Mallory asked.

"She teaches second grade and coaches high school basketball," Aaron answered. "Before you ask, the eldest brother is still a computer geek, so some things never change."

Listening to them, I felt like a knife had sliced through me. I was jealous of the shared history between Aaron and Mallory. There was nothing intimate about the stories, but it was something I couldn't compete with. It didn't help that Pete was part of the conversation; that was almost a bigger betrayal. I thought we were friends with a deep bond, but their history wiped that away.

"All right, so back to where we were. You guys can reminisce, and the two of us will sit and wait for someone to show up," Sherrie said. She always has my back.

"I thought I told you guys to leave." Hailey walked up behind us. "I'm sure your shift is done, Sherrie. Just go."

"I told you we can't!" Sherrie snapped. "Get it through your head."

"Why not? I'm not giving you a pass like Nana did. Her fragile memory is what's saving her from asking what you guys are really doing in her home, acting like this is some kind of sick party."

"Listen, we can't leave. Get a hold of Holton," Sherrie said.

"He texted. He's on his way."

The group let out a collective sigh.

I retreated to the seating area and started picking up our Styrofoam cups, noting everyone had finished their beverages except Mallory. I dumped her portion into the base of a same fake tree where some of the ice was still sitting from earlier this evening.

Sherrie collected the bottle and crackers and took everything to the kitchenette area. Pete returned all the chairs to their original places.

I decided the floral-print chair was fine where it was and secured my butt to it. Sherrie resumed her position on the arm of the couch. Aaron stood near the front row of viewing seats, Mallory was near the front window, and Pete was in the doorway with Hailey.

She asked, "Are you guys going to tell me why you need Holton here before you leave?"

"I would like to know that too." Jonathan had come up behind Hailey. He ushered her and Pete into the viewing room. "Earlier, I mistook you as patrons, but Hailey corrected me. Yet she couldn't explain what all of you are doing here."

"Mr. Carlin, I don't know if you remember me, but I'm Mallory Douglas. My uncle used to live next door to you."

Jonathan was clearly trying hard to recall her. "Henry Douglas, of course. You can never forget the Douglas clan in River Bend." Like a slick politician, neither admitting nor denying he remembers her, he deflected the conversation to a safe place.

Mallory continued. "Next to you is Pete Morris. I believe you met the girls earlier, and that is—"

"I know a Rhoimly boy when I see one. I have one shot—fifty-fifty odds of you being Chuck or Aaron. Unless there are more of you since I left River Bend."

"It's Aaron." He stepped forward to shake Jonathan's hand.

"I must stop by Peach's before I leave." He was losing his charm with each cheesy line.

Aaron played along. "It's a must for everyone in town. Are you here for the holiday?"

"I'm sure he's not staying that long," Hailey said.

She got an icy glare from her father. The art of deflection continued as he ignored the shot from Hailey. "So what is it that's keeping you all here so late in this nasty weather?"

That simple question seemed to deflate any sense of hope we'd raised when Hailey had told us Holton was finally on his way.

"Just some things came up, and we need to explain it to Holton before we can leave," Aaron replied.

I leaned into Sherrie and whispered, "Since when is Aaron our spokesperson?"

She whispered back, "Since you started dating him and/or the moment we begged him to pick us up or—"

"Ok, I get it."

Aaron kept talking. "I suppose Holton will need to talk to you as well. Can I ask how you got in here? Was the door open, or did the ladies let you in?"

"I don't understand why you're asking. I

have a key. Why am I answering these questions? My grandmother lives here." Jonathan raised his voice. "This might be funny to you, being in a funeral home, but this is also my family's home, which I have keys to."

"We understand that. It's that things came up, sir," Aaron said, his calm fully intact.

"You already said that. Do you mind clarifying for me what's going on?" He looked at each of us and then turned to Hailey. "Is this what has Nana so upset?" When she didn't answer right away, he raised his voice again. "Someone answer me!"

"I don't know. They won't share with me what's going on," Hailey said, whining.

Either Hailey hit my last nerve or the brandy kicked in. She needed to pick a side. She had played the poor-me, I'm-a-victim, my-dad-left-me-for-another-family, I-hate-him routine for so long, and now, she suddenly a whipped around to pitting us against the two of them.

I stood and took control. It might not have been a hotel, but I could still tell people what to do. "Sir, listen, we mean no disrespect, but Sherrie, Pete, and I were here to do a job for Harold. Things happened, and we needed assistance from Aaron and Mallory. We sat and listened to Maribel's conversation, which we could not follow nor should anyone be subjected to, but we did it upon the request of your daughter and respect for Harold."

I was only missing a soapbox, otherwise I was doing just fine. "We have stayed because we are decent people trying to do the right thing. We're tired, hungry, and would love nothing more than to leave. I just know everyone that walks in these doors will have to fill out a police statement."

"What are you talking about?" Hailey said.

No one moved except Aaron when he turned toward me. "You might as well tell them."

I nodded and simply put it out there. "There is a body down there."

"This is a *funeral home*," Hailey snapped.

That voice of mine returned. That special voice I had for talking to Hailey or customers who thought they were right but were not, but I still couldn't tell them to jump in the lake. It was that singsong voice—calm with a hint of pettiness. "Yes, Hailey. There is a body down there, but there's a second body that doesn't belong here."

"The funeral home receives bodies any time of day. It is a twenty-four-hour business," Jonathan said.

"Harold sent everyone away. I am to direct anyone that shows up here to the place in Kirkasaw," Sherrie said.

"That's impossible. My father would never miss an opportunity for business."

"Something happened that changed his mind."

"Impossible," Jonathan said. "Unless—" He turned and took off out of the room.

People in a funeral home: All of us, plus Jonathan and still no police

CHAPTER THIRTY-ONE

Jonathan headed towards the stairs.

"Dad, wait for me. Where are you going? What's wrong?" Hailey said, taking off behind him.

We all followed close behind. I was a little slower than everyone else. Mallory was up front right behind Jonathan and Hailey, followed by Pete and Sherrie. I was moving fast, but the stairs would slow me down.

I let out a yelp when Aaron swept me off my feet and cradled me in his arms. His face was inches from mine.

"If I have to watch you hobble down the stairs, I will go crazy. It'll be faster this way."

I was mad at how good it felt to be in his arms. His breath was redolent of brandy. I wiped a saltine crumb off his chest. Anything to keep me from yelling at him or, worse, kissing his neck.

He carried me down in silence. We passed Sherrie holding the door open for us and entered the hallway.

Halfway down the hall, he whispered something I couldn't understand. He put me down just outside the embalming room door, which Pete was holding open for us. I shuffled in to the right with Sherrie next to me and Pete next to her. Convenient for Aaron, he was standing next to Mallory. Maybe not convenient because it was the logical order based on how we had walked in, but the little girl in me wanted to scream.

The odor from Two creeped into our nostrils. It was faint but distinguishable, so I kept my hand to my nose.

Jonathan walked between the two metal tables, then to the desk. He picked an empty plastic tray that held paper, swung his arms wide, and then turned to Sherrie and me. "I see no body here."

This man was getting irritating.

He rubbed his shoulder like he was working out a muscle kink.

"I appreciate the obvious. The man I delivered in is the first space. The surprise guest is in the second one."

"Are you telling me you're here because of a body in the embalming room getting ready to be prepped for a funeral service?" Jonathan said.

"It was not here yesterday. The entire staff except for me has been given the week off. Please look, something is not right," Sherrie pleaded.

Jonathan put down the tray and moved along the metal table towards the refrigerator drawers. Sherrie, Pete, and I scrambled to cover our noses. Jonathan donned a pair of rubber gloves and stepped up to drawer one. I motioned him to the second drawer.

The metal door handle clanked open. I looked down and braced myself for the smell that I thought would have stewed into something more potent since we could smell it just hanging in the air from the last time we opened the door. I didn't need to see the body again, but it was not an option.

Jonathan swung open the door and shut it just as fast. Swiftly moving down the line, he opened drawers three and four before he returned to drawer one.

"I don't know what you're trying to do here, but this is not funny. There is one body here."

"What?" I looked up.

Aaron and Mallory were looking at the three of us. Sherrie, I guess, had looked away as I had. Pete looked like a deer in headlights. The three of us lurched forward.

Jonathan did not stop us. Sherrie snapped the door open.

We were smacked in the face at the sight of

an empty table.

Sherrie and I mumbled, "Hells bells."

Pete rested one hand on my shoulder and the other on Sherrie's. The three of us stood in this embrace, trying to focus on what we were seeing — or not seeing.

The odor was stronger near the drawer but not overwhelming. Sherrie opened drawers three and four and found them empty. I turned to drawer one and placed my hand on the metal handle.

"Think this one is gone too?" Jonathan said.

I ignored him, opened the drawer, and retrieved the paperwork then turned to the group. "Listen, I don't care if you believe us or not. There was a second body there. You can still smell it. I have no obligation to, but I will also tell you this paperwork does not match that body. I don't intend to lose it."

Jonathan ran his hands through his hair. "I still don't understand what is happening. You can't keep track of the number of bodies, yet you can tell me the name of the certificate does not match the deceased. What did you do? You are right, no one is leaving until the police get here and arrest you for loitering and tampering with a corpse."

"Sir," Pete said, "listen. we did no such thing. We are trying to do the right thing and got trapped in this mess, but you will not accuse us of any wrongdoing. We don't care if you believe us or not, but don't come after us. Like it or not, you are now part of it."

"He didn't do anything," Hailey said, her voice whiny.

Mallory made the mistake this time of placing her hand on Hailey's back. "Because he's here in the house, he is part of the story now, and so are you."

Hailey took a half step forward, removing herself from Mallory's touch. "Leave me alone. Leave my family alone." She stormed out of the room, and Jonathan followed.

We stood around looking at each other and saying nothing. Mallory filed out first, and we quickly followed.

We saw them in the corridor in front of the heavy hallway doors. Jonathan was holding Hailey's shoulders. They spoke in whispers and Hailey's upper lip quivered but no tears fell.

Jonathon saw us and tossed Aaron his set of keys. "Lock that room and make sure the outside door is locked." He looked at the three of us. "Tell me how you know the paperwork is not valid."

I spoke for the group. "Valid? I don't know about that, but the name does not match the body."

"You can't get that from the transport paperwork," he said.

Pete cleared his throat. "You can when the name is Anthony Coletti."

Jonathan went a shade whiter. "Wait, don't lock that door."

Hailey tried holding her father back, but he shook her off.

"Go check on Nana," he said, then leaned in and whispered something.

She seemed unsure of what to do, but he opened the door to the hallway and guided her through before closing it back.

He led the way back into the embalming room, and we followed right behind. His actions were swift. He went to the desk, opened one drawer before moving to the second filing cabinet, and looked at the files. He raced over to the metal cabinet for a pair of gloves and a cream, which he placed under his nose.

"This body is embalmed," Sherrie said.

"Growing up, I used to spend a lot of time here. My father was trying to groom me for the business, and I had to work in this room for more hours than any teenager—or even most adults—should be allowed to. Just the smell of chemicals triggers resentment." The honest statement was more jarring than the smell.

He opened the first drawer and slid the table out. It was morbidly refreshing to see One still there. Jonathan touched the body, presumably to determine which way One had gone in—feet first was the conclusion. He grabbed the zipper and pulled.

Mallory came forward to make her own observation, but he closed the bag too soon for her to look.

His eyebrow drew up, but other than that, Jonathan's expression never changed. He slowly pushed the table back in and closed the door, keeping his back to us as he removed the gloves and wiped the cream from his nose. He dropped this stuff in the small trash bin and motioned us out of the room, then retrieved the keys from Aaron.

We waited while Jonathan locked that door and checked the outside door. Everyone moved towards the stairs to go back up to the viewing room, the silence deafening.

Aaron came to my side and started to pick me up again.

I held my hand up to stop him. "I'm fine walking up on my own."

He surprisingly did not argue. "I'll go behind you in case."

We stayed in the rear of the room, and no one took a seat. Jonathan was the last one in.

He stood in the center aisle and started to speak but stopped. He paced a little before stopping in the middle of an aisle and finally collected his thoughts enough to ask, "Can you start at the beginning?"

Sherrie gave a quick, abbreviated version of

the story. She left a few details out but Jonathan understood the situation.

"I don't mean to sound condescending, but how are you going to explain the sudden appearance and disappearance of a body? If the cops smell the alcohol on your breath, you are going to lose any credibility you have."

"We had one drink," Sherrie said.

"And a nonexistent body," Jonathan said.

"Are you suggesting they don't report the missing body?" Aaron asked.

"You took care of Hailey and Maribel, so I just want to look out for you."

Back to his politician spin, I thought.

"I call BS. You are just like your father. You are both all about business. Can you imagine how it would look if word got out that someone went missing from a funeral home?" Sherrie said.

"Business? You think I care about the business? I walked away from all this. It cost me my marriage and my relationship with my daughter."

"Then why get us to lie to the police?" Sherrie asked.

"I would not ask you to lie. Just understand what you're going to say," he said.

"Why is Holton not here yet?" I asked.

"Figure that out while I check on Hailey and Nana." He stormed past us and stopped in the doorway, then turned back to us. "Just get your story straight. You don't even have Anderson to collaborate what you three drunks saw."

We let him go, and my ears started ringing.

Sherrie finally said, "Holy shit, we're in trouble. Let's leave and drive to the police department."

"I'm in," I said.

"Me too." Pete was collecting our jackets. "Where are your shoes?"

"I left them by the couch."

"I moved them to the wall radiator earlier," Aaron said. "Hey, you guys are not seriously bowing down to this guy and changing your story, are you?"

Pete shook his head. "Hell no. But that guy is trouble, and we should not be here with him."

Aaron looked puzzled. "What are you talking about?"

"Didn't you hear him just now?" Pete said.

Aaron gestured to the door Jonathan had just gone through. "He had some weak attempt to discredit what you guys saw."

"Aaron, it was more than that," Mallory said.

I couldn't believe she'd caught on before him. Damn—funny, empathic, and kinda sharp—she was really starting to annoy me.

"You don't even have *Anderson* to collaborate what you three drunks saw," Mallory

said.

I guessed I had to spell it out for him. "Sherrie never said Anderson's name. She referred to him as the guy doing a historical profile on the family."

"He knows more than he's saying and is trying to get them to back down," Mallory said.

"Do we leave without Hailey? What does she know, or is she in on it too? Did she lure us upstairs to talk with Maribel so someone could remove Two?"

"I'm ready to go. Claudia, you can have my shoes. I'll walk barefoot to the police station if we all don't fit in Aaron's truck. It's not too far from here," Pete said.

"One point four," I said automatically.

Sherrie's head whipped around so fast towards me, and she broke out in a cackle. "You just did not do that?"

Pete and Aaron laughed too. I hadn't meant to break the tension, but it was well needed.

"I don't get it," Mallory said.

"I can't help it. The police department is one point four miles from here."

"It's her new and special talent," Aaron explained.

We suddenly grew quiet.

I finally broke the weight that had fallen on us. "Well, do we go, or do we stay?"

People in a funeral home:

Give me a minute to count . . .

The original three of us, Aaron, and his friend make five.

Hailey, Maribel, and Jonathan bring us to eight.

Add One but not Two. I think we are at nine with (still) no police.

CHAPTER THIRTY-TWO

The viewing room could drain the energy out of a person, void of personal touches, with sterile banquet chairs surrounded by garage-sale-worthy living room furniture. The dull-olive-colored accordion wall reflected the overhead light, giving it a dizzying affect. Another overhead light illuminated ten feet of open space in the front of the room like a retail store's sad, empty display window. Something had to change.

"Are we going or are we staying?" I said.

"Hailey said Holton was on his way," Sherrie reminded the group.

"If he was, he would have been here by now. Can we trust her?" I asked.

"Remember, I'm the one who sent the text from her phone."

"What did you say?" I asked.

"Are you saying I had another 9-1-1 moment? It was something to the effect of *Come here, police attention needed*," Sherrie said.

I asked, "Did it say *here* or—"

"I said *here*, not the gazebo, not the boat launch, but here. I think I know where we are."

Pete covered his face. Aaron was holding strong, but his smile was cracking. I didn't care enough to look at Mallory.

"Did you type the word *here*, or did you provide an address?"

Sherrie actually stumbled back a step, shaking her head, and uttered, "*Here*."

"So Holton is on the way to Hailey's house or some prearranged sex rendezvous spot," I said.

She just shook her head.

I turned to Aaron. "Can you try Wyatt again or come up with something to say to 9-1-1? Something better than *We had an extra body but lost it. Please come quick.*"

I sat down and looked at my phone. Maddie from the hotel had called and sent a text asking that I call. I really didn't want to worry about the hotel right now, but I called her back.

She picked up immediately and rambled out one long sentence that covered everything from Gloria being impressed with all the preparations for the storm and forbidding Karen to bring any more food in a Styrofoam container, but the highlight was hearing that Norm was out of the hospital. I managed to squeak "Great news about Norm," in between her breaths, but I had missed her point.

"You're not listening," Maddie screamed. "Norm left of his own accord before they could even examine him."

"What are you talking about? How do you know this?"

"I called to check on him, and the lady in Admitting would not give me any information, but I told her I was calling from the hotel and needed to know where I should take his stuff, you know, like his car keys. I knew I got her with that one, but she didn't put me on hold when she asked the person next to her. I heard the whole story. What do you think that was about? Did you make his delivery? Sorry, I don't know what to tell you about returning his van."

"It's ok, there is nothing to worry about." No need to tell a lie when I had no van to return. I hung up and relayed the information to everyone except Mallory, who was near the front windows on the phone.

Sherrie and I sat down on the mahogany chairs in the corner. Pete took one of the viewing room chairs, flipped it around, sat down, hugging the back of the chair, facing Sherrie and me.

Aaron rolled the floral chair over and eased himself into it. "I don't know how you guys managed to take the weird event and twist it into something even more complicated, and that's without you being at the hospital with Norm."

He reached out to me, but I pretended not to see it. I closed my eyes and tried to picture myself somewhere else. Anywhere else. Odd thing was this crazy bunch was with me in each scene—a beach, ski chalet, or EG's porch.

Unsurprisingly, Mallory broke up my day dream. "So what have we got?"

Sherrie filled her in on Norm missing from the hospital. "So maybe he planned it all along."

"What do you mean?" I asked.

"He faked the heart attack. Got someone else to complete the delivery because he knew who he was driving. He didn't want to be seen at a funeral home associated with Coletti. Somehow, taxi, Uber, or perhaps a partner drove him here to get the van back and hightail it out of town."

"Was Coletti *that* bad of a guy?" I asked.

Mallory nodded. "Yes. And then there is the mystery. People want answers to a lot of things. The feds want him. If they can't nail him for a crime, they want to make sure he's dead. He has ruled the streets for years in hiding. Some say he died a few years ago and young Russo Coletti does not have the cojones to lead and think he is making empty threats on behalf a dead guy. Any association with the family is not good. Anyone could be watching this place."

"Norm is just a delivery person," I said.

Sherrie looked at me pointedly. "So were you."

"Fair point. Can we talk about Jonathan's reaction down there?"

"There was no reaction!" Pete said. "You're right. It is strange. I don't care how long you work in this business, when you open a body bag, you should have some type of reaction."

"It's like he knew who to expect," I said, and I lowered my voice. "What do you think they are doing up there? How much attention does Maribel need? Tuck her into bed and fix us dinner while we wait."

"Would you stop talking about food? It won't help," Sherrie said. "Is Hailey even upstairs? Jonathan could have told her to leave, or she could have done that on her own."

"I don't know what it is, but she seems to be sincerely concerned and have a special bond with her nana, although the lady is not worthy of loving attention. Even if she had something to do with Two disappearing, where is she going to go?" I said.

Pete started laughing silently and couldn't control it, his whole body shaking. "Here, maybe she will call 9-1-1 for directions to *here*. For all the crazy shit tonight, you providing guidance on where one should go is top of the crazy pile."

"Whatever." Sherrie kicked Pete's foot and laughed at herself with the rest of us.

"Great, you turned your party into a comedy routine. Don't you have something better to do?" Jonathan said as he and Hailey walked in.

Sherrie's phone rang. She sat up straight like she was suddenly onstage. "I think it's a work call. It's coming through the answering service."

She stood up and stepped away from the group but was still in earshot.

"C&C Companies, this is Sherrie."

. . .

"Yes, I will take the call from him."

. . .

"This is Sherrie."

. . .

"Yes, it's me. I'm working."

. . .

"Actually, Hailey and Jonathan are with me. Can I—"

. . .

"She is here too. What's going on? Everything ok?"

. . .

"Police business? You called me!"

. . .

"We are all here together." Her voice twitched.

. . .

"We won't go anywhere. Wait, do you know where we are?"

. . .

"Yes, the funeral home. Text me and I will let you in the back door."

. . .

"Pete Morris, Aaron, Mallory Douglas, Maribel."

. . .

"Hello? Hello, hello?"

"I guess he hung up," Sherrie said to the group, shrugging.

"What was that all about?" I asked.

"Believe it or not, that was Holton. He's on his way, and no one should leave. That means everyone."

"Who was he looking for?"

"That was the strange part. He called the office line, and the phone service put the call through to me, but I don't know who he expected to answer. He asked if a Carlin was available and then asked about you, Claud. He sure as hell was not expecting me to answer."

"Call him back and ask him to pick up some burgers," I suggested.

"He was all official. If you weren't in the

same room with me, I would have thought you were dead with the way he was asking about you."

People in a funeral home: Same as the last count, but this time I really think the police are on their way.

CHAPTER THIRTY-THREE

"I'm alive and kicking. Did he say where he was or when they would get here?" I said.

"Did he indicate why he wanted to talk to us?" Jonathan asked.

"No clue. He didn't ask for anyone in particular, not even Harold, just someone from the Carlin family."

Jonathan picked up his phone and walked out of the room but not far enough away. "It's me again. You need to call me. The police are on their way. I'm at the funeral home with Hailey, Nana, and others. I'm serious; you need to call me back."

Jonathan had one foot back into the viewing room when he stopped and looked down the hall. "It's about time! Where the hell have you been?"

We waited, as did Jonathan, for someone to

answer.

"I didn't expect you," Harold said to Jonathan as he walked in, carrying a brown paper grocery bag. He surveyed the room before speaking. "I certainly did not expect you to be here so late, Sherrie, much less with all your friends. Maybe we had a breakdown in communication."

"Things came up, and I needed help, sir," Sherrie said.

"You can all go now. I can assist Sherrie in whatever came up to keep her this late." He looked at each of us before turning to Sherrie. "Please wait here for me. I need to take this up to Mother. I will be back in a moment."

Sherrie took a step forward. "Sir, I'm sorry, but they can't leave."

"Sure, they can."

"Actually, she's right. We're not supposed to leave," Hailey said. "Give me that stuff and I can take it up to Nana."

"I will take this one. There's another one at the back door that you can grab. I don't understand why they can't leave. The weather has let up."

Jonathan was neither part of our gang nor the Carlin clan and stood in the doorway like an outsider. "I have been trying to get in touch with you. As Sherrie mentioned, things have come up."

Harold looked around and seemed to size up the situation. "Let me take care of this, and I will be back."

He left the viewing room and went back down the hall instead of heading towards the stairs. Hailey carried another bag past.

Suddenly, the lighting adjusted, and the chandelier now had a soft glow. The spotlight was off the empty space in front, and the wall sconces provided a blush tone on the beige walls, bringing a little life to the room. The vent behind the chair started blowing warm air that I swore was scented with nutmeg. The sound of violins flowed from the speakers, filling the space with a soft tempo.

Harold passed the doorway, ignoring us, and then disappeared to the staircase. Jonathan was no more acknowledged than any of us of in the room, and I was pretty sure Harold knew his son's name.

"I don't know if this night can get any stranger," Pete said.

"You want to bet?" Aaron asked.

"Absolutely not." Pete shook his head.

We sat around like it was a doctor's office, waiting for our names to be called and unsure what to do. We couldn't leave and had been promised repeatedly that the police were on their way.

"I suppose this is all gold for you," I said to Mallory.

"It is not what I expected and everything I expected at the same time," she said. "Yet I don't have what I need."

"I don't think it's over. I'm sure you'll get some type of story," I said. "But remember the agreement we made earlier about us."

No response.

"The agreement. There is no mention of us without all of us agreeing," I said.

"I am sure she understands—"

I raised my hand, cutting off Aaron. "There is no doubt she understands, but does she still agree?"

"I agree," Mallory said. She opened her mouth again but declined any further comment.

I wasn't sure, but from the corner of my eye, I thought Aaron was shaking his head, probably warning her not to engage with me.

"What are you guys agreeing to?" Hailey watched the entire exchange from the doorway. She stood three feet away from her father, but it might as well have been fifty.

"We don't need or want our name in any news article," Sherrie explained. "Mallory is in town doing a story on the Coletti family, and we don't wish to be a part of it."

"Why didn't you say something? You're sitting in Nana's house and she welcomes you into her room, and you are just trying to use her!" Hailey shouted at Mallory.

"You're a reporter?" Jonathan asked. "What

about the rest of you!"

Harold strolled back in like this was a normal day at the office for him, but his voice was sharp and directed at Sherrie. "You let a reporter into the family home? You had explicit instructions."

The smell of nutmeg was replaced with something faint but distinct.

"She did not let me in. I forced myself along."

I didn't know if she was defending Sherrie or proving her own talent. Either way, it was annoying.

Harold handed Hailey her purse and coat. "You can leave. I will stay with Nana."

Hailey took her purse and coat but refused to move. "If you're writing a story about the Coletti family, then why are you here?"

Jonathan seemed desperate to control the situation. "Mr. Coletti was a onetime business partner of the Carlin family. That ended decades ago when he left and made his life in Chicago. He died and returned to River Bend to be buried with his family. That is the end of the story."

"If that's the end of the story, then why did a van get stolen and a body go missing? Why is there a padlock and chain on the front door and cement barricades in the parking lot? What I really want to know is why am I still sitting here taking crap from this family?" Sherrie demanded.

"I think we can take care of that situation right here," Harold said. He stood there in a gray sweater over a white-collared shirt and gray dress pants that were wet around the cuffs.

I got lost for a moment, wondering if his socks were wet and if he hated cold feet like I did.

Sherrie stood with her arms crossed and one leg swinging a little. This was a miniature nutcracker move where she was figuring out a puzzle, but now, she was caught inside the puzzle.

"I was wrong before. You can all leave," Harold said.

"I just told you a van and a body went missing, and you are dismissing me?"

"I don't care to discuss this here and now. If you like, we can talk about it when the office opens in a week. Now, if you would excuse us, I believe Jonathan has some things he would like to discuss with me."

"We are not leaving," Sherrie said.

The four of us stood and moved closer to her side. Mallory actually just stood. Maybe because she was in a row of chairs; however, she was still an outsider to the group, at least to me and Sherrie.

"The police are on their way. You need to listen to them," Jonathan said.

"Ah, yes. You return home and start giving directions and trying to take charge. It's about time.

If you would have done this years ago, you would not be in this mess." Harold didn't raise his voice when he spoke to Jonathan or when he turned to Hailey. "I think your nana is fine for the night. Why don't you head home?"

Hailey toggled between her father and grandfather. She suddenly looked so small in her big fuzzy boots and peach sweater, so big it could swallow her.

Jonathan stopped her from having to respond to her grandfather. He threw up his arms and started yelling. "Stop it! Stop it. Just stop telling Hailey and everyone what to do. Stop trying to make things perfect."

Harold's face turned red, but he steeled his voice to an even tone. "Watch what you say, Jonathan. I can only do so much to help you."

"I never needed your help. I just needed you, and you couldn't provide that. You were too busy making sure everything at work was perfect when nothing at home was perfect. Mother drank herself into the grave, and you ignored that, as you did with me at home. It was about being Nana's little perfect son. You forgot you had a son at home. You only saw me as a mini you and I played along too. Then it all came out one day. I wised up and left. I came back now, and I did what I had to do to protect this family, but somehow you found a way to—"

"Jonathan! Keep your mouth shut," Harold shouted. "I'm warning you."

Did Jonathan just confess? What did he have to do to protect this family?

"It's too late." Jonathan talked like we were not in the room. "They know."

"No, they don't. Our word against theirs. I took care of it," Harold spit out.

"There is someone else. Someone I brought in," Jonathan said.

"Stop it. Why are the two of you always fighting?" Hailey cried.

Jonathan reached for his daughter, but she pulled back.

She didn't let up. "You yell at him, but at least he's around. You left and walked out on me and Mom. We don't need you here now."

Jonathan's face changed from violet red to a sunken pale-ash color. "This is not how you should learn things, but I guess you're going to now. Your mother threw me out when I refused to play my part in the Carlin family regime. She cared more about being accepted in some pompous society she thought came with being a Carlin in this town. I begged her to come with me. I fought for you, but she threatened to let it all out."

"I don't believe you," Hailey said.

Jonathan was wringing his hands. "She—"

"Don't do it," Harold said, his fists balled at

his sides.

"Enough of the secrets," Jonathan snapped, but his voice was calm when he spoke to Hailey. "Your mother gave me an ultimatum; leave quietly without you, or if I fought, she would go public with what she knew. Your mother knew Harold would stop providing for you, and she would not be able to protect you. Your nana would be devastated, and it would pretty much end any quality of life you may have had." He was visibly shaken and needed a minute before he continued. "I thought it would be better for you to be with your mom, in a home and get a decent education than come with me to the unknown. It broke my heart leaving you, but I did what I thought was best."

Harold stepped closer to Hailey. "Too much has been said. Go get Nana and bring her to my house. You will have a hard time getting her across the street to your car, but just tell her she's visiting her son. That alone will make her move mountains. Just tell her that her son wants to see her." Harold's eye twitched, and his fingers combed through his hair over his right ear.

"I don't understand. She can't hear anything up there. She's fine." Hailey's hands were shaking. "Why take her out in this weather? You can visit upstairs with her."

Harold and Jonathan both looked down and

then mirrored each other without even realizing it, sweeping a hand over their ear like they were pushing the stress away from their temple. Hailey did the same thing when she was uncomfortable, but after looking down, she pulls her hair back. Three generations of Carlin with the same tick.

"Go tell Nana what I said, and move quickly. I don't think we have much time," Harold said.

"Don't confuse her," Jonathan pleaded.

"I think it's best for you to be here with her." Hailey was clearly scared, yet she stood firm while protecting her nana.

The four of us and Mallory were watching the family drama play out, and I nearly forgot to breathe. I shifted uncomfortably and stuck my hands in my pockets to keep from reaching for Aaron. I felt the picture that Maribel had dropped, and it all clicked into place for me, well some of it did.

"Hailey, you will not tell Nana any of that. It will confuse or upset her more," Jonathan pleaded.

"I don't understand. Why don't you just go talk to her? Here?" Hailey was begging Harold by this point.

"He's not talking about himself," I said.

The whole room looked at me.

"He is—"

I couldn't believe I had put it together. I just

didn't know if I had the answer or had created more questions.

People in a funeral home: The four of us, Mallory (she is still not part of the group), too many Carlins, yet no police.

CHAPTER THIRTY-FOUR

My voice cracked, but I was pretty confident in my conclusion and started again. "Hailey, Harold is referring to his brother, Nana's other son."

"What are you talking about?" Hailey said. "Nana only had Harold. Well, there was another child, who died shortly after childbirth."

"I think I'm right, and your father will back me up." I stepped forward, and Sherrie stayed at my side. "Do you know what Maribel was talking about upstairs? Us paying our respects? You said she has become more agitated lately."

"She's having more memory issues. She's old, but she is still fine," Hailey said.

"It's more than that. She's upset. I don't think her son died after childbirth. I believe he recently died and is downstairs. I think that's who

I drove here."

"You're crazy. I don't have an uncle." Hailey looked at her father and then at Harold. Neither one of them denied it. "Tell her she's wrong."

"She is absolutely right. Pretty good conclusion. How did you figure it out? Did Sherrie finally break into the file cabinet in my office, or was it when she agreed to receive the body when the care facility called?" Harold looked at Sherrie. "I instructed you that all the businesses were closed. If that home can't send him here then no one will follow. Did that lady explain it to you? That bitch at the place screwed it up from the beginning, blabbing about him being sick." He turned back to me. "All you two had to do was just put him inside and leave. Tell me how you figured it out. Morbid curiosity? You had to look at the body?"

I stepped past Harold and gave Hailey the photo. "Maribel dropped this upstairs. It's a picture of her holding an infant, and I think that's five-year-old Harold in her other arm. Upstairs in the bookcase is a photo of the same baby with the sunken eyes and dark hair with a rosary draped around the frame and a small brass cross and a candle. It's like a shrine."

"I don't get it," Hailey said. "I know that shrine. But why be upset now?"

"Memory failure? Loss of time? I really don't know," I said.

310

"So where did this uncle go, and what is the problem with being buried in River Bend?" Hailey was trying to connect dots; she was not fighting against the information.

It did not surprise me when Sherrie spoke next. "It is not your uncle that has everyone here freaking out; it is the name on the death certificate. Anthony Coletti. I have a feeling the second body that was down there is Coletti and he was using the death of the person Norm and I drove here as a cover in faking his own death."

"Not bad," Harold said. "You ladies almost have it figured out."

"Dad?" Hailey looked at him for confirmation, but Jonathan remained silent.

We had cracked part of the mystery, but there were a lot of missing pieces. Each minute standing inside the funeral room, I felt more and more part of the story.

Harold looked at Jonathan. "Still too weak to confront anything. You can't even answer your own daughter. The company and this family were all the better the day you left." Harold could have been in a classroom giving a lecture, using such a simple tone as if explaining the difference between a verb and an adverb.

"After what you did, there was no family or company left," Jonathan retorted.

"What is going on?" Hailey howled,

stomping her feet like a toddler.

Harold continued with his story. "About three years ago, I get a phone call from a care facility in Kenosha talking about this man there. I was listed as a secondary contact, but I didn't know anything about him. This was right before my dad passed away, and I asked him about this. I figure that was as good of a place to start. At first, he refused to tell me anything. Him saying nothing was enough to know this was something big, so I told him he could tell or I would keep digging.

"He explained that my mother gave birth to a son. The minute he was born, you could tell something was not right. If he survived, he would never have a normal life. It devastated my mother. She said it was her fault. Because of the affair, she was penalized with an agonizing childbirth and with a child that would not live."

Harold stopped talking. I didn't know if he expected us to connect the dots.

Jonathan turned to Hailey. "You need to learn no one in this family is perfect. Not even Nana. Sorry, honey."

Hailey's eyes were watering, but she was holding back the tears. She asked her grandfather, "Is this true?"

He didn't answer her, and Jonathan prodded him. "Finish the story, Harold."

"Nana had an affair with her husband's

business partner, Anthony Coletti, and became pregnant. Alvin found out about the affair and somehow manipulated the books and cut the partnership from a fifty-fifty profit split to giving him just some land in the Chicago area. He made it look like an even buyout. Alvin cut Anthony out of the logging and manufacturing side of the business, really everything here in River Bend. Somehow, he did it legally and in a short amount of time. When Coletti found out, he threatened revenge, but then, one day, he disappeared.

"He left town and took his son with him. My mother had just given birth and been told the chances of her son living were slim, so when Anthony kidnapped his own child my father told his wife the baby died six days after child birth. My father thought he was settling the score. I don't know what stories are true about the man that moved to Chicago, but I know he took care of his son. He had a birth certificate made and gave him his own name of Anthony Coletti. He cared for him the best he could and eventually set him up in an adult care facility and got him the best treatment possible. Junior could never live on his own. He had the mental capacity of a child and needed supervision."

"Why did that make you leave?" Hailey asked, begging Jonathan for answers she had been waiting decades for.

Jonathan turned to his father. "Don't stop now when you're actually being honest."

Harold continued. "When I found out everything, I went down to see my brother, and I learned something else. I discovered where Coletti—senior—was hiding and how the feds could find him. He had trusted the director at the facility with the information. That guy assumed I knew and gave me the file to review."

Sweat poured out of me. I was too stunned to be shaking.

Jonathan said, "This is the part where Harold gets to tell you he took a payoff from Anthony Senior. Turned out, Alvin was not a brilliant businessman without his former partner around and the logging business shut down. When Harold took over, he too struggled to keep the business going and was in the hole. He took Coletti's money for his silence. The day I found out was the day I decided to leave. Jessa refused to go. She did not want to start over." Jonathan was now a foot away from Hailey. "The other part of the deal Harold made was as long as Coletti was safe, so were you, Hailey. Coletti said if he suspected Harold had turned him, he would come after you. When the news reported Coletti being sick and that the feds intensified their push to find him is when I hired Anderson to watch you. I thought Senior would use one of us to help hide him or ask for a final big favor."

Just when I thought I knew where this was going, Jonathan threw that out.

"I couldn't tell you what was going on or put you in hiding because I didn't want a bigger target on you."

"So that story is bogus about him doing a profile on our family," Hailey asked.

"I am afraid so. He set up the meeting with you in the bar and made up that story so he could come to River Bend and be close to you without suspicion. The problem is, he's not answering my calls now. When you wouldn't return my calls last night and today, I couldn't tell you what that did to me."

"I have a fool for a son. You don't have to worry about Anderson anymore. Why would you hire an outsider to take care of family business? It's just more stuff I had to clean up."

"What did you do?" Jonathan yelled.

Harold shook his head. "It doesn't matter."

Tears streamed down Hailey's cheeks. "Is he the second one you keep mentioning, you know, the other one down there?"

Jonathan and Harold were strangely quiet again, so I said, "No, remember the timeline. Anderson was with us when we were down there, and you were up with Maribel. I have to ask, who was it that had you bring us upstairs?"

"I don't understand. You guys came up on your own."

"I'm talking about when you had us come meet with Maribel."

"Anderson texted that he would be back. He said to get you guys talking and let Maribel tell her story naturally instead of a question-and-answer interview."

I looked at Jonathan and Harold. "It wasn't really Anderson—it was one of you?"

"What are you talking about?" Jonathan said.

Sherrie asked him, "When we told you there was an extra body downstairs that was not there before, why did you go straight to the embalming room? We never said where it was. Why not check out the coffin sales room? Why go straight to the workroom?"

"You ever been around death before? I told you before I worked in this home. There is an odor that comes with death, and if anything had been sitting in that room even for a few hours, I would have known the minute I walked in that hallway." Jonathan paused before he confessed. "Plus, Anderson had already told me."

Pete figured it out first. "It was you he called and not 9-1-1."

"Well, he tried. The signal was crappy, and I couldn't understand him very well. When he left the house, he told me what was going on and that Hailey was safe."

"Then why were you not shocked when the body was missing? If Anderson told you what was going on, you would have expected two bodies," Pete said, clearly doing a little calculating on his own. "You already knew he was gone or knew enough to know what was at stake. Anderson told you that was old man Coletti down there."

Jonathan remained silent.

Pete asked the real question we had been missing the whole time. "We have been focusing on where the body went; we never asked how it got there. It was you. You killed him and then brought his body downstairs. You never expected anyone to open that drawer. It is the perfect place to commit a murder."

"That is crazy," Hailey cried.

"Don't say anything, Hailey. They don't know what they're talking about," Jonathan begged.

Harold said, "Let me see if I have this right. You say there was a body down there. Yet have no proof. On top of all that, you really suggest that nonexistent body is that Anthony, the Pigeon, Coletti. I see to no crime scene here."

"People with experience taking care of the dead might have knowledge of how to clean up a murder. You just forgot to replace the rug," Pete

said.

Harold wasted no time settling on Pete's conclusion. "Why are you doing this? Is it fame or reward from the FBI? Are you trying to impress the reporter friend of yours? You are going to have to have some proof."

This was our turn not to say anything.

Jonathan spoke to Hailey again. "I am not sure what's going on—not sure if Senior is dead or if that was just another victim that they say was down there. Take my car and go. Here's my phone. Anderson's number is in there. He'll help you."

"I am *not* leaving," Hailey said.

"You have to listen to me. I have not always been there for you, but let me help you now."

"Get away from me. I mean it," Hailey screamed.

"Listen to him," Harold said. "But Anderson can't help you now. You have to do this on your own. Go."

"I didn't do anything, and I am not leaving Nana. I'm tired of this family. It's either all fighting or all silence."

"Damn it, Hailey. Take your purse and go," Harold said.

I couldn't figure out why they were rushing Hailey out. They had already spilled the family dirt in front of us. I couldn't imagine there being much more to hear, and then I realized they were protecting her.

Mallory, who had been quiet this whole time, finally spoke. "Hailey, where were you last night?"

Hailey looked stunned. She turned from Mallory to Pete, then quickly looked down before she ran her hand through her hair. "Me? Why are you asking?"

"*Just go*," Jonathan begged her. "Get away from here."

Here? Does Johnathon believe Senior is still a threat or Harold is pinning this on Hailey or Hailey is capable of murder?

Hailey must have made the connection to Mallory's question. "No way! You think I had something to do with whoever was down there? Who do you think you are coming here and saying that?"

"Tell us where you were last night and this morning," Mallory said.

"I don't have to say anything to you. You think you're such a hotshot reporter. You don't even remember seeing me this morning at the damn breakfast and telling me I look good in peach. It was the same line you said when you got here. Just sucking up for a story or another fake person trying to use me."

Mallory stared at her pointedly. "Tell us the rest of it."

Mallory was trapped behind a row of chairs, and Aaron was blocking one end, and the other side was ten chairs away.

She suddenly seemed to want to be in the middle of the action but was confined to only her words. "It's only making you look bad."

Hailey swayed and chewed her thumbnail. "I don't need to say anything to you."

Jonathan repeated, "Honey, just go. We will finish up here."

Something was not right. All evening, Hailey had been too calm, and she was too poor of an actress to have been playing us. Jonathon's biggest concern all night was Hailey. He'd hired Anderson to protect her. That was two of the four Carlins in the house, and Maribel had the gumption but not the aim or strength to hide a body.

"It was you!" I stepped forward between Harold and Jonathan, a foot away from Hailey. It wasn't her; it was him. "You killed him and moved him downstairs."

"Stay out of this." Harold shouted and pushed me away, but it took little force to make me wobble back.

I tried catching myself, and Sherrie lunged forward to grab me. Instead of extending my hand to her, I threw the cane and landed on my butt. She backhanded the cane away from her face, causing it to fly at Hailey.

Hailey raised her arms for protection and then swung them wide to deflect the flying cane. Her left arm pushed the cane away. The right hand hit the doorjamb hard, and she dropped her purse.

The cane clipped Jonathan's shoulder, but it was the gunshot Jonathan's leg that got everybody's attention.

People in a funeral home: Forget the police at this point. Now we are waiting for an ambulance.

CHAPTER THIRTY-FIVE

Shock was on almost everyone's face. Jonathan's jeans turned crimson red.

Hailey ran to her father's side, screaming, "What's happening!"

I didn't know if it was shock or disbelief that kept Sherrie and me frozen. Between losing the van, a body missing, a disappearing reporter, an old lady talking about imaginary people, hunger pangs, and now a gunshot left me content on the ground where I had landed.

Sweat poured out of Jonathan. He held on tight to the chair.

Harold pulled Hailey away. "Pick up the gun"—he gestured to the weapon, which had misfired when Hailey's purse hit the doorjamb and now lay next to her purse on the floor—"and leave,

Hailey, *now*."

"No!" Aaron screamed. "Don't touch it. Go get some towels."

He ran to Jonathan and got him to lie down. He pulled off his sweatshirt and applied pressure to Jonathan's wound.

Sherrie pulled me up, and we shuffled to the doorway.

Pete went to the hallway, blocked the path to the back exit, which Harold was eyeing, and pulled out his phone. "I'll call 9-1-1 for an ambulance." He was slow and methodical when explaining the situation and the address. He verified they were sending someone and said he would remain on the phone with the operator until someone got here.

Hailey returned from upstairs with kitchen towels, looking sickly. Jonathan reached for her hand, but she pulled away.

"I have to go back upstairs. Something is not right," she said.

"What's wrong with Nana?" Jonathan shrieked in pain and concern. He looked at Aaron. "What are you doing?"

Something shifted in Aaron. He went from casual observer to an authority figure. No panic, only swift, controlled actions. Aaron held him down, and without resentment, he said, "Taking care of you. I can only do so much until the paramedics get here. You need to lie still and let me control the bleeding." He ripped Jonathon's jeans open, using the small towels and his sweatshirt to control the bleeding.

You can take the man out of the military, but you can't take the military out of Aaron, I thought.

Hailey stared in the middle distance, wide-eyed. "It's—"

Harold cut her off. "We will take care of it." He grabbed her by the arm, picked up her purse and fled upstairs.

We turned our attention back to Jonathon when he tried to stand. Aaron held him down with his knee on his shoulder without further resistance from Jonathon. We were focused on the two of them, so we barely heard the scream from upstairs.

Sherrie and I looked at each other for confirmation before we went for the stairs.

Pete yelled to Mallory, "Go to the back door, and let in the ambulance or police. No one else." He tossed her his phone. "Keep them on the line. We can't lose contact this time."

Sherrie was on the tenth step, and I was on the third when Pete came to my side and picked me up like I was his three-legged race partner.

We made good time going up the stairs, and Sherrie cranked open the second hallway door. We saw nothing out of the ordinary.

An overwhelming smell of gasoline

smacked us in the face.

Hailey's muffled cries came from the kitchen. We ran in and found her on the floor in the fetal position, crying.

A fireplace iron lay next to her. Cold air swept in from the open patio door by the kitchen table.

Pete ran to the door. Sherrie went to the living room, and I knelt down next to Hailey.

Pete returned first and went past Hailey and me to find Sherrie.

I rubbed Hailey's back. "Are you ok?"

I got only silent cries. She held her face in her hand and rocked herself forward, almost knocking on the floor.

The two super sleuths returned, and Pete did not look happy.

He said, "If he was out there, he's gone, and we don't think he's back there unless he's hiding in a secret closet. Maribel's sleeping in her bed."

Hailey didn't seem to hear anything around her.

I held her steady so she would stop rocking. "Hailey, the ambulance should be here any minute. I think your dad should be ok, but do you want to see him?"

She looked up and noticed us for the first time. It seemed to take her a minute to understand.

"Do you want to see your dad?" I repeated.

She jumped up and ran down the hall. The three of us followed.

At the top of the stairs, Sherrie leaned over to me. "I know it's my turn to carry you, but I'm sure as hell not picking you up."

Downstairs, Hailey was at her father's side. The ambulance lights flashed through the front curtains.

Pete went to the padlocked door. "You have to go around to the back door!" he yelled.

"He's gone. He tried to get me to go. I can't believe . . ." Tears poured down Hailey's cheeks.

Jonathan held his daughter's hands. "You will be safe. Someone will watch Nana. I'm sorry I ever thought you were involved."

Two paramedics pulling a stretcher and Holton walked in, Mallory following them.

"Everybody get down," Holton shouted, his gun drawn.

"What?" I mumbled.

"You have got to be kidding me?" Sherrie said.

Aaron looked up at him. "Holton, can you—"

"Get down."

We should have dropped to floor the immediately and been frightened and overall more cooperative and less put-out, but I was reaching the end of my rope. This did not even warrant a "hells bells" from Sherrie and me.

Pete, Sherrie, and I slowly got to the floor, mostly because we were tired and hungry, and it was better than standing.

Pete was kneeling and about to lie down when he whispered, "I should have listened to that afterschool special that was on television."

Sherrie whispered back, "What are you talking about?"

"Never get in an unmarked van. It is always trouble. Five hours later, and here I am."

Sherrie and I suppressed a laugh.

I whispered back, "I can't believe I'm lying on the floor in my one hundred and thirty-seven dollar sweatshirt."

Mallory had her head in her phone and didn't seem to hear Holton until he was practically in her face.

"Get down," he repeated.

A voice of reason finally shot out. "Relax, Officer Patrick."

I barely recognized her. The last time I had seen Detective Angie Decorah, I'd interrupted her Saturday night out. She'd had enough makeup on and hair spray in her hair to last the entire weekend, in contrast to now. It looked like we had woken her up from a winter hibernation.

Aaron stood and stepped back after the paramedics took over. They let Hailey hold her father's hand until they lifted him onto the stretcher. She asked to go with him, but the detective said no. Before she gave an uneducated statement, she got confirmation from the paramedic that he would be fine.

"Gunshot wound to the thigh, but the bleeding was contained."

It was no proclamation from a doctor, but it seemed like it would be a good outcome.

Detective Decorah responded to the paramedics, "Officer Drew is out there. Tell him to ride along and get his statement. If he has a problem with that, too bad, and he better know not to come in here asking me. The three of you on the ground can stand up, but stay where you are."

The paramedics kept doing their thing, attending to Jonathan, radioing ahead to the hospital, and finally wheeling him out.

I didn't know what to expect next, and I surely didn't think I would laugh, but when the door was open, I heard one of the paramedics yell, "Drew, Dad wants you on the bus. I wouldn't question it."

Holton looked aghast at the detective who was treating this like a potluck gathering and not a crime scene so he took the lead. "Miss Middleton, come with me please."

"Me?" No one called me Miss Middleton. Not even at work. I was on my stomach, inhaling floor dust, and cranked my neck to look to Holton. "Where?"

That simple question seemed to throw him.

"Where?" I asked again.

"You need to come with me and answer some questions."

"You want us to give our statements?" I asked.

"No, just you. They can make their statements here."

"Here? Where am I going?"

"Is she giving a statement or being questioned?" Aaron asked.

Detective Decorah rolled her eyes and then removed her gloves, hat, coat, and sweater, tossing them on the velour-covered bench, revealing she was no hibernating bear but as slim and fit as I remembered from a few months ago.

"I don't see the weapon," Detective Decorah said almost to herself.

We weren't sure if we should answer her while she surveyed the area.

Finally Pete answered. "I think Harold grabbed it before he fled upstairs."

Detective Decorah was blocking the pathway between me and Holton, so I stayed where I was. The detective's hair had dropped on her shoulders when she'd taken off her wool hat, and she wiped away the last of the mascara smeared around the corner of her eyes. I couldn't help but think her feet must have been cozy and warm in those boots, which were thicker than her puffy coat and had a three-inch rubber sole.

"Sorry, you have to give me a minute. I'm coming from another scene off the highway."

Holton was still on a mission of his own. "Miss Middleton, this way."

"Hold up, everyone. Stay put. That can wait. I need you, Holton, to clear the upstairs and downstairs. I will take this from here until the other guys show up."

"Nana is upstairs," Hailey said.

The detective held Hailey back.

"She's sleeping. Don't disturb her. She won't hear you, so don't startle her. Can I go up there?"

"Not now. If she's sleeping, she'll be fine. Holton is just going to make sure no one else is here," she said in a gentle tone before barking at Holton. "Go."

Holton was clearly agitated for being dismissed but refrained from speaking.

I was not positive, but I thought I heard her mumble "Dumbass" before she told him to get a move on again, and he ran up the stairs.

She called after him, "This time, stay on the property." She turned to us. "Ok, I know most of you, so let's get on with this. Everybody get up. For the record, I am Detective Decorah. Are you ok,

Aaron?"

It was only then that I saw blood on his hands. I was surprised there was so little on him. His jacket was on the floor, and his sweatshirt was missing.

He looked at his hands. "I'm fine. You met Claudia and Sherrie, and you know Pete. This here is Hailey Carlin, daughter to Jonathan, the man that just left."

Mallory still had her head in her phone, cursing under her breath.

Aaron gestured to her. "That is Mallory Douglas, reporter." He emphasized the latter.

"Thank you." Detective Decorah said and assessed us and the foyer area. "Miss Carlin, is Maribel Carlin your nana who is upstairs?"

Hailey nodded.

"Is there someone you can call or someplace your grandmother can go? She's not in immediate danger, but that's an active crime scene." When Hailey nodded, Decorah continued. "Have them go to the rear door, give me the name, and I will have an officer escort them upstairs."

Hailey pulled her phone from her pocket and walked into the small family sitting room down the hall.

"All right, let's move into the room so we can sit. Aaron go clean up and come back. They will need to take statements from each of you,"

Detective Decorah said. "I love when we can wrap it up in one night."

Sherrie, Pete, and I walked into the viewing room. On the way to the restroom, Aaron nudged Mallory. She pulled her head out of her phone and followed us in.

Holton returned from upstairs and had a quiet conversation with the detective before heading downstairs.

What does Holton want to question me about? We were all here together and so why not all of us?

I was going to ask, but our next guest that showed up was surprising when he should not have been.

People in a funeral home: Does it really matter, because the police are finally here.

CHAPTER THIRTY-SIX

We walked back into the viewing room in single file. Pete, always the gentleman, stopped in the doorway and let us pass. I took my position back on the couch. Sherrie took the arm of the couch.

Mallory walked in, stopped in the corner, reading her phone again, but Detective Decorah motioned her forward. She marched towards the group and took a chair from the viewing section and turned it towards us. Pete brought back one of the mahogany chairs but remained standing behind it.

Hailey came back and said her mother was coming, but she didn't know if Nana would be ok to leave in this weather and time of night. Detective Decorah said they would figure out something. She told us to stay put, and she was going to talk to her team. Holton returned from downstairs and followed the detective down the hall.

Aaron returned and stood next to Pete. Hailey took the floral chair next to Sherrie. The Scooby-Doo Trio was back again in this room, but the gang now included Aaron, Mallory, and Hailey.

"Are you ok, Hailey?" I asked.

"I don't know." She sat with her arms on her lap, looking caught between wanting to slink farther into the chair and wanting to run out. "I'm not even sure I know what happened. I took Nana food, and the next thing I know you guys are running around here like crazy people, my friend leaves, my father and grandfather are here. My grandfather shoots him."

Mallory leaned forward, touched Hailey's knee, and cleared up the situation. "Anderson was never your friend. Harold didn't shoot your dad, but he put the gun in your purse. When the purse went flying, the gun misfired."

"I shot my dad?" Hailey recoiled her knees and wrapped her arms around her legs.

"No. It was an accident. You didn't know the gun was there and could not have predicted a cane flying at your head."

"They are not going to believe I didn't know about the gun," Hailey said, biting her thumbnail.

Aaron tried reasoning with her. "I'm sorry to say this, but I think Harold was trying to get you to carry the gun out. He knew the police were on their way and didn't want it found on him."

"Does that mean he . . . I don't know what that means." Hailey dropped her legs to the floor in what looked like exhaustion.

Sherrie said what no one else had to courage to explain to Hailey. "It means it was probably Harold who shot Coletti sometime last night or early this morning. He was waiting for me to leave so he could dispose of the body and didn't think or at least hoped we wouldn't open the wrong drawer."

Mallory was still trying to complete her story. "Why would you not say where you were last night? You stopped short in defending yourself."

Hailey didn't say anything.

Mallory kept fishing for answers. "The police are going to ask you."

"I was with Anna," Hailey said quietly.

"Unless you were robbing a liquor store, I think that's ok to share," Mallory said.

"We were with some guys, at their apartment."

Pete shifted uncomfortably. "It's ok. We broke up. Kinda surprised she didn't tell you. Although I learned she is good at keeping secrets."

My head spun around to Pete and Sherrie froze, but the rest of the group could not have cared less.

Hailey finally looked at Pete. "What do you mean?"

"You can stop covering for her. I could not care less who it is; I just know she was seeing someone else," Pete said.

"Sorry about that. She is my friend, but what she was doing was pretty crappy. Cheating on you and all that is not right."

Shouting came from down the hall. Aaron and Pete went to investigate but quickly returned.

Detective Decorah stomped in behind them with a new guy. "Let's go wait near the front door." She came with us and remained silent.

What is happening right now? I thought.

A minute later, the guy left the viewing room and headed towards the stairs. Before Hailey could protest, Detective Deborah told her he would not disturb her grandmother, and she pushed us back into the viewing room.

We followed her up the center aisle. Mallory walked to the front window. Sherrie sat on my left with Pete and Aaron on my right. I felt like we were schoolkids being ushered around.

Detective Decorah pulled out a chair and sat facing us. "Thank you for your patience. They just cleared the house and removed the bugs."

"Damn it!" Mallory said to her phone.

"What's up? You got problems?" Sherrie

didn't hide the sarcasm, nor did Mallory pick up on it.

Sherrie turned back to Detective Decorah. "Bugs?"

Decorah gave no response.

I thought I would try.

"Listening devices?"

I also got no response.

"Some other fool got the story," Mallory hissed. She continued to pace by the window. We watched her for a minute before she realized she had an audience. She looked at Hailey and mumbled, "Sorry, I know this is bad for you and your family; it's just that I wasted a lot of time."

"Whatever." Hailey rolled her eyes. "What's going on now? Can I check on my dad?"

A male voice came from the back of the room, sounding vaguely familiar. Detective Decorah was about to speak but instead stood up and gave them her attention. "My team will take over. I just need one of your guys posted by the back door until the crime scene guys clear the place."

The black glasses and backpack were gone, but the blue jacket with FBI written on Anderson's back was a surprise. Jonathan had hired one hell of a bodyguard for Hailey.

"Officer Drew LeDuc will be at the door. You got my number. The rest of the team and I will be out of your way," Detective Decorah replied.

Irritated or relieved, I wasn't sure; I didn't know the detective well enough to read her face.

Anderson responded. "Thanks. I need you guys to stay in here and someone will take your statements."

"What the hell? You're an agent?" Mallory stormed after Anderson.

We listened to her scream until she was out of earshot.

"What is going on? I am more confused than ever," Sherrie said.

The detective sat back down. "It's an ongoing investigation that now belongs to the feds."

"Can't you give us more?" Sherrie said.

"Investigation, my ass. It's all over the news," Mallory screamed. She stormed back and stood in front of the window drapes.

"Care to explain?" I asked.

"There was an accident on the freeway. Inside a burning van, they found a body believed to be Anthony Coletti," Mallory said.

"Who was driving?" Sherrie asked.

"I'm trying to get the details. It's just headlines at this point. My boss is all over my ass for not being the lead on this."

"You are a witness," Detective Decorah said.

"I wanted the story! Can I go? You will have

all their statements," Mallory snapped.

"Remember, it's no longer my investigation."

"Thanks but no thanks." Mallory walked out of the room.

Detective Decorah spoke softly. "If that one would get her head out of her ass, she would realize she knows more than anything being reported. While she is worried about being the second person to report on this story, let me ask, are you guys ok?"

We mostly nodded and mumbled yes.

"Are you able to tell us anything? I think there are a few missing pieces," I said.

Before she could answer, a new lady screamed from outside somewhere. "Let me see her. This is my family's home."

"Mom!" Hailey jumped up and ran to the door.

"Sounds like I need to intervene out there. Excuse me," Detective Decorah said.

Pete stood and stretched. Aaron leaned back, pushed his heels in the floor, looking like he was doing the dead man float on a chair.

Someone walked in, and we froze in our positions.

I closed my eyes. "I am too tired to look or care who it is."

Sherrie turned her head to look.

"Friend or foe?" I asked.

"Friend, I hope." Wyatt walked down the center aisle and shook Aaron's hand. "I owe you one."

"What do you mean? We should be thanking you, the police, for finally showing up," Aaron said.

"I managed to get this whole week off for hunting, and that ruffled some feathers in the department with my low seniority and the holiday coming up. When I got your call, I was able to report what was happening. We had a jump on it before the feds, or so we thought. Technically, I'm off duty. I got here in time to see Carlin trying to shimmy down the wall from the patio and hit the pavement. I've been out there waiting for the ambulance to pick up the old guy. He took out his ankle and probably tweaked his back," Wyatt said.

"Good, that old ass will be in pain when he's in court pleading his case. So much for the slick getaway," Sherrie said.

"Sorry, I cut into your hunting," Aaron said.

"No sweat. It was crappy weather. The guys drank all the beer last night and were starting in on the schnapps and some cheap whiskey. I was looking for a reason to get out of that cabin. That's the problem when you only go thirty minutes away; everybody and their stupid brothers want to join you."

"Not to be pushy, but can you tell us what

happened out there?" Sherrie asked.

"I only caught part of it." He looked at Aaron, holding eye contact.

Aaron responded to the unspoken question. "They're good. They will keep their mouths shut. It's the other one out there pacing around you gotta watch."

"A vehicle on fire was found in the ditch twelve miles out on County Road 29, about a quarter mile to the on-ramp. Inside it, they found a body in the driver's seat, gasoline all over the cargo area, and one not so happy federal agent handcuffed to something in the back. I wasn't out there. I was just listening to the radio. If I have it right—" He stopped talking to the four of us and turned to Pete. "What the hell are you wearing?"

"It's hip with the kids, move on," Pete said. No matter what room or what lighting the split-pea-colored sweatshirt looked hideous.

"The van in the ditch was staged. The body in the driver's seat was clearly not the driver. The guy had died some hours before. Gibson was cuffed to the back door."

"Gibson?" Aaron asked.

"Yeah, that guy that was just in here."

"Anderson is really Gibson?" Sherrie asked.

Wyatt shrugged. "I don't know about that."

"I might be pushing this, and I don't want to get you into trouble. Why am I being questioned?"

"Then don't ask the question," Detective Decorah said. "You can go now, Wyatt."

"Don't worry, I didn't say anything, Dad," Wyatt said.

"If he can't answer that, can you answer why they call you Dad?" Sherrie asked.

"D. A. D., Detective Angie Decorah. I'm ok with it. It is part of the reason I wanted to switch from street cop to detective. It was worse being Sergeant Angie Decorah. No one would call me SAD directly, but I heard it behind my back. Only those who really know me know it's ok and say it directly to me. I found it's a measure of trust if they can say it to me. That's why I know I can trust that Wyatt didn't say anything he wasn't supposed to."

"Let's hope you can do the same," Anderson/Gibson said, walking into the viewing room. "I need to speak to Miss Middleton."

"That's me, but who are you?" At this point, I was too hungry to care that some agent wanted me for questioning.

He just stood there.

The violin music Harold had put on an hour ago started mocking us. The tranquil strings scratched at my nerves.

Without expression, he answered, "I'm Agent Andrew Gibson, FBI. I need to get Miss Middleton's statement first and then the rest of yours. Please do not discuss anything that happened tonight."

I followed Agent Gibson into the family sitting room and was asked to outline everything that had happened. I started with Norm and the van and then stopped.

"I know this is a one-way conversation, but I have a question. Why did Holton come blazing in here, wanting to take me in for questioning?"

Agent Gibson looked at me, stone-faced and silent.

"I'm going to find out sooner or later."

"Good for you. All I need is your official statement. I think we could be done quickly, if you cooperate."

"No, I'm not. Does this mean we're in a standoff here?" I didn't know why I was in a one-way deadlock with an FBI agent. Maybe I should have chalked it up to being hangry.

Agent Gibson shook his head in disbelief. "I thought you were the smart one. We can play your game, or we can play mine and you get out of here faster. Can you just give me your statement?"

"Fine." I recounted everything from the moment Norm walked into the hotel to the minute I walked into this room. I finished with my first question. "Why am I wanted for questioning by Deputy Hound Dog out there?"

"The van with the body was the same van Norm left you with. That was not some random auto theft. Your wallet was found in there. If I had to guess, it probably fell out during your drive to the funeral home."

Damn, I didn't notice it was missing. "Hey, did you find a pair of socks in the van?"

Agent Gibson did not answer.

I was still skeptical. "Why are you just taking statements? I can't believe I'm going to say this, but I would think you would need more."

Agent Gibson shook his head again, and I finally put it together.

He just listened to me piece it together verbally.

"You know everything. You put in the listening devices, the bugs. Each time you walked away from us, when you were supposedly checking if anyone else was here you were actually checking or adding the bugs, or you were telling whoever was listening what to do or what you just heard."

"See, you are the smart one," Gibson said. "Can you figure out the next one?"

"Do you want to give me a topic, or am I just going to solve the entire case for you?"

"I don't have to tell you squat but thought maybe you could figure out what happened in the janitors closet."

That got my attention. I loved a good puzzle and was mad I had missed something I should have seen.

"You got ten seconds, or I'm out of here," he said and held up his hand in a waving motion, trying to tell me something.

Wave, hand, fingers? What could he be telling me?

"I got it. You weren't being a chauvinist pig about the electrical panel. You didn't want me screwing up the fingerprints. But whose fingerprints? Who killed the power to the drawers?"

"You don't get all the answers. You just need to know I am a good guy. Nice working with you, Miss Middleton," Gibson said with one foot out the door.

"Wait," I said.

He looked back.

"Can you confirm that when we opened the drawer and looked at Two, which we now believe to be Anthony Coletti, it was no mistake that you dropped your phone into the bloody wound? You did it to get the DNA."

"That's not bad Miss Middleton. I can't confirm or deny anything about an open case." He was about to leave again when he said, "Have a pleasant holiday, and maybe you should get out of the hotel business and think of being a career in law enforcement. You already have a nice FBI profile going." He left.

That last statement hit me like a ton of bricks. It was a reminder that since I had been in River Bend, I had been involved in a shooting at EG's house with Sherrie getting hit in the arm; I had caused a fire in her house; and I'd killed a man. Six months, and I'd had multiple run-ins with police, criminals, stupidity of an ex-boyfriend, some mentally unstable people, and now, two installments with the FBI.

An icy shiver ran down my spine. It was too much to think about in the moment.

I hobbled my way into the viewing room. A never-before-seen agent had just asked Aaron to give his statement, and we passed without saying anything to each other. That left just Sherrie and Pete sitting next to each other in the viewing room.

People in a funeral home: All that matters is Pete and Sherrie are alone again.

CHAPTER THIRTY—SEVEN

Sherrie asked Pete, "Ok, we just have to give our statements, and this night will be over. Can you finally tell me the issue you have with salad?"

I stayed in the back of the room because I didn't want to interrupt and didn't know where else I could go, and to be honest, I really wanted to listen.

Pete chuckled. "As you heard, Anna and I broke up. I was going to do it sometime ago. It's really shitty of me that I didn't do it sooner, but now I don't care since I know she was cheating on me."

"If you don't mind me asking, how did you figure it out?" Sherrie asked.

"I had my suspicions when she started to be more possessive about her phone. Once, I hit the screen just to see the time, and she freaked out. A month before, she had given me her phone while she went to the bathroom at a concert. She has a fear of dropping it into a toilet."

"Amen to that," Sherrie said.

"It was the sudden shift of attitude. I knew for sure the other night at the bar when we were doing the drinking contest. She hates that fruity cocktail I made, and I got her vote because she was feeling guilty. One of the reasons I liked her in the first place was that she was confident in who she is and wouldn't just give a pity vote to the guy she was dating. She had actual opinions and stuck to them." He paused.

I really tried standing still and hidden in the back of the room so they would keep talking.

Pete finally continued, sounding a bit flirty. "She's kinda like you in that way. Confident and does what she wants, independent, not a follower."

"Oh, I guess I'll take that as a compliment," Sherrie said.

"I only meant it as a compliment. Words are not always my thing."

"You're right. About you not being good with words. I asked about salad, and you gave me a breakup story." Sherrie leaned over, shoulder to shoulder with Pete, and nudged him to tell him she was kidding.

"The reason I didn't break up with her

sooner is because she signed us up for this cooking class that I really wanted to go to. I know I was using her for the silly class, but I would miss the class if I broke it off. I figured if she was cheating on me, the least I could do was get to go to the class even if it was with her. Anyway, we went, and all we made was this stupid Niçoise salad with seared tuna. I learned nothing, not one technique, not one new spice, no new cool kitchen gadget; we made a salad. I guess you could say I was equally disappointed in the class as I was at her cheating. I just did not want to think about her so I bitched about that lame meal. I waited three weeks to make a damn salad. It served me right for using her."

"I don't know if what you did would be considered using a person, but I get it. I'm sorry you guys didn't work out."

Pete had been looking straight and suddenly turned to Sherrie, and he dropped his shoulders. "You're disappointed I'm not with her anymore? I didn't think you guys were friends."

"What? No, we're not friends. I mean, she's nice, minus what she did to you, but I'm saying sometimes breakups suck," Sherrie said, her legs swinging under the chair. "Other times, breakups are for the best."

Pete hesitated before he spoke again. "The other reason I was so mad was because I didn't want, I don't want you . . . I was worried what you would think of me."

"Me?" she said, slowly bouncing in her seat, between the legs kicking and her swaying.

I thought this must have been her flirting mode in a chair. She bumped shoulders with him again, and I knew I had to retreat. Any sign of me being in the room would break their momentum.

I turned in the foyer and saw the agent and Aaron exit the family sitting room and head towards the back door. Aaron stepped into the kitchenette, and the agent continued to the rear of the building.

I walked towards the restroom but stopped when I heard Mallory and Aaron talking. I stood outside, listened.

Damn, now I'm spying. Maybe I should consider a career in law enforcement.

"Did you get your story?" Aaron asked.

"Not the one I wanted, but I guess I have details that no one else has, so it might be something."

"Since you were not the one to announce that Coletti is dead, you could do the human-interest side of the story."

"Just like you to try and turn a mob story into a sappy Hallmark Channel story about a daughter and father reuniting."

"Nothing wrong with that," Aaron said.

"I have to try some angle, or I'm dead in the

water. I'm assuming the four of you guys and the feds are going to void most of what I have to say until it's all sorted out in the courts."

"I guess so. I'm sure you'll come up with some story and barrel-burn out of town."

"Wow, it has been several hours since you last took a shot at me in the bar," Mallory said.

"Well, that is your MO. Crash, burn, and skip town." Resentment suffused his words.

Resentment is feelings that are still raw and festering. Is he hanging on to some feelings for her?

"We are not doing this here and now." Mallory's voice was angry, but she shifted to defiant. "So tell me, how long have you been seeing blondie?"

"What?" Aaron said, sounding like he was trying to deny it.

Frickin A, he is denying it. Is he trying to get her to stay?

"Oh, come off it. Since I got to town this time, you have been reserved and been giving me one-word answers. Anytime I asked anything remotely personal, I got less than one-word answers."

"Is that what you think? I don't answer or jump for you; it must be someone else."

"You weren't so quiet last time I was here." She laughed.

That laugh implied a lot. I wondered when

was the last time she was here and what happened.

Mallory kept talking. "I'm not dumb. The minute we walked in here, you distanced yourself so much from her, which you don't even do to strangers in your bar; I knew something was up. Well, tell me, I am wrong?"

"Ok, you want the honest answer? Careful what you wish for." Aaron was angry. "I have been dating Claudia for several months. Yeah, I kept it from you. She doesn't need you infiltrating her life. You leech on to things and use them. Pretend to be their friend to get what you need. Just like you did with Hailey back there. Faking concern, asking her where she was last night. Like it was in her best interest to tell you because the police are going to interrogate her. You were writing your story."

"What's wrong with being a reporter?" Mallory sounded incredulous.

"Right there—you don't even see it. I said you were using Hailey for the story, and you cannot acknowledge it. You're defending your job, but not defending your moral code. If I tell you I'm dating Claudia, you will try to be her friend, get close to her just to mess with me. She doesn't need my protection. The thing is that woman has more guts and grit and would spit you out before you knew what was happening. Maybe I just didn't want to watch it happen again. I would say you nearly destroyed Chuck and me, but that's giving you too much credit. Infiltrate and suck people dry. That's your method of operation before you move on."

"You mean I still stir up some emotions, and you can't handle it. You just don't toss away old feelings. Why did you bring me here if you hate me that much?"

"You heard me on the phone. You knew where I was going, and you were stubborn enough to follow me. Ten minutes, we would have been digging you out of an icy wipeout. You didn't give me much choice when you jumped into the truck."

"You wanted me to meet her. You needed to see her and me in the same room to figure out your feelings."

"You are so full of yourself."

"So good witch versus the wicked witch. She wins at being a good one, but that doesn't mean you still can't have feelings for the wicked witch. We had some pretty good times together. You could almost call them naughty times. And, recall, you enjoyed the devilish side of me."

My gut twisted, my head pounding, and my heart was drowning. She was flirting and hitting on some emotional history they shared. I wanted to run but couldn't. I wanted to at least hobble away fast, but it was like a car accident; I couldn't turn away. I had to see the wreckage of my relationship play out.

"I also enjoyed smoking weed before work, having bonfires in the fields, and having a contest to see who could bring the stupidest thing to burn, and letting out the air of the tires of Principal Hogan's car every Wednesday back in high school, but that is well in the past. If I want something, I would go for it. I don't play games."

"You don't let go that easy."

"You're right," Aaron said. "Hurtful memories linger, but I enjoy happy times now."

"So come with me. You're more than this town."

"I don't even know what that means. Small town or big city does not make the person, and surely, it does not make a relationship, much less one that burned out a long time ago. I'm done rehashing this. You want to continue down this path, call Chuck I am sure he would love to reminisce."

"That was a low blow. You don't even know the story. I'm sure Chuck is too decent to have ever told you the truth, but I think I'm back to that point in my life," Mallory said.

What is she talking about? This is all so confusing. What happened with them, and what point is she at now?

Aaron said nothing. I imagined him standing there with his arms crossed, glaring at her.

"I could use a friend. We could start there,"

she said.

"You think we could have a friendship? You are unbelievable. I hate to think how you treat your enemies. Now, if you excuse me, I want to check on my girlfriend. Not because she needs me to, but because I want to."

There it is. That's all I wanted to hear.

"Sure, run away from me again," Mallory said.

"Stop playing the victim. It gets old," Aaron said. "I can't even say it was good seeing you this time, but I will say, take care of yourself." He stomped out of the room.

Oh, crap.

I was about to be busted for eavesdropping. I shuffled myself back ten feet into the family sitting room and pulled myself inside just around the entryway.

Aaron walked past, so I snagged his T-shirt and pulled him into the room with me, drawing him close.

He didn't fight it or question me. I took in every muscle pressing against my body, his thighs, our hips, and chest leaning into each other. My hands ran along his upper arms and shoulders.

I leaned in closer, feeling his breath on my neck, and inhaled his scent. He brought his lips to mine, and the kiss exploded down my body.

I withdrew only to catch my breath as his

hands wondered down my back, and he lifted me up. I wrapped my legs around him and kissed him again. We staggered back and collapsed onto the small sofa, only to miss it by half a butt cheek. We ended up sliding down to the floor, laughing.

Aaron broke the laughter first. "I don't know what inspired that from you, but I will apparently take it anytime and apparently anywhere."

We looked around, suddenly conscious we were in a funeral home, and we started laughing again.

He rolled me on top of him and kissed my neck, nibbling my earlobe, and softly said, "And apparently I love you." His lips hit mine again.

His words slammed inside of me as he kissed me. I had not been ready for him to say that and, thankfully, didn't have to respond because everything came to an abrupt halt when a pair of socks came flying at me.

"Seriously, you guys are going at it here?" Sherrie said.

She and Pete were standing side by side, not as close as Aaron and I had been standing moments ago, but it was closer than I would stand next to a friend.

Hmm, I guess we both have stories to share.

I rolled off Aaron. Sherrie tossed my shoes at me, and I hoisted myself onto the sofa. Aaron stood and made room for Pete and Sherrie to step inside the small room.

Giving us a slight wave, Hailey and her mother, Jessa, escorted Maribel out of the funeral home. I couldn't imagine what tonight, tomorrow, and the rest of their lives would be like.

People in a funeral home: Fewer and fewer and, hopefully soon, not us

CHAPTER THIRTY-EIGHT

Pete and Sherrie gave their statements and were dismissed with strict instructions not to discuss the investigation with anyone. We all made that promise and felt comfortable in our commitment; however, that lasted twenty-seven minutes.

We made our way to Aaron's truck. He wanted to carry me, but I felt that could be too dangerous on the ice, so Aaron and Pete walked at each side, making sure I didn't fall.

I was busy maneuvering my butt up on the seat without slipping, and I let out a scream when Rita licked my neck.

Nothing is better than the love of a golden retriever after a long, long, long evening, but a little warning would have been nice.

Sherrie was not happy. "Oh my god, she

must be freezing. How could you do that to her?"

"Whoa, easy on me, please. She's happy in the back seat. I tuck her in under blankets. She's warm in her happy spot," Aaron said.

We all gave Rita some chin scratches, and I eased myself into the truck.

"Unfortunately, there's no room back there because of the equipment. We'll have to all squeeze in front," Aaron said.

Sherrie hopped up next and waited for Pete to get in and sat on his lap and gave me a shy smile. She and I started debating our best option for food at this hour. She thought Towne's would be open, but I thought they would be closed due to the weather. She said truckers always drive, and truckers always eat.

"You two could probably debate this for hours, but I think I've got the best option," Aaron said, but refused to give up his food source.

He was driving only twelve miles an hour, either because the roads were still bad or because there was no way for me, Sherrie, and Pete to use a seat belt. Aaron had one hand on the wheel, and the other was holding my hand. I used my other arm to clutch Wilbur for a little extra warmth. Four bodies and a dog seemed to be the only source of heat.

All we had was each other, and it was all we needed.

We drove around the town square. No one

was out. The bars were closed, but the neon signs and holiday lights slowly erased all the misery we witnessed. The sparkle from the lights reflected on the windows and the ice, giving the town a sherbet-colored glaze.

Sherrie suggested driving to the boat ramp so we could watch the Mississippi. Short of having a campfire to gaze into, the second-best option was watching the river. Watching the water flow and seeing barges float past was usually pretty zen and something we could lose ourselves in while we decompressed. Everyone agreed to the detour. Our hunger could wait until we found a moment to collect ourselves.

I even broke my no-Christmas-music-before-Thanksgiving rule. We listened to "Silent Night, Holy Night," the single angelic voice filling the truck and soothing our tired and weather nerves.

Unhurried, Aaron continued the drive slowly, and as the hymn ended, he pulled into the lot.

We all vetoed the plan when we realized that, without the moon shining with ice covering the parking lot lights and too much ice on the boat ramp, we couldn't get close enough to enjoy the purring roar of the river.

I turned off the Christmas music, and Aaron was back on track to his mystery destination.

We finally pulled into the alley behind Peach's. Aaron told us to hop out, and Rita followed. As we exited the truck, he reached over into the glove box and pulled out a new set of keys.

Sherrie and I squealed in delight. We were being led through the back door and into the inner sanctum of all that is holy with baked goods. Not only does Peach's have the best baked goods in River Bend, they have the best baked goods for three hundred miles. We'd heard about a place in Chicago that was pretty good, but we didn't know if it could compete with Peach's.

I was disappointed when the smell of cleaning agents covered the sweet aroma I was accustomed to when walking through the door.

Aaron punched a few buttons into the security system, and our eyes adjusted to the soft lights. There was one overhead light in the kitchen and one near the register. The large glass windows let in a little light from the streetlights, but the dining room was otherwise dark.

My second disappointment was that there was no powdered sugar anywhere. I envisioned everything covered in layers and layers of delightful white dust. I was hoping to write my name on the metal worktable, but everything was sterile.

"Why don't you guys have a seat in the corner? If someone is foolish enough to be out at this hour and in this weather, I don't need them knocking on the door to be let in."

"Are we good being here?" I asked.

"Of course, Aunt Jan wouldn't mind. She probably won't know. We'll be gone before she gets in. Freddie will open up in a few hours, but he and I have a deal."

"A deal?" Sherrie asked. "You do this often?"

"Not so much now. Claud, can you grab the specials board and write on it: *Shut up, don't rat us out. Long night. All good. Coletti dead.*"

"What?" I asked.

Aaron disappeared into the cooler. Sherrie and I fiddled with the sign, and Pete went to help Aaron.

They came back a minute later and dropped some stuff on a metal workstation. Aaron directed us to the register and had us look up into the corner at the security camera. He held up the sign and told us to wave.

Aaron's phone beeped. "Ok, Chuck got our message. We're good."

"Does he have every place in this town wired with some high-tech security system? Couldn't you just text him?" Sherrie asked.

A few months back, Sherrie had learned about the bar's extensive security camera system when Chuck confessed he had a recording of her dancing around while she set up before opening. The same system saved Aaron, Pete, and me from further harm and possible arrest for murder when I shot a man in the bar. I guessed I was ok with being on film.

"It's different if the message comes from just me or all of us. Just be happy we didn't have to stand there for an hour before he saw us. When I turned off the alarm, with it being so late, I knew he would get an alert. I was hoping we weren't disturbing whatever assignment he's on." He laughed a little to himself. "Also, I wouldn't do anything dumb or embarrassing in Phil's store or the flower shop on Main."

"So what's the deal with Freddie?" I asked.

Aaron talked as he went back into the kitchen. "As long as I clean up and I don't screw up inventory or make a mess of things, Freddie stays quiet and I keep my keys to the place and I throw him a free pizza or beer at the bar."

"Free pizza Freddie!" Pete said. "I have not seen him lately. You must have been behaving and staying away from this place at night."

"At least six or eight months since the last late-night visit. You guys have a seat. I'll have something ready in a few minutes," Aaron said.

"I'll do drinks," Pete said.

Aaron looked at Rita and said, "Sofa," and she led us to the far corner and plopped down between the coffee table and sofa.

This corner of the dining room had two sofas and a throne for a chair. Sherrie and I each took a seat on a sofa opposing each other. She was smiling, clearly wanting to talk to me in private. I was suddenly reeling when Aaron's words came rippling through me again.

I love you; he said it. I still had not processed all of that.

We took off our coats and got comfy. Before we could exchange a word, we heard another voice and froze. We couldn't make out if it was a man or woman. The minute Aaron left Mallory in the kitchenette at the funeral home, I had not thought about her or how she was going to get anywhere since Aaron had been the one to drive her to the funeral home. I was ok not thinking about her now. Just because Aaron was done with her did not mean she was done with him.

Pete came over to us carrying a tray of mugs and following behind was Wyatt. I just about peed in my pants with delight. It was a weird reaction to sudden happiness, but hell, at this point, nothing during that evening would have surprised me. It was not so much joy of seeing Wyatt as it was the joy of it not being Mallory. He took off his coat and sat on the grand chair between the sofas.

I wrapped my hands around the mug and stretched out on the sofa. Sherrie and Pete sat close to each other, so their knees were touching.

Aaron came in with sandwiches, quiche, scones, plates, forks, and knives. He set up everything as a buffet, and we tore it apart. There was sharing, dividing up remaining portions, and very few thank-yous were said to each other as we passed food around, but we were cordial and respectful of each other's hunger. There were quick offers to have the last of some foods, but not much time was allowed for an answer before the one offering it devoured it themselves.

There was not much talking while we ate. The tea was excellent, and Pete refused to tell us what he had put in it. He said it was Mary Seward's recipe. Mary was Anna's mother, and Pete said even if Anna didn't have morals, he would still keep his promise to Mary about the secret tea.

Wyatt helped Aaron clean up the mess, and the two returned with pumpkin pie.

"Pete, this tea is good, but I was hoping for something stronger," I said "Too bad we're not at the bar, or did you sneak out Maribel's brandy?"

"Well, maybe I can help." Wyatt reached under his jacket and held up a bottle of liquid brown goodwill. It was the second time that night I felt joy for the stuff I usually steered clear of in bars.

"I'll get the glasses," Aaron said.

I shook my head. "Forget the glasses."

We all slammed whatever was left of the tea

and held our mugs out to Wyatt.

"When I got the text from Aaron saying where you were headed, I figured you guys may need something. But on the other hand, I didn't know what kind of state you guys would be in, so I didn't pull it out right away. I snagged the good stuff from the hunting cabin when I left."

Sherrie raised her mug, and we all followed suit.

She started the traditional Thanksgiving Day mantra. "I'm thankful that when I'm stuck in a funeral home, my friend is the one delivering the body."

Aaron said, "I'm thankful Maribel does not remember it was me twelve years ago who tore up her rose garden and ruined her chance of winning River Bend's best garden seven years in a row."

I shifted in my seat. "I'm thankful Pete was foolish enough to get in that unmarked white van with me and didn't steal it himself."

Pete gave me the side-eye and said, "I'm thankful Wyatt showed up with this bottle."

Wyatt nodded solemnly to Pete. "I am thankful for being included in this midnight fest. It's been years since we have done this here. Seriously, thank you for the phone call and finally settling one of River Bend's infamous tales."

"Cheers," everybody said in unison.

It was strange when Wyatt referred to times

he and Aaron had snuck into Peach's. It made me want to learn more about Aaron, opposed to when Mallory had been talking about their past and I'd wanted to shove an arrow through her skull.

I lay against the armrest and stretched my legs over Aaron's lap. Sherrie and Pete were sitting comfortably close again, and Wyatt sat, wide-eyed, looking fresher than the four of us combined.

"Again, I don't want to impose, but can you fill in some of the gaps?" I asked.

"I can try. When I was at the police academy, we did some cross-training with the feds. Believe it or not, one of those agents I met was on-site tonight and provided some details. I think you guys know more than I do. What do you want to know?" Wyatt asked.

"Jonathan said he hired Anderson — Gibson — but he isn't a fed?" I asked.

"Jonathan didn't know Gibson's true identity. They have been watching Harold on and off for years, but when talk increased about Coletti being terminally ill, the feds stepped up their surveillance on old associates. Harold must have known something was up with Coletti, and he reached out to Jonathan. So Jonathan got worried about Hailey. He thought Coletti might use Hailey as a negotiating tool for Harold to carry out some final big plan. I guess Jonathon went to a security company to find someone to monitor her, and the feds slipped in Gibson. This agent said Senior wanted to settle up in River Bend. They thought it was to settle the score for being kicked out of the business.

"I don't know about that guy Gibson. One minute, you think the guy is brilliant getting close to Hailey and getting inside the old family home, but then he is dumb enough to get himself handcuffed to the van door."

"So who stole the van?" Pete asked.

"This guy they picked up speeding out of town. Gibson was able to provide information about the getaway car because it was following the van. It was some associate of Coletti named Hauge."

"Hauge?" Sherrie asked.

"Norm! Norm Hauge," I said.

"You know him?" Wyatt asked.

I exchanged looks with Sherrie and Pete, and Wyatt caught me.

"C'mon, I've been telling you guys what I know," Wyatt said.

"Sorry, habit. All night long, we have been figuring out what to say as a group. I apologize. There was no intention of leaving you out," I said.

"Ok," he said.

I chuckled to myself. *Simple one-word answers from guys, and you know you're back on their good side.*

"Norm was delivering a body. He stopped

at the hotel, and I believe faked a heart attack and made me promise I would finish the delivery," I said.

Wyatt replied. "So I understand Claudia driving the van and picking up Pete but how did you and Sherrie end up at the funeral home? Happy accident or are you looking at a new career?"

"That was no accident. The whole reason all this started was because of the body he was driving," I said.

Sherrie nodded. "Last week, I was working the phones for C&C and took the call for the funeral home. I didn't know what I was doing and just said I would accept the business."

I finished the story. "The body in the van was Maribel Carlin and Anthony Coletti's son, Junior. She had an affair. Coletti kidnapped his own kid when old man Alvin Carlin ran him out of town and severed the partnership. Maribel, still in the hospital because of complications at childbirth, was told the baby died a few days later. I'm speculating on this part, Coletti came here to tell Maribel the truth or maybe give a final goodbye to his son. Harold had probably hoped to keep the younger Coletti from returning to River Bend and in turn keep Senior away. The facility where Junior lived called Harold because Coletti Senior could not be reached, and the lady didn't understand the gravity of the situation or what Coletti Senior had worked out with the administration about privacy."

Wyatt rubbed his face, sat back, then leaned forward to pick up his mug. He took a big drink. His face tightened up, the liquid clearly burning his throat. "Wow, old lady Maribel getting it on back in her day. The way she walked around town telling everyone how act, and she was the one stepping out on Alvin. Wait, don't we have an extra body?"

We chuckled because we understood keeping track of bodies, Coletti's and Carlins, can be challenging.

I said, "The body Norm Hauge drove here and is currently in the funeral home is Junior. The body in the driver seat was Coletti Senior who was killed sometime last night."

"Can't believe you guys have been sitting with that information. I had the back story on Gibson you guys know the fate of Anthony, The Pigeon, Coletti. River Bend's most notorious former resident. Remind me never to play poker with you guys. The way you guys hold your shit together is a little unnerving."

"When Coletti took his son and left River Bend, he had a fake birth certificate made and gave the boy his name," I explained. "It wasn't Coletti Senior who was ill but his son. If Coletti could get people thinking he was really dead he might come after Harold for extorting him all these years for his silence."

"Are we positive it was Harold who killed Coletti last night? Why not Jonathan?" Sherrie asked. "It seemed like he would truly do anything to protect Hailey."

"It's only my guess, but I think Harold did it," Wyatt said.

"I agree, Jonathan would do anything to protect Hailey and even cover for her if she murdered someone. Harold was using Hailey to get rid of the gun," I said.

"Then what about Hailey. Could she have done it?" Sherrie asked.

"I don't think she's dumb, but I don't think she has what it takes to pull it off and act that naive about everything happening around her," I said. "I think Harold was going to burn the place down. Hailey was too upset when we found her upstairs when Harold tried escaping."

"Remember, she will have an alibi from Anna and the guys they were seeing last night," Pete said.

Wyatt said, "Harold reeked of gasoline when they loaded him in the ambulance."

"How did Harold get away from the van and Gibson? Did he walk?" I asked.

"Hauge. He was following the van in a car,"

Wyatt said. "They—or at least I—don't know where he is right now. He dropped off Harold here and took off. The best part is Holton leaving the scene. He was first to respond and found Gibson and wouldn't release him from the door immediately."

"He didn't know he was a fed, did he?" I asked.

"Not right away, but the van was on fire when he arrived and found Gibson cuffed to the back. Somehow they worked it out, and then Holton took off when he got another call. It seemed to be a personal problem because Gibson heard nothing from Holton's car radio when they were waiting for the fire department. Holton left, leaving Gibson standing on the side of a country road with a dead body and a van on fire."

"Oh, shit," Sherrie said, so matter-of-fact almost no one paid any attention to her.

But then it dawned on me what she meant. "It was your text from Hailey's phone. The one asking for help. I shouldn't laugh, but even I know that's a stupid move. Leaving one scene without even calling for more information. Does he have that big of a need to be seen as a hero?"

We sat around, talking for a bit, and laughed at the absurdity of the evening and speculated at our role in history. We were all content with not being part of the folklore.

Then the elephant in the room appeared. No one could see Mallory, but we were all thinking of her.

I figured I would be the one to break the silence. "Are we positive Mallory will keep us out of any story?" I asked.

Wyatt answered before anyone could take a shot at her. "Gibson shut that down. He threatened her with all sorts of legal crap if something gets printed before they settled it in court."

Then he hit us with something else. "I will let you know, my cousin Zoey is friends with her. Actually, last month when Mallory was in town, the two of them went to Minneapolis for shopping. Zoey will tell me if Mallory is writing an online piece or a book."

"She would rat out her friend?" Sherrie asked.

"Two reasons I would say absolutely she will rat out anyone: Zoey loves playing the spy regardless who it is. I actually told her that the police are looking at Maggie in the library as a drug dealer who is using the library desk to deal. It's totally fictional, but Zoey has checked out fifty books in the last two months, hoping to report on something." Wyatt laughed.

"That's awful," I said.

He shrugged. "She is always on me to give her some police dirt, so sometimes I just make shit up to get her off my back."

"You said two reasons, what's the second?" Sherrie asked.

"Zoey is pissed at Mallory. I guess she bought a leather jacket and then Mallory got the same one with asking."

"What?" Sherrie and I said together.

"Easy, ladies, there are plenty more if you like the jacket. You just have to drive to an H&M Store," Wyatt said.

"H&M!" Sherrie said.

"Yeah, it's like the Gap of Europe according to Zoey," he said.

Sherrie and I giggled like seven-year-olds.

"She tore the label out of a jacket to make it more cool," I said.

Aaron was silent on the subject of Mallory, but so was Pete, but I decided to not read into that any more than I should. Aaron had been quiet all night, and I let that go too. He hadn't been there from the beginning, but he'd had a long night and a confrontation with an ex.

Let's hope he's not stewing about her.

Before we knew it, it was nearly 2 a.m. I hobbled my way to the restroom and came back to find everyone standing up.

Pete winced in pain as he grabbed the tray of mugs. "I guess my wrist is a little tender."

"Sorry I never made a splint for your arm.

After all, you made me a cane," I said.

"How is the ankle?" Pete asked.

"Not bad. I can stand but can't put too much pressure on it. I don't need to go to the doctor. The swelling should be gone in a day or two."

Sherrie carried the cups into the kitchen area and started doing the dishes. Pete went to help her.

Wyatt was having fun with the chalkboard sign, writing messages to Chuck. I got in on the action. We had no idea if Chuck was watching the security camera in real time or not, but it was fun. Aaron sat on the couch, watching us.

Some of the messages included:

Wyatt: SOS I have been kidnapped by the Pillsbury Doughboy, he is holding me ransom for some of Jan's peach pie.

Me: River Bend town motto: boring as hell until you live here

Wyatt: No liquor license, no problem

Me: Just a working-class girl with a brown bag lunch and whiskey in a mug

Wyatt: Get a life if you are still watching us. Do your security defense job in the Middle East, not the Midwest.

Me: Lesson #1 - If Sherrie is ever talking too much, just take her to a funeral home. She will keep talking, but it will be a whisper. Much easier to block out until you piss her off, and then she is back full force and full voice.

Wyatt: Don't adjust your screen. Pete's sweatshirt is really that ugly.

Me: Don't stop watching. With my luck, we may need you to recuse us.

Wyatt: You were always my favorite Rhoimly.

Me: Wyatt is just kissing your butt so you don't rat out our late-night feeding frenzy. His favorite Rhoimly is your cute cousin Krista.

Wyatt: Is she still single? I would make you best man—not your brother—if you fix us up.

I was getting chalk all over my $137 sweatshirt, so I stopped.

I could see into the kitchen a little bit, around the espresso maker. Sherrie and Pete were putting away the plates and mugs. Suddenly, they were only partially visible, but I knew they were facing each other and intimately close.

I imagined they must be kissing, and quietly sang "Right Here, Right Now" by Jesus Jones until Sherrie screamed. The three of us flew into the kitchen.

Pete was covered head to toe in powdered sugar.

I had been mistaken. Sherrie and Pete had not been kissing. Sherrie had tried to put the tray on the top shelf, and Pete had gone to help but knocked over the powdered sugar in the process. There was nothing but laughter from everyone, including Pete.

Always the sensible one, Aaron took control. The noise sent Rita to Aaron's side, but he quickly and smartly sent her back to the sofa area. "Pete, step away and touch nothing. Stand by the back door. Wyatt will drive you home. We'll clean up. We don't have much time. Freddie will be here soon and if he sees it like this I will be feeding him for a month."

"No way," Wyatt said. "He is not getting in my car. I'll take the girls, and you get him."

We couldn't really argue with him. Sherrie grabbed everybody's coats and Wilbur. She and Pete pulled out some cash and tossed it by the register, Sherrie covering my portion because I didn't have my wallet.

She asked Aaron, "Will you make sure that gets in the register so whoever is opening doesn't think they get a tipped just for showing up?"

"That is kind of you guys but unnecessary. Jan has a key to my bar."

"Then why the panic about Freddie talking?" Sherrie asked.

"He talks to my mother, who gets on my case. I just can't handle her griping, and god forbid if she knew Rita was in the kitchen."

Wyatt went back to the chalkboard for one more sign. He made Pete walk in front of the camera and hold up the board, which read

"Pillsbury Doughboy actually showed up looking for a little sugar."

Pete held up his middle finger along with the sign.

Aaron was lost in a mess of powdered sugar. I kissed him and only got a smidge of it on me.

After ending an evening like we'd had, I wanted to hug Pete for ten minutes. The guy had stuck with us, and never for one second did he think to leave us. It was pretty amazing what he and I had been through together those last few months, but instead of a hug, he got a high five, and I got powdered sugar dust floating over my head.

Wyatt was out the door before Aaron could change his mind about taking powdered-sugar-covered Pete home. I turned in time to see Sherrie and Pete high-five and their hands fall together, interlocking their fingers before she stepped away.

Number of people no longer hungry: All of us

CHAPTER THIRTY-NINE

Wyatt drove us to the hotel so I could retrieve Debby, my car. My foot was still tender, I let Sherrie take the driver's seat. Wyatt, always the gentleman, waited until my car started. Anytime someone saw it, they were amazed it still ran, much less starts right up in this weather. We gave him a wave, and he left us in the hotel parking lot.

The second his headlights were out of sight, I turned to Sherrie. "I was right! I don't need details; I want them, but I want to hear I was right."

"Maybe you were right, but there are no juicy details to share."

"You are lying."

"Unlike you, I don't go at it with a guy in a funeral home before our first date," Sherrie said.

"So there will be a first date! And by the

way, do I need to remind you about you making out with Chase in the art building on campus after the senior exhibit when we were freshmen?"

"Let me remind you he was hot, and it was *not* a funeral home."

We sat there another minute, letting the car warm up. I looked at the hotel and realized Maddie would shit the bed if she knew that Sherrie, Pete, and I cracked one of River Bend's most notorious mysteries. She had been one game of rock, paper, scissors away from seeing a real-life mobster. I felt like I owed her dinner for having taken the opportunity away from her.

Sherrie put the car into drive. "Let's get out of here."

I asked, "Do you want to drive past his house?"

"What? Are you asking if I want to drive past Pete's house like I'm sixteen years old and hoping to catch a glimpse of him? Are you nuts? I don't know where he lives, and if I did, we could easily get caught if Aaron was able to clean up fast," Sherrie said.

We giggled halfway to EG's house. Pure exhaustion hit us on the last mile.

We walked into the house like robots. The cold was no longer a factor, each of us longing for our beds. We walked in the back door, through the kitchen, and living room.

Sherrie stopped short at the bottom of the stairs. "All right, girl, I'll give you a piggyback ride up. Be gentle when you hop on my back."

"Thanks for the offer. I think I'm good, but let me go first in case I stumble, so you can break my fall."

"No way. I was offering a ride. I am not an airbag," Sherrie said and ran up.

I followed slowly behind and sat on the couch in her room, waiting for my turn in the bathroom. I thought if I put on my pj's and waited on my bed, I would fall asleep before I could brush my teeth. I wasn't that far off with that prediction, because I fell asleep within ninety seconds of sitting on Sherrie's sofa. She and Aaron were the only two people I knew who actually brushed their teeth for the full two minutes as recommended by dentists everywhere.

Sherrie must have covered me with a blanket, and sometime during the night, I shifted from sitting to lying on my back with my neck curled into my body. I woke us when I tried stretching and fell off the sofa. I must have looked like a fool scrambling to get up faster than Sherrie because I wanted to beat her to the bathroom. I was successful, but not because of speed, but because she rolled over and slept for another thirty minutes as I showered and got dressed.

I managed just fine around the bathroom

and my room. Going down the stairs was slow, but I could put some weight on my foot. I got the coffee going and plopped myself down at the island when Sherrie came into the kitchen smiling like crazy.

"Perky morning people are annoying," I said.

"Cynical people need more time in a funeral home with their boyfriends." Sherrie grabbed a mug and joined me at the island. "I figured we got to bed around four a.m., and with six hours of dead sleep, I feel pretty good."

Sunshine was streaming through the kitchen windows, and I went to the kitchen sink, looked out to the driveway, and saw no evidence of the ice and snow from yesterday. The window was cold to the touch and the wind was howling, so not everything from yesterday was gone.

"Oh, crap. We got a problem." I went to the refrigerator, to the stove, and then I quick-stepped it—an improvement from yesterday's hobbling—to EG's room. I stood in the doorway. Sherrie was behind me, holding her coffee and looking confused.

"What's up?" she asked.

"It's gone and EG's not back." I stood there in my jeans, my twenty-six-dollar sweatshirt, and fuzzy socks with a look of bewilderment on my face.

"Whatever it is, please don't say you lost a

body. Been there, done that." Sherrie walked back into the kitchen and filled up our mugs. "What's up?"

"Perky Sherrie is kinda of annoying. I tell you something is gone, and you make jokes."

"After yesterday and losing a body, not much can faze me."

"I don't think you are suddenly so cool under pressure. I think you're daydreaming about your new beau."

"Well, what has you all up in a tither?"

"The turkey is missing. Yesterday, I put it in the sink, and now it's gone. EG is not back yet, and I don't see it anywhere." I looked at Sherrie, wanting an answer.

"Don't look at me. I lose bodies, not birds. Well, I guess I lose my job, actually maybe jobs."

"What do you mean *jobs*?" I asked.

"I am pretty sure C&C is going to be cutting back on some things. In case you forgot, Harold, the owner, is wanted for setting a van on fire with a federal agent in it and is probably wanted for killing a mobster. That does not make for good business. And I will probably cut way back on my hours at the bar. Maybe I can get more shifts at Bumbles or just worry about getting through finals and find something in January."

"Why are you cutting back on hours at the bar?" I asked but knew the answer. "Is it because you don't want to date a coworker, so instead of not dating him, you are just going to get new coworkers?"

"That's pretty good detective work. Now only if you could figure out what happened to a turkey." Sherrie got up and went to the fridge and looked around the counters. "Also, add my potatoes to the police report. They are missing too."

Before we expended too much energy into this, I got a text from my mother asking if we were up yet and just say the word, then someone would come get us.

"Who, where?" Sherrie asked.

I was as confused as she was.

I called, and Mom picked up immediately. It was hard to hear her with all the background noise and her having to shout at me. She finally understood that we were dressed. I told Sherrie I didn't know any more information than I had before the call, but I thought we should be ready for someone to pick us up.

We went upstairs and finished getting ready, and five minutes later, a horn honked from the street.

Sherrie shouted from her bedroom, "Why is your family so angry?"

"Not a clue, but let's go. I'm too tired to figure any of this out."

The sidewalks were clear of ice, and I had an

easy time making it to the car. Sherrie was at my side for each step should I need her. I opened the front car door but moved to the back when I saw it was my brother, Connor, driving. He hit the horn again.

"What are you doing here? I thought you guys were stuck at home. How is Mom's wrist and your foot? What's going on?"

"I'm fine. My leg is a little sore, and Mom will never tell you she is hurting, so I have no idea."

"So where are we going?" Sherrie asked.

"Wherever I drive you." Connor smirked at her.

I leaned over the seat and grabbed his ear. He kept on driving and ignoring the pain I was inflicting.

"Answer the question," I said.

"I don't have to. You hurt me, and I will tell Mom and Dad you forced us off the road."

"If you—"

Sherrie cut me off. "Stop. Why do the two of you regress to ten-year-olds when you're around each other?"

"Like you are so levelheaded with your brother," I said.

"Seriously, you are coming after me. Ease up, and go find yourself a funeral home and get lucky. You need to get yourself some action," Sherrie said.

"Shut up, please stop talking," Connor said. "I can't hear about my sister's dating life. Just sit back. We're almost at the bar."

We remained silent for the rest of the ride. We pulled into the alley behind the bar. My brother's parking job next to the dumpster was questionable, but I was feeling the holiday spirit and let any comments slide.

We walked in and found my mom, dad, and Phil, from the hardware store, moving tables and chairs around.

"What's going on?" I asked.

"We are doing Thanksgiving here. Now," my mom said from across the bar. She said it so casually, it was like I was supposed to know.

Sherrie and I looked at each other, seeing if we knew what that meant.

My dad came over and gave me a hug and whispered in my ear, "Just go with it." He looked at Sherrie and me. "How are you two doing? I understand it was a crazy night. I thought I was going to have the big story of driving into a ditch and helping pull people out of a wreckage, but from what Aaron tells us, you girls had a whopper of a night."

Before we could answer, my mom came over and hugged me before moving on to Sherrie. "How is the foot, honey? Can you move or do you need to sit?"

Aaron was behind the bar cleaning glasses. Connor was trying to get football on the TVs.

Aaron's mother, Lesley, walked in, with an armful of linen, greeting everyone. "Aaron, your dad will be here in a few hours when the turkey is done, and Jan will be here in five with dessert."

Sherrie and I stood in the center of activity, confused.

"What is going on here?" I asked overly loud so someone would have to answer.

My mom said, "We took over the Thanksgiving meal. Last night, when you stopped sending out instructions, date requests, menu options, etcetera and didn't get upset when we told you about our little roadside incident, I knew something was wrong. I texted Aaron, and he filled us in, so I started a new text chain and came up with this plan. I also learned just an hour ago Aaron left out a lot of details about last night." My mother raised her voice at the end and looked at Aaron, who was doing his best to avoid eye contact with my mother and me.

"So you came to the house and didn't wake us?" I asked my mom.

"Don't be silly. We got to town thirty minutes ago. I sent the O'Briens over to get the food. They will be here when their turkey is done. Honey, it takes more than a day to defrost a turkey—" She looked towards the door. "I think someone is knocking on the door. If they should be with us, let them in, otherwise tell the folks that Draw Bar is open to the public. Sherrie, can you wait by the back door? Jan will be here and will need help bringing in the dessert."

I let EG in the front door, and she handed me a box with several bottles of wine and went back to her car for another box with more wine. She came in practically dancing and looking fresh. Hair swept back over her shoulders, clothes not wrinkled after the drive from Chicago and a ball of good energy, just like my mom.

"Aaron, I know you have the bar covered with beer and booze, but I thought we could enjoy some wine with dinner. It shouldn't be up to you to serve us your inventory since we took over your place."

Aaron walked out from behind the bar, taking the wine from EG. "That is the nicest way someone has ever told me that my wine list is not up to par. I hope the drive was not too treacherous from Chicago."

"I started driving yesterday, but it got too bad so I stopped in Madison for the night. Actually, I might head back there if the weather holds out in the next few days," EG said.

"What about your cruise?" I asked.

"Maybe some other time," EG said.

My mother was quick to add, "Let me guess,

you met a new fellow who lives in Madison, and he is sitting on a higher priority list than the cruise ship captain."

"Maybe, maybe not." EG smiled with delight and finally confessed. "Yup, cuter and closer to home than the captain."

My mother put her to work, and I let Kay and Jenna in. They immediately went to my brother, who was wearing some new tennis shoes they thought were cool. The look on my brother's face was priceless because he had the attention of twenty-four-year-old women who were not his sister or his sister's roommate.

A few more people came in the back door, some on the original list and a few new ones. The weather held some here in River Bend, and others it forced them to rearrange their plans for the week, but all looked happy being part of the big group.

I took a seat in the booth to the right of door and hung back, watching everyone set up for the feast, talk, hug, laugh, and enjoy the holiday spirit. The only disagreement was the balance of music to that of the football game. My mother and brother would be at the volume controls all day and night, and my father would spend most of his time avoiding that discussion. If he liked Aaron, my father would teach him to stay away from that argument when there was no chance of winning, regardless if you want music or football.

Everyone I cared for and more were in this room for the sole purpose of celebrating a holiday that is full of everything good. I should have felt happy, but I felt a little helpless or hapless. Last night, I had stood strong and refused to leave when I knew the right thing to do was to stay. For lack of better words, I fought the good fight, but I felt now like things had happened without me.

I shouldn't need to be in charge to have a good time.

The more I thought about it, the more I felt like something had been taken away from me. I knew this wasn't my dinner, but I suddenly felt lost inside the crowd.

I should see it as a sweet gesture that my boyfriend talks or texts with my mom.

But does he think I couldn't handle multiple tasks? Do I need taking care of? Does he see me as someone who needs to be rescued?

I then remembered what I'd heard him say to Mallory, that I didn't need protection and I had guts and grit. It made me smile, but I still couldn't help thinking if he thought I was soft.

Or was it me—was I looking for something more challenging? I was having trouble enjoying this party, but was it the same thing with my relationship?

Do I need it to be challenging for it to be exciting? Why did hearing my boyfriend say he loves me leave me shocked and wondering what that means? It is pretty clear what that means for him, but what does that mean for me?

Is this relationship too easy? What is wrong with easy? I am confusing easy *with* convenient.

I needed to leave these thoughts behind and go enjoy my family. I thought about Hailey and what that family was going through today. I doubted she and her nana will be at the country club on Thursday for Thanksgiving.

I got up from my hidden corner and walked over and gave my mother a hug, thinking how lucky I was to have my family. I enjoyed the moment and appreciated everyone around me. My mother broke into my smiling daze when she sent me upstairs to Aaron's loft to get some supplies that were up there.

"With my sore foot?" I protested.

"He said you would know where everything is and you have the code to get in." She left me to my tasks while she rearranged the tables for the fifth time since I had been there.

I went through the front exit and walked three feet over to the entrance to the upstairs apartments. I punched in the key code and quickly stepped inside. A row of metal mailboxes were lined up on the wall, threadbare carpet, and one stairwell eight feet from the door. It was either head up or back outside. One minute in the cold outside was one minute too much, so I made my way up the stairs, using the handrail and going at my slow but steady pace.

Six steps up, I heard the door open behind me. There were six other lofts that shared this stairwell and upstairs hallway. I had met a couple of other tenants, mostly college students, but I didn't know everyone.

I didn't turn around; I just said, "It's ok to pass me. I'm moving at my own pace."

No one responded. Cold air rushed past me. I could sense one other person. My hand shook a little. Why didn't they speak? I was scared to turn around, but maybe they didn't hear me. I stopped walking and turned around.

A man in a black thermal top, black jeans, and combat boots with steel-blue eyes looked directly at me. He had a small spiderweb tattoo peeking out from the shirt. Although his shirt was so form-fitting one might have thought it was a tattoo also. For some unknown reason, I wanted to reach out and check if, in fact, he had a shirt on, but I refrained.

I motioned for him to pass, and he stayed put. Cold air radiated off him, and I took in a pine scent. I didn't know if he had used a code to get into the stairwell or if he'd grabbed the door behind me. I had never seen this man before. I didn't know everyone in River Bend, but outsiders were easy to spot.

We were two feet apart, and I was two steps above him, but it felt like inches. There was no reason to trust his man, but I didn't feel threatened. The feeling surging through me was electric. He did not speak, and his eyes never left me. He left me breathless. I forced my hand down. My fingers wanted to trace his spiderweb tattoo. I instantly wanted to know more about this man..

"You don't need to wait. I can make it up the stairs," I finally said.

He stepped to the left, leaving little space between us, and continued up the stairs at a faster rate than me but in no hurry. He stood at the top and waited. Anyone with common sense, anyone who knows the feds are in town looking for the mob, anyone alone in a staircase would have known enough to turn around and get out, but that was not for me, so I continued up.

I went slow, not because of my ankle, but because I didn't want to be out of breath when I got to the top. I had two more steps, and he was watching with his arm crossed and his lips pressed closed.

I felt intimately aware of every move, every breath, every motion I made. It felt like everything was alive, like the handrail would grab my arm, the stairs would grab my legs, and the walls were ready to swallow me whole. The man's gaze made me aware of everything.

"You really don't need to wait. I am not going to fall."

He waited until I lifted my leg for the last step and bent forward, speaking into my ear. "Maybe I just wanted to catch you."

He turned, walked left, and opened a door. Every nerve tingled down my body. A surge inside me made me want to follow him into his apartment and let him catch me.

Instead, I turned right and made my way to Aaron's apartment, only to realize I didn't have a key. I was about to turn around when the door opened and a hand reached out for me, yanking me inside.

Aaron pressed me against the door. "I missed you," he said, and he kissed me. "Are you ok? You seem a little shaken."

I didn't know who I was kissing. I knew I was kissing Aaron, but the scent of pine lingered around me, and I pictured the man from the stairwell.

"Oh, you just startled me" was all I could come up with. Why couldn't I tell him about the strange encounter in the hallway?

Aaron moved his lips around to my neck and to my ear, giving me little kisses along the way. I thought about the spiderweb and if there was a spider tattooed underneath that shirt.

"Oh, how I missed you," he said.

"It's been ten minutes since I saw you."

"Yeah, but it's been twelve hours since we were this close and my hands were able to do this." He ran his hands down my back, and his lips came back to mine. He pulled away slightly, only to bend down and cradle me in his arms, and carried me to his bed.

"What are you doing? We can't do this now! Our families are downstairs." I could barely get the words out because he was on top of me, and I was melting.

"I bought us some time. I told your mom it might take some extra time searching through the storage space. There are so many people there, they won't notice if we aren't there."

His hands ran down my side and legs and back up. He pushed up my sweatshirt and kissed my belly. His fingers lingered there, dancing across my stomach, and his mouth returned to mine. I was lost in the moment, and he was winning his argument. Every touch and every kiss felt new and exciting.

Images of the man from the stairwell floated in my head. "We can't do this," I said. "Our families are downstairs."

The weight of him made me feel safe, and I wanted more, but my mind was reeling between two men. One of whom was a stranger.

Mallory suddenly popped into my head.

"Are you sure you want me to stop?" he said.

I shifted, so we were lying on our sides, and our legs were intertwined. He kissed my neck again, his breathing heavy. "So, should I stop?" he whispered.

"We need to stop. We can continue later." I was trying to convince him and myself that this was not a good idea. "What has gotten into you?"

"I just missed you," he said.

I couldn't help thinking if I inspired these desires or if seeing Mallory did.

I pulled away and turned my head to avoid any more contact. "We'll have more time later."

"I don't know about that. With your family here, this might be the only time we have together." He kissed my neck.

Why does that make me melt?

"They won't be here forever." I took one last kiss before I finally had the willpower to stand.

"I see I lost the battle." Aaron smiled.

Our fingers were locked. I attempted to pull him up and he tried fighting it, but he eventually stood up. We were again dangerously close, so I stepped/hobbled back.

"Let me throw cold water on my face before we head back down," I said.

"I need a cold shower." Aaron laughed. "We

have to head outside. You will be fine. Let's go."

"What are we here to get?" I asked "I don't see any food."

"The storage area is at the end of the hall. We can use the dumbwaiter, but it's old and not reliable, so one has to be upstairs and the other person has to be on the other end," Aaron said.

"You have storage up here. You have a dumbwaiter? Why don't I know these things?" I said.

Aaron was at the door to the loft waiting for me. "Let's go. If you don't hurry, I am going to lock this door behind us and send everyone a text saying we skipped town and won't be back until Christmas and then throw you on that bed and get back to where we were a minute ago."

He took a step towards me, and I knew he was serious.

"We can't start up, and no more talk about that in the same conversation as my parents being downstairs." I fiddled with my hair. I was sure I looked like a mess, and Sherrie would be the one to bust us, so I would have to avoid her for a bit.

As I walked to the door, I realized I wanted a glimpse of that man to make sure he was not a mirage.

I walked through the doorway and dared to glance down the hallway. I knew it would be empty, but I couldn't help feeling disappointment.

Aaron locked his door, and we headed down the hall, away from the stairwell and away from the mystery man's door.

Aaron pointed to a door. "Every unit gets a storage locker in there. The last door here belongs to the bar. That thing here on your left is the dumbwaiter."

"I never noticed it," I said.

"You come up these back steps often?" Aaron laughed. He opened the door on the right, and inside was a metal cart loaded up with small boxes and, beyond that, larger boxes and crates filled with restaurant supplies. "Most of this stuff is left over from the previous bar owner."

Not surprisingly, since it was Aaron's storage area now, there was no dust or cobwebs anywhere. A broom and dustpan hung neatly to the right and everything was organized, labeled, and neatly stacked. A clipboard hung on the wall with the current inventory list.

I looked at the cart and said, "Is that it? Can't we just carry it down?"

"Those boxes are just some of it, and they are heavy. The forks and knives weigh a ton, plus I want to take the good wineglasses down."

Aaron stepped back into the hallway and pressed a button on the far wall. There was a window-like unit with a wood shade that rolled up, revealing a three-by-four space. Aaron put three boxes of wineglasses in the unit, and I handed him the unusually heavy utensils.

"Give me a few seconds to get down the stairs. I need to make sure the shaft is clear, and nothing is leaning on the frame down there. This thing is sensitive, but it works. I will send a text, and you just have to keep the metal window frame clear of any debris and, most importantly, your arm." Aaron locked the storage door behind him.

"Did you really need me up here? That did not take us long," I said.

Aaron came over and pressed me against the wall. We were nose to nose. He didn't kiss me but smiled and said, "I know. We still have time before we have to be back."

A door opened down the hall, and I was flooded with relief when I saw it was Izzie and Madison from apartment two.

"Get a room," one of them shouted, not waiting for a reply as they ran down the stairs.

I loved that Aaron was comfortable enough with me and himself that he hadn't jumped back. He had no burden of embarrassment. I wondered what I would have done if my mystery man had opened his door.

Aaron reached into the dumbwaiter and ran his hand along the interior wall and then ran his dirty hand across my thighs.

"What are you doing?" I yelled.

"Giving you a cover story, making you look legit. You were to be up here helping me sort through the old stuff, looking for what we need. No one will believe you if you come down there all nice and clean."

I reached in and rubbed my sleeve against the wall. "That should do it."

Aaron had not moved, and I was losing my willpower to head downstairs. We were eye to eye, and he finally stepped back and reached into his pocket and held something in his hand. I realized it was a key. He used his back to push open the metal door to the rear staircase, and he pulled me towards him with his fingers in my front pockets. His right hand dipped into my pocket.

This guy won't let up. I was really losing any resolution I had left, and then it felt like he dumped a bucket of ice on me.

"Give up Wilbur, it's time to put him out to pasture. God, I sound like Sherrie." Aaron laughed. "Forget having a drawer; I will get you your own dresser," he said, and then he was gone.

Give up Wilbur? What was he saying? My hand drifted down into my pocket, and I found his apartment key.

Did Aaron just ask me to move in with him?

The beep on my phone broke me out of my trance. I turned and pressed the green button on the wall. The window door closed, and the old gears

404

started grinding, and the dumbwaiter tumbled down. I waited until the motor stopped, and after a few clangs and a thump, I pushed open the metal door.

Before it closed behind me, I looked one last time for my mystery man to reemerge. Sadly, he did not until much later.

I went down and exited the stairwell and found Kay outside on the phone, pointing to a vestibule behind the dumpster. I walked over and found Aaron there with Phil pulling out the goods I had just sent down. They didn't need my help, and I was glad to have a minute to myself in the cold.

The idea of the cold, fresh air being a good thing lasted about forty seconds before I made my way inside. About six more people had walked in since I'd gone upstairs. The room was filled with the savory aroma from all the appetizers. Turkeys had yet to arrive.

I decided we had room for one more, and I texted Maddie an invite.

She had texted me sixteen times with questions about the hotel and her speculations on what had happened to Norm. I told her to come to the bar after her shift. That would allow me some time to figure out how much I could tell her. I figured we would be eating all day, and people would be coming and going.

Jorge was there, sans the girlfriend, but he seemed to enjoy talking to Patty, Phil's wife, and her neighbor, Sophie. I guessed Patty had never made it out of town to her sister's place. My brother was seated at the other end of the bar in Earl's seat, looking too comfortable for a kid his age. He and money-hungry Jacob were fixated on the football game. He held tight to the remote so, I assumed, my mother couldn't adjust the volume.

My father came dancing by carrying the appetizers I had seen Eva and Charlie bring in. He was singing "Red, Red Wine," by the band UB40. He placed them on the bar before pouring himself a glass of wine. Phil was carrying in the stuff Aaron and I had pulled from storage and went back for more.

My mother, EG, and Lesley each held a Bloody Mary and were discussing if they needed to change the table layout one more time. I was doing my best to avoid the discussion, so I did a little therapy for myself.

I stood in the spot where four months ago I had killed a man, and I replaced that imagery with everything set out before my eyes. Family, friends, a few unknown but friendly faces. The room buzzed with joy, laughter, football announcers, but not too much music. I needed and wanted to freeze-frame this picture.

This was not Thanksgiving Day, but it had

all the right trimmings, so later, when someone mentioned Thanksgiving, I would look back at this year and, this would be the day I think of.

My parents' actual Thanksgiving Day would be spent volunteering back home in St. Paul, and I would be working. It would also be the year Maddie had given me a special gift when I was invited to her house on Thanksgiving after my shift.

Her mother hosted every employee from the hotel who had nowhere else to go or missed their families' get-togethers because they'd had to work. Maddie's mother, Tina, used to call it the orphan-holiday-place and then changed it to EDubs. It took me two years of attending Thanksgiving there to understand that stood for E-W, Everybody's Welcome. Years later, it got slightly ridiculous when hotel guests were angling for an invite so they wouldn't have to go see their own families.

I broke from my spot when I saw the ladies eyeing me with a potential new assignment, so I turned to look for Aaron.

Sherrie and Pete were coming out of the walk-in cooler.

"Oh my god, here with everyone forty feet away!" I said.

"Relax, we just carried in some wine," Sherrie said.

Pete said hello and wouldn't look at me

when he walked past.

When Sherrie passed me, she confessed in a whisper, "At least it's not a funeral home!"

Aaron came up behind me, slipping his arms around me, and put his head on my shoulder. We were cheek to cheek, swaying to the barely audible music.

Phil carried in the last box of flatware. He saw EG for the first time and greeted her with a big hug. "It's always nice when you're home."

"I see you got to keep your wife home this holiday," EG said.

Patty walked over and gave EG a hug. "I will go next week to help my sister when the holiday is over and Phil is busy in the store. It's good to have you here. You fly away on all those trips, but you know to return when it counts. Same thing with your sister. You folks are like some type of homing pigeon, always knowing when it's time to come home."

"Gotta love being home," EG said.

Aaron dropped his arms from my waist and moved his hand over my front pocket with the key in it and echoed EG's words to me. "Yup, good to have you home." Then he kissed me behind my ear on my neck.

I thought of the spiderweb tattoo I'd seen on

my mystery man's neck, and I pictured myself surrounded by pine trees.

Number of people at Thanksgiving: Everyone that mattered. Maybe one too many in my thoughts, but I couldn't tell anyone that.

GIBSON'S STORY

FBI AGENT ANDREW GIBSON
BADGE NUMBER XXX-XX-XX-XXX-XX-XXX (YOU DON'T
NEED THAT INFORMATION)
ALIAS ON THIS CASE: ANDERSON

It is not much of an alias using Anderson when my name is Andrew Gibson. I am good at my job, very good, but sometimes I forget the name I give people, so I have to keep it close to my real name.

I don't have to review the case with you, but I will fill in some details that Scooby-Doo bunch left out. I have to give them credit for how much they figured it out in a short amount of time.

The biggest question left out there is who shot Coletti Sr.? Let's eliminate the obvious starting with Hailey. I don't know if she has it in her. Even

411

if she was protecting someone she loved, she doesn't have the mental strength to pull the trigger.

Maribel, back in her day, I would have no doubt about her capabilities, but she did not do it. Harold and Jonathan have no idea she knew about Coletti Jr. After Jonathan left town, she started digging around and found out the truth. She even found a way to contact Coletti Sr., and she visited her son without Harold and Jonathan knowing. The son she had named Archibald Carlin.

That poor lady mourn the death of her son shortly after child birth and years later when she stopped visiting him when she realized he would never accept her as his mother. He just did not have the mental capacity to differentiate her from the nurses who took care of him on a daily basis. Being unable to connect with this man on an emotional level was too painful. She told herself from then on that her son had died and Anthony Jr. did not belong to her. It is sad to see her mind failing her, but not as sad at how much her family failed her.

I don't know enough about her now to know if she fully understands that her son returned home and her other son tried to kill me and dispose of her former lover.

As messed up as this family is there are few who would do anything to protect it. Jonathon would do anything to protect his daughter, Hailey, but I vote him most likely to shoot himself in the foot before being able to shoot a man he'd never met and who imposed no direct threat to him. It was not shocking he was the one to get hit when the gun misfired.

If it's not Hailey, Maribel, or Jonathon, you expect me to name Harold as the killer. You forget there was someone else who had a lot to lose if C&C was associated with Coletti. The IRS would be all over company books and maybe freeze the assets to get Harold to lead them to Coletti Sr. Jonathon's wife Jessa is about the money.

Jessa wanted her place in the Carlin family legacy. Not only did she walk right in during the investigation, she had easy access the night before. She wanted everything she did not have growing up—money, status, and for people to know who she was. I could go into more details we've collected about her, but it would be a waste.

Jessa had motive and opportunity, but she also had an alibi. She did not do it, but it was fun making you think she did. I needed to have a good laugh after that weasel Harold managed to handcuff me to the back door on that van. I don't know how that slippery sucker did it. He is such a moron he could not even properly set a vehicle on fire. I don't know why that makes me upset, because I would have died, but the guy was an idiot.

I will give him credit for using Coletti's

phone to manipulate Hauge. Hauge faked the heart attack on his own and had the perfect exit plan from the hospital when Harold texted him Coletti's car was in the hospital parking lot. Harold told him where to park the car and to get the van back and hide it until he was ready.

Harold even got Hauge to flip the breaker switch to kill power to the drawers. Harold thought it would mess with decomposing Coletti and the time of death in case he couldn't get the body out of the funeral home.

He eventually texted Hauge to return the van to the same lot where he left Coletti's car earlier. The small lot where Hailey and I had parked Harold had been directing Hauge with Coletti's phone but had no idea what he looked like.

I went out the door a few minutes after Sherrie and Pete but I turned right and saw Harold pushing Coletti up the ramp. He just assumed I was Hauge. Together we pushed the gurney across the street to the van. Hauge jumped out of the van and clocked me on the back of my head and told Harold to cuff me to the van.

One of several mistakes Harold made was confessing most everything to me as we drove out of town. He had no plans of letting me live.

Coletti showed up Friday night. He was upstairs talking to Maribel when Harold walked in, and at some point, a disagreement happened and he ended shooting Coletti. Harold was lucky Coletti drove himself and did not bring anyone for protection. It must have been purely personal for Coletti finally to see Maribel again after all these years for him to come out of hiding.

After Harold shot Coletti he spent most of the night cleaning up. Harold even laughed when he said how easy it was cleaning up a shooting in a funeral home with all the chemicals to remove the evidence.

As he confessed he purposely drove the van into the ditch, moved Coletti's body up front to the driver's seat, and poured gasoline under the hood. He lit the fire under the hood, thinking it would eventually spread to the whole van, thus giving him more time to get away from the scene before it blew up. Harold did not count on the fire panel between the hood and dashboard to limit the fire's spread. I'm assuming he expected Coletti's body to be burned in the fire, hiding the gunshot wound, and Coletti would be blamed for my assumed death, who in theory would have died handcuffed to the door."

Those girls were smart, but they missed a few things. They didn't realize the gurney was gone when they went into the workroom with Jonathan. Harold was making up contingency plans one after another on account of Sherrie,

Claudia, and Pete wanting to do the right thing.

Hauge got fifty miles out of town before my team picked him up, driving Coletti's car eighty miles an hour on the freeway. He was lucky he didn't end up in the ditch.

I had to let Harold take the body out of the funeral home and work himself deeper into trouble. We got the listening devices in there too late. I needed Harold to confess to me as much as possible.

If you think you heard it all, you are missing one piece of information. I am not even sure of the answer. I am doing some math and counting back the days, but until the end date, I can't or won't confirm anything.

I met Mallory in a bar in Chicago one night when I started working for Jonathan. We were both there to see Hailey. Mallory had been following Hailey on Instagram and knew where she was headed and designed the accidental run-in with her.

She was angling to do a story about Coletti, diving into his old ties to River Bend, and figured Hailey might get her some inside information, or at least put in a good word with Harold. Mallory knew the Coletti Senior was the Cole part of C&C but never could have guessed about Junior. So I did what every good federal agent would do; I slept with her and used her reporter angle. She had no clue I was a fed, but she is competitive and set out to write a better story than me.

I almost felt bad for leaking the story to Clark. He's not much more than paparazzi with gossip-style tendencies in his writing, but he has associates on the wrong side of the law. We have been friends since sixth grade and occasionally do each other a professional favor.

He heard Jonathan was looking for someone to watch out for Hailey, and he gave me the heads-up. I tossed him the story about Coletti being dead when that cop left me at the scene without backup.

Sometimes I think I should have been a reporter because I'm good at research. I know Mallory has been to River Bend several times over the last few months. I know she has an ex-boyfriend named Aaron she had run into several times before this week, and I know she has a pregnancy test in her bag. I just don't know if it's him or me—like I said, I am waiting for a due date before I can do the backwards math.

Number of women pregnant: One

BOOK CLUB DISCUSSION QUESTIONS

Is Claudia morally responsible for finishing Norm's delivery?

Would you complete the drive after discovering what was inside the van?

Claudia says "Dead is dead." Why do bodies make people nervous?

Sherrie agreed to accept the delivery of a body because she thought that was standard practice for running a funeral home. Was she obligated to stay after she found the front door padlocked and the barricades placed in the parking lot?

Is Claudia attracted to the stranger in the stairwell, or is she finding ways to not get closer to Aaron?

Is setting up a friend on a date ever a good idea?

Is dating a coworker a good idea?

ACKNOWLEDGMENTS

If you are family or friend, you may find your name or some variation of your name in the book. Large and small characters, heroes or villains, endearing or annoying, just know there is no correlation between you and the character. I needed a name, and I chose from what I know and what means something to me. Just know the name was used out of love and familiarity.

Thank you to my sister, Heidi, for inspiring me to read that Mary Higgins Clark book many, many, many years ago. It started my love of reading and eventually led me to writing.

Thank you to my editor, Starr Waddell. The story and mistakes are mine, but Starr helped smooth out the rough edges.

I never thought I would be a writer, much less writing about a funeral home. I write for entertainment purposes. I hope my descriptions match what is found in reality and that any liberties I took fit the story and do not offend you, the reader.

I sought help from two professionals in the industry, Lindsay Schraad and Jessica Ceille, for details and appreciate their candid answers about the funeral home business. Any errors are mine. Thanks, Lindsay and Jessica!

Thank you to my beta readers for the feedback—Bridgit, Molly, and Mel.

I don't always know where I get my story ideas from, but occasionally someone hands you a gift. Thank you, Scott Dluzak for providing the inspiration for the salad story. Listening to you tell the story of your French cooking experience stuck with me. You provided us with laughter and it was great to know while we were hiking the French mountains you tried expanding your cooking skills — well; you learned how to make a salad.

A special shout-out to Molly Stretten. I don't have enough words of appreciation to express my gratitude for all the roles you cover—beta reader, social media coordinator, and for always answering the weird and mundane questions and for all the encouragement.

Most of all, thank you to my husband, Brian, and son, Alex, for their love and support.

ABOUT THE AUTHOR

After graduating from the University of Wisconsin-Stout, TJ embarked on a career in the hospitality industry, which led to multiple moves across the country. An avid marathon runner, TJ turned to writing after her knee eventually gave out. The author lives in Kansas with her husband Brian, son Alex, and dog, Reba. When not writing, TJ can be found hiking our national parks or traveling with her book club.